T

Morning

After

Memoirs

Kate Michaels

PUBLISHING

Published by Ago 2015

A CIP catalogue record for this book is available from the
British Library.

ISBN 9780993258008

Cover Design by Steven Dobson
Cover Illustration by Jemma Coffey

Ago Publishing, London
www.agopublishing.com

To my family and friends.
We're in this for life — you know too much...

Contents

CHAPTER ONE

The Morning After

It was dark. There was ringing. There was also searing pain. I shifted my weight enough to establish I was lying down. Not so much out of choice, I realised as a wave of nausea came over me, but because there was no other feasible option. I took a deep breath and exhaled slowly. I heard a moan. It may have come from me.

My eyelids were heavy. I concentrated all my energy on prising them open. One relented and stuck fast in a half moon. Still nothing. Just black. As I contemplated possible kidnap scenarios – me stuffed in the boot of some pervert's car, locked in a basement with nothing but a potty chair, transported to Eastern Europe as part of a sex slave ring – my hands groped at what seemed like comfortable surroundings, which suggested I was, in fact, just blind.

A voice called out. Did I recognise it? I couldn't

tell. It seemed to be stuck in a thick fog. Shapes materialised from the darkness – one looked like a small dinosaur. "Jess?" murmured a deep man's voice. "What are you doing?" I painfully rolled myself in the direction of the noise, as my brain slowly attempted to connect the dots. Of course, it was Ben. The dinosaur was his guitar. And I was his eternally hungover girlfriend. I stared dreamily into his deep blue eyes, ready to wish him a Happy New Year... Only they weren't blue. They were brown. And it sure as hell wasn't Ben.

Twenty minutes later, when I'd finally extracted my head from its porcelain pillow, the real panic set in. How had this happened? And where the hell was Ben? As the room spun around me, I felt like Alice after following the 'Eat Me' instructions on a tab of LSD. I remembered getting ready and being aware I was overdoing the glitter (hey, it was New Year's Eve and I was still under 30, so the takeaway guy could bite me). I remembered wiping my smeared mascara on the muscular arm of a sympathetic doorman. There was interference... I was going to be sick… I was in the corridor by the toilets. Ben was shouting. His eyes were steely. He handed me some keys and walked away.

There was a knock at the door. "Jess?" Not-Ben whispered through the cheap wooden paneling. "Should I just go?" My response was automatic, like my brain wished no further part in this fiasco and my body had taken over. I felt bile rising in my throat. I threw up whatever was left of my stomach lining until I was dry heaving pitifully as I wept. Not-Ben let himself out.

Over a sugar-free, milk-free, caffeine-free (let's face

it, coffee-free) coffee and a small, disfigured grapefruit, I listened to my friend Charlie explain what seemed like the end of my life. This was far from the way I'd expected to spend New Year's Day and I berated myself for removing any temptation from the house in anticipation of my January detox. Now, as my stomach lurched and my head throbbed, it seemed like some sick form of self-abuse. Instead of making a start on my long list of New Year's resolutions – I was fighting more of a losing battle each year – I was listening to the intricate details of a relationship meltdown that appeared to have taken place overnight. One luke-warm debate about marriage (I was on the side of waiting until Ben could afford a ring from somewhere other than Argos) and one drunken slobber over a man I didn't even remember had ruined my life. That's right. *Ruined my life*.

It's always the most together friends who seem to group around in times of crisis. What they don't realise is that they're making it worse. What I wanted right now was to speak to someone whose life was more ridiculous than mine, someone who's such a mess they can barely get themselves out of bed in the morning. Someone who would get drunk, spill a drink on the woman who'd interviewed her for a job the previous week, accidentally go home with a man who was not her live-in boyfriend of four years, then wipe the whole sorry experience from her mind. Since that mess was now me, I had to relent to the sympathetic tones of Check-List Charlie for over an hour.

Check-List Charlie – 5'10", long brown hair, blue eyes, likes baking, dislikes time-wasting – was officially the most sorted member of our social circle. She had married, bought a house and thrown herself into a high-powered job while the rest of us were still trying to extract ourselves from bed before noon. While we earthlings looked for some sign of unstable foundations, she continued to outshine every single one of us at every single thing. She was the tallest, the prettiest, the most successful, the only one who could actually follow the dance steps on Davina McCall's workout DVDs...

While my check-list had previously come around second place (a feat I'd felt sufficiently smug about), somehow the planets had turned, the cosmos realigned and the social ladder had been pulled from beneath me, leaving me with nothing but broken dreams and a bad case of the shakes. I stared forlornly at my breakfast, thinking that if any of my New Year's resolutions were going to come to fruition under this disastrous new moon, I was going to need a much bigger grapefruit...

"OK, well, call me. I love you." As I put down the receiver I tried to block out the fact that this was the 29th call, one for each sorry year of my life, that I'd placed to Ben's stoic mobile that day. What's worse, I had to make them in secret, away from the judgmental eyes of Charlie who, worried for the sanity of her newly-pathetic buddy, had appeared on my doorstep two days ago and refused to leave until I "got it together". I wondered whether she understood this was likely to be a long–term project and at what point I could feasibly start charging rent...

What she hadn't understood when she called me into the bedroom that Sunday was that she was asking,

4

at the same time, that I relinquish my long-term project of gradually merging my entire being into the ass-print on Ben's side of the sofa. "You're back at work tomorrow, so I've laid out your clothes for the next week," she said, heinously perky, "washed and ironed and ready to go." Ready to go to what, I wasn't sure. Here was a pile of trouser suits that hadn't seen the light of day since I'd sweated my way through a handful of hopeless post-uni interviews. There were also old-lady trousers I'd purchased on a whim after my trusty denim skirt had received the hundredth withering look from my mother during a lecture about dressing age-appropriately and always for the job you want, not for the job you have. I hadn't mentioned that after a visit to the safari park I'd decided zoo ranger seemed like a perfectly legitimate career path, so if she'd like me to slip into a camouflage boiler suit before heading into the office it would make for interesting viewing.

Either way, the dregs of wardrobe society that were being displayed in front of me were not appropriate for an environment where even the boss was unwilling to relinquish his ten-year-old denim. I remembered with a shudder the day Jill from accounts appeared in a black bodycon dress and spent the afternoon fielding questions about her 'hot' date that night (if you met Jill, you'd know she probably didn't have one). The onus was on casual and 'creative', which, for most of the men in the office at any rate, meant comedy movie T-shirts and sweater vests. Women could choose between casual and slutty, but smart had been sidelined along with the campaign for a water-cooler that spat out something other than cloudy, luke-warm refreshment.

Charlie sat down on the sofa (in Ben's ass spot) and patted the cushion beside her. I obediently yielded like a dog. I didn't get a treat, but I did receive my third sideways pity-look of the day. "Do you want to talk about it?" she ventured nervously – my hair must have been even more alarming than I thought. "You've hardly said a word for days." I let out a sigh that seemed to go on for hours while I made the decision – get it all out in a healthy, cathartic montage of sobs, stories and photo albums or bottle it up and drink through it? As soon as she'd left I could sneak the emergency holiday liquor out of its hiding place... I wondered which memories I'd sniffle about most, the time Ben and I went to Euro Disney and he thought it would be funny to steal the hat off one of the Seven Dwarfs, only to be chased around the park by the 'dwarf's' six-foot father. The time we went to Spain with his family and his sister ran into the bedroom outraged because somehow her vibrator had been mixed up with her step-mother's – it turned out they had the same preference for purple sparkles. The time we'd had to shave off his pubic hair because I'd failed to get rid of my chewing gum before giving him 'a birthday treat'. I realised I'd been stonily silent for a good five minutes, and even Charlie seemed to have lost the will to live, so I just said no, and we sat in silence. Girl's day in was proving pretty fun.

"How about we watch Bridget Jones?" she suggested excitedly. "Or we could make cookies? I have a great, low-fat recipe at home..." Now, I like a cookie as much as the next person, and I've been known to

6

engage in many a chick flick in my time, but she was missing the point of the one thing I actively wanted to do. Wallow. I didn't want to be cheered up. I didn't want my mind taken off the situation. I wanted full-fat, non-organic chocolate. I wanted a duvet that hadn't been washed in two weeks. I wanted to watch Top Model while eating a week's worth of calories before passing out in an alcohol-fuelled slumber every night for at least a month. It wasn't asking too much. "We could play a game?" she said hopefully.

There was no doubt. She had to go. If I were to enjoy a normal healing process I needed to get this Stepford friend out of my house and fast. "You know what," I said casually, "I'm feeling a lot better." Charlie looked at me doubtfully, so I went in for the flatter-bomb. "I think you fixed me!" I said with as dazzling a smile as I could muster without provoking any further laughter lines.

"OK then," she said skeptically as I pushed her none-too-subtly out of the living room. "There's Quorn lasagne in the fridge and three nights' worth of organic lentil stew in the freezer." She stopped to give me another sideways pity-look. "You'll get through this much more quickly if you stick to your new diet. Healthy food makes you *so* much happier." With that, she attempted to squeeze my organs out with a bony bear-hug, picked up her Kate Middleton handbag and crossed the threshold back into the land of the sane.

I picked up the phone. I couldn't tell whether I was depressed or relieved that I'd completely given up calling that bastard Ben. Charlie had filled in a few gaps from New Year's Eve. She was pretty sure Ben was about to propose before our fight, and that I must have acted like an complete dick for him to do a complete 180. I, on the other hand, was pretty sure *he* must have acted like a complete dick for me to elope with a man who wore day-of-the-week socks (one was still staring accusingly from under my bed and it wasn't even the right day). I sure as hell wasn't going to be the one to apologise. Instead, I flew in the face of my wheat and three veg menu and called my trusty friends at China Garden. They knew how to show a girl a good time.

By the time my Set Menu For 2 (don't judge me) arrived, I'd already started feeling the food guilt. I was about to rack up an extreme diet fail and I wasn't sure if my self-esteem could cope with the Kung-pow comedown. I discarded it heartlessly on the sideboard and headed to the lounge to find something more productive to do. Rifling through my (mostly unwanted) Christmas presents I discovered a retro-style step aerobics set – it was the latest in a long line of gifts I'd requested in anticipation of a fabulous new me. Last year it had been a Piloxing (yes, Pilates mixed with boxing) DVD and the year before that an exercise ball, which had actually stopped me exercising for two months with a sprained ankle after I tried to walk on it like I was in the circus. The step came ready assembled, so I manoeuvred it onto the floor in front of the TV and sat on its (surprisingly comfortable) top while I forced the DVD into the player. Within ten minutes I was hooked, watching a crazed blonde jump around like the Energizer bunny's bubbly second wife – all the while sitting comfortably on my new step, devouring my second main course…

8

Exercise has never really been my thing. Well, not since turning 13 at any rate. Until then I'd been the perfect little athlete, joining every team on offer and wowing the parents (OK, *my* parents) on sports day by being what I would be described on my report cards for years to come as 'a good all-rounder'. While my folks were encouraged by their daughter's ability to turn her hand to any subject thrown her way, I was aware from an early age the dark truth behind that backhanded compliment. I was destined to be 'good' at most things, but I had a sneaking suspicion I was 'great' at absolutely nothing. Still, I rushed around in an obscenely short gym skirt, like a slightly dumpy version of a Japanese businessman's fantasy, full of energy and the joys of life. From the ages of 13 to 29 I had moved very little.

Eventually Monday morning reared its ugly head and, after a successful weekend of barely moving at all, it was time to face the real world. I cursed my parents for not being rich, landed gentry, or at least new-money millionaires whose success could support me through a lifetime of lunching and attending charity galas. Something about working a nine-to-five and looking forward to a holiday for about 50 of the 52 weeks a year seemed tawdry compared to the life plan I'd had as a kid. Though my profession had changed regularly – a singer, an actress, a waitress on roller skates (the prevailing choice between the ages of six and 12) or a lawyer (more specifically, Ally McBeal) – my imaginary lifestyle had always been one of laughter, free time and shiny new things. It turned out my 'career' in marketing allowed for none of the above.

In the absence of anything clean, I was forced to

fashion office wear from the carefully selected dress-up box Charlie had lovingly put together. Half an hour after I should have been at my desk I'd rejected the entire 'breakup collection' and was rummaging through my washing basket in hope of something that could be revived with a few spritzes of Febreze. After seizing a black jumper and a pair of slightly-too-tight jeans I attacked the winners with some freshener and bolted for the door. It wasn't until I was squashed on the Tube with a face full of a giant woman's wiry black hair that I noticed a gravy stain on my left leg. My day got steadily worse from there.

After claiming a bad-luck onslaught involving boiler issues, a broken train and, in lieu of a dog to eat my homework, 'family issues', I skulked over to my desk and opened my emails, hoping to ease myself back into working life gently. What I hadn't prepared for was a message from Ben. After stalking him relentlessly on his mobile it transpired he had changed his number. He was also fleeing the country. Well, he was "going travelling" now that he "had the opportunity" – apparently I'd been holding him back from a life of heavy backpacks and tropical diseases. If I'd needed confirmation that I hadn't been wallowing over nothing, this was it. If we'd have been married, this would be the day the divorce papers came through. The day I was expected to accept that within the space of just over a week, I had gone from comfortably coupled-up to alarmingly single. Dumped without further ado – your heart will be posted back in due course as per the terms and conditions of the original agreement (that fateful night four years ago when we got to second base by the quiz machine in the corner of the Old Red Lion). He signed off casually with, "I'll be by to collect my things at the weekend and I think it'll be easier if you're not around."

I stared at the screen for the best part of 15 minutes before the IT guy asked if I was alright. At which point I found it appropriate to burst into tears at my desk like some drama queen in a two-a-penny rom-com. As I was ushered into the kitchenette (a small sink and a fridge cordoned off by a dirty grey display screen), I felt like I'd truly hit rock bottom. I was being comforted by someone whose name I've never even bothered to learn, who I steered clear of in the pub through fear of being damned to eternal boredom, whose life was supposed to be *much* worse than mine.

My boss stomped in, looked about as uncomfortable as a ferociously heterosexual male with very little experience of the emotional spectrum outside of anger and intimidation can and, after absentmindedly handing me his digestive biscuit, suggested I take the rest of the day off. A gesture that would have seemed unusually kind had he not punctuated it with, "I don't want HR on my back."

Once safely back at home my break-up breakdown really set in. Huddled under the covers, fully clothed in coat and shoes, I sniffled my way through nearly six hours of staring at the walls, the ceiling, the carpet – anywhere that would avoid direct eye contact with anything that reminded me of Ben. At some point I stopped pining long enough to relocate to the sofa, which felt like quite the achievement.

I flicked through the movie channels and landed

on Sleepless In Seattle, a film that would support my theory that love was never easy (I'd turn it off before the end). But, instead of consoling me, it inspired me to phone the local radio stations one after another dedicating songs to Ben like some kind of lovesick teenager. By the end of the night I'd resorted to angry Pink songs and the gruesome strawberry holiday liquor I'd been hoarding "in case of emergency". Well, here it was.

My greatest achievement over the next few days was making it through work without having a meltdown. That's if you didn't count the mild tirade I launched at the sandwich guy when he ran out of chocolate two chairs before my desk. It was like he was deliberately trying to break me.

I spent my days warding off sympathetic looks and my nights warding off nightmares about New Year, interspersed with vomit-inducing dreams of Ben and I snuggled up on the sofa, laughing in the twilight or frolicking through the countryside. I felt like the walking dead. I didn't look much better, according to a Skype conversation with my charming friend Matt – 6'1", brown hair, brown eyes, likes Cheestrings dipped in Marmite, dislikes small dogs with tongues longer than their tails – who was currently hiding out in Hong Kong.

Charlie had returned and taken more of a bad-cop approach, which seemed unfair since there was no good cop to compensate. She forced me into the shower, cleaned up my flat (which I now had a month to leave unless I wanted to pay double the rent) and told me in no uncertain terms that I was boring the crap out of her and everyone else.

I could empathise. I'd already bored the crap out of myself. She was halfway through building a new healthy eating regime for me to follow in her absence when I got a call from Selina.

Selina – 5'6", blonde hair, blue eyes, likes vodka, dislikes going to bed before 3am – is one of those friends you only see a couple of times a year. Neither of you really bother to stay in touch during the interim, but somehow when you do hang out it's always a blast. She said she was coming to London for a week and could I escape the humdrum of coupled-up life to accompany her to a new cocktail bar tomorrow night? Clearly she hadn't heard about Ben, so I filled her in, ready for my rush of sympathy. "Oh my God!" she exclaimed. Here it comes... "That's good timing. I can just stay with you then! Shall I head over about 5.30?"

One of the great things about Selina is she doesn't go through the motions. She's one of the few people I know who admits that sometimes she just doesn't care. There was no, "I thought you guys were made for each other," or "I'm completely here for you." When she arrived at the flat there were two dramatic air kisses quickly followed by excitement over how much 'break-up weight' I could lose and how amazing it was that we could go on the pull together now.

At this point, somehow I was too exhausted to argue. I was willing to try a new approach to my misery that didn't involve cutting out sugar or putting on trainers. As misguided as it seemed, at least Selina's plan sounded fun. After hanging her multitude of short dresses and revealing tops in Ben's side of the wardrobe, she popped open a bottle of champagne (OK, prosecco) and I was well on my way towards another morning of regret.

Considering it had been some time since I'd been 'out out' – my social life for the past four years had involved mostly house parties, barbeques and dinners (all with Ben in tow) – I once again found my wardrobe lacking the appropriate attire for the task in hand. Before I'd opened my mouth to defend my choice of woollen jumper dress, leggings and Ugg boots, Selina had half undressed me and was shoving something sequined in my direction.

After a good five minutes of struggling into it ("Which is the head hole?") I emerged from my room to a horrified shriek. Having thought I'd pulled off slutty chic pretty well, I ran back to the mirror to reassess, Selina hot on my heels, grabbing at my legs. "Oh my God! Shave your legs!" she demanded with an outrage usually reserved for child-molesters. My response was a random feminist tirade about society's expectations and media pressure on the female form, wrapped up with a less-convincing, "Anyway, it's freezing outside and I need the insulation." We compromised on thick black tights, although halfway through the evening I looked down and saw a blanket covering of tiny brown hairs poking through the fibres. I thought it unwise to mention.

As the waiter, whom Selina had groped no fewer than three times already, inched over to the comparatively safe zone of my side of the table with our fourth pitcher of margaritas, I looked around and realised that, despite my initial desire to return home as quickly as possible and shoot myself in the face, I was actually having fun. Sure, the décor was brazen, the drinks overpriced and most of the clientele under the age of 18, but somehow the teacher at the school disco feeling was gradually subsiding in favour of a powerful desire to throw some shapes on the dance floor.

Anyone who knows me will know that dancing and I don't mix. Just ask my friend Paul, whose nose I broke during a questionable rendition of Night Fever. Or the waiter from our local Italian restaurant whose fertility I put in severe danger while dancing to New York, New York on my birthday. Alone. Considering my mother was a ballet dancer until she was 25 (yes, she was onstage at the age I was completing my eighth stint of useless work experience) my coordination was that of a blind, drunk clown.

But, alcohol being the ultimate confidence booster, I discarded my straw, downed the remainder of the margarita (gagging on a few mint leaves along the way) and strutted my stuff towards the centre of the dance floor. Now, it was 8.30pm, the place was half empty, and the rhythms I'd been nodding my head to for the past hour were actually those of low-key background music. But none of this mattered as I launched my arms in the air and swayed precariously, gazing up at the glitter ball as though it held the meaning of life. I was in the zone.

While I'd noticed a few sly glances – youngsters clearly jealous of my moves – there was one figure that seemed to be approaching my dance class for one at great speed. "Jess!" said a deep, sexy voice, as I tried to focus on three tall, dark, handsomes headed my way. I

15

twisted into what could have been an elegant spin had I been blessed with style, coordination or, indeed sobriety, but my brain made the rookie mistake of forgetting to mention the plan to my feet. As my panicked extremities attempted to right the wrong, I felt myself tipping slowly but surely backwards, landing sharply in what I can only assume to be an advanced yoga pose. My brain, the turncoat, forced a loud guffaw out of my otherwise horrified lips.

The three handsomes helped me up with their one giant hand. "We must stop meeting like this," said its magical voice, as I was propped up against a leopard-print sofa. I was struggling to place it, but before I could register, well, anything really, one face came into view and its plump, kissable lips said, "So, how was the rest of New Year's Day?" Somehow, I'd found my way back into the arms of Not-Ben, and I was too drunk to establish whether I liked it.

Liam – 6'2", brown hair, brown eyes, likes guinea pigs (apparently his was called Rose), dislikes hair gel (from what I could tell from his sexy/messy mop) – lived in Greenwich and "worked in TV", which could have meant anything from a runner to the head of the BBC. He seemed like a normal-enough guy – rodent obsession aside – but as I listened to him talk about his volunteering summer in Iran and his do-gooder itinerary, I started to think about how I'd always hated this kind of self-righteous drudgery. How Ben and I rolled our eyes when our friend Kate had bored us for an entire dinner party about the huge amount of difference she was making with the one hour a week she volunteered at the old people's home.

16

My eyes narrowed as I realised Ben and I might still be making fun of kind people had this designer-stubbled imposter not singlehandedly ruined my life. Though my reactions were a little slower than usual, I went from naught to raging maniac in 60 seconds and, throwing my ice cubes at him (in lieu of any remaining drink) I launched into a slurred rant, accompanied by the dramatic throwing of beer mats, about how he was a sexual predator who should be locked up and never allowed to speak to decent, law-abiding women ever again. It was maybe two minutes and three choruses of my blame song later that I was asked – very impolitely, actually – by the bouncer to leave.

Standing on the curb – not the steps, which were, apparently, still the bar's precious property – I rummaged in my bag for Selina's number. She had seemingly been MIA for the past half an hour, and I didn't want to leave her stranded. After the tenth attempt I left a message saying I was going home and walked nonchalantly in the opposite direction of the Tube stop. Like a ferociously inbred homing pigeon, two hours later I finally arrived back at château du lonely to what I assumed was a future episode of Crimewatch. The flat door was wide open and banging was coming from inside. I grabbed my gas-powered hair tongs for protection, attempted to light them, gave up, and proceeded up the stairs. An axe-wielding, rapist burglar was just what I needed.

As I hugged the wall – more for balance than cover – I peered around the corner of the lounge into the bedroom and relinquished my grip on the hair accessory-come-weapon. It turned out the barman had

17

finally fallen victim to Selina's charms and, once convinced, he was giving the evening's entertainment his all. Attempting to erase the hairy-assed image from my brain by closing my eyes and shaking my head furiously, I soon found myself toppled on to the floor and crawling towards the sofa, accepting it as my place of slumber for the night. It would turn out, after my good friend's "back injury" from this very evening's fun, that it would be my place of slumber for the next week.

Although I hadn't given up on alcohol as the answer to my woes, I'd definitely given up on Selina for now. Since arriving in my flat she'd commandeered my bedroom, spilled red wine on my carpet and brought me face-to-face with the very man I was determined to blame for my whole pathetic situation. I needed a new way to deal with my break-up bereavement, but first, I needed some sleep.

CHAPTER TWO

On The Hunt

Birds were chirping, the sun was shining and, as I opened my eyes on that Saturday morning I was ready to face the world. Well, someone in the flat above was drilling, it was raining so hard I thought the window might break and I felt like I'd slept for less than an hour, but I was trying to Disney this up and make the most of my weekend. Selina had left the night before to the usual squawks of, "We must do this again soon," and I was determined to get my life back on track.

An hour later I was standing in the kitchen surrounded by mess and wafting a towel at the fire alarm. I shot an accusatory glance at the cocky TV chef who'd convinced me making a tomato and mozzarella tart would be the quick, healthy solution to my lunchtime woes. Bastard. The amount of smoke suggested my concoction had actually caught fire, but when I extracted the singed remains from the oven, I wondered, "What would Nigella do?", chopped off the blackest bits and headed into the lounge – seductively licking my fingers for the benefit of the one-eyed pigeon taking refuge on the window ledge.

I sat down to flick though the local paper – something I've literally never done before. I figured throwing myself into the community might help take my mind off things. In the events column there was the predictable motley crew of fun runs, megastore protests and car boot sales, but an ad illustrated with a sofa and a glass of wine grabbed my attention. A relaxation class. What could be a better activity than doing absolutely nothing?

I was more than willing to make the five-minute trip around the corner in order to sit and indulge myself in my favourite pastime. But who could I drag along on my self-help mission? Charlie would think it ridiculous. I was definitely ready for a break from Selina. I settled on Lisa – 5'11", Kardashian-brown hair, Disney-Princess eyes, likes sparkling cocktails, dislikes men with tongue studs (it's a long and painful story) – who was willing to try most things as long as they were followed by at least the same amount of time in the pub afterwards.

Lisa was a stripper-turned-investment banker. Two years ago she'd swapped dancing for high-powered men to making them dance for her. Something about her mixture of bombshell looks and ferocious intelligence had the majority of her co-workers completely at her mercy. In Lisa's opinion there were three things that made the world go round: money, sex and cocaine. She'd learned this in the strip clubs and had it confirmed in the world of city bankers. Although she still earned slightly less than during her "days of naked ambition", her lifestyle wasn't actually that different. Now she seduced people with hedge funds and a dazzling smile, instead of diamante crotchless panties. Luckily she was still happy to slum it with the rest of us when the situation demanded (which, when she was hanging out with me, was most of the time).

I phoned and arranged our first session, which would be at 2pm the following day. The woman's painfully slow speech was underscored by the tinkling of what I can only assume was a wind chime, but for some reason this raised no alarm bells. I was determined to embrace a new outlook on life, no matter how annoying. Lisa was relieved to hear the class was in the afternoon and asked if I wanted to go shopping for "relaxation gear". I was pretty sure I had that fashion down, so I declined and vowed to do something constructive with the rest of the day. I went in search of the toenail clippers. I returned empty handed. I played with my phone. I flicked through the TV channels until I landed on a Hallmark movie about some kind of fairy godmother trying to set up James Van Der Beek with that girl from Being Erica. At some point I fell asleep.

Sunday morning arrived and Lisa and I approached the battered school hall in which we were to become calmer human beings with only a mild amount of pessimism. However, it increased dramatically when we were greeted by a pack of women who looked like they believed strongly in attachment parenting, but definitely not make-up. One of them had broken the cardinal rule about wearing tracksuits in public when you're not engaged in exercise (i.e. don't do it). Another was actually sporting flip-flops on one of the coldest days of the year. They all looked like they drank tomato juice, squeezed by hand from their vegetable patch. These bitches meant business and as I peered through the window at the finger paintings on the walls, I was pretty sure this was a dry school.

Of all the places people need to drink, schools are top of the list. Whether it's the teachers at lunchtime – the poor, misguided souls – or the parents learning that the only As their little princes will ever get are for effort, schools should definitely have bars (albeit with child locks on). I wondered whether I could sneak a hip flask under my jumper on our next visit – even the playground was making me want to scream.

We hung back to avoid speaking to anyone – I'd brought a friend, I didn't need to make any more, thank you – and when I turned around Lisa had a cigarette held firmly between her lips, so I settled on the wall to wait it out until 1.59, when we'd make our grand entrance.

We walked in and were ushered towards a staircase to the left, which led to what smelled like a musty dungeon. The stairs themselves were decorated with the kind of kids' paintings that wouldn't even have made the fridge in my house. There had clearly been too much, "Tell me about your picture," and not enough, "What the hell is this?" going on and I was concerned that the children's core skills were suffering as a result. We snickered our way down, loudly remarking on how lame this was going to be, when we turned the corner

22

to find ourselves immediately faced with our fellow relaxees. They were sitting in tight rows of wooden school chairs – not a sofa or glass of wine in sight.

I thought about reporting them to the Advertising Standards Agency as, heads down, we mumbled our apologies and shuffled to the only two remaining seats – bang in the centre of the first row. I was directly in front of the teacher, knees almost touching, trying not to stare at the ugliest pair of shoes I'd ever seen. If I'd have been asked to draw a picture of a self-help leader, Brooke – 5'7", mousy brown hair, creepy green eyes, likes all the elements equally, dislikes hairdryers (by the look of it) – would have been spot on. She had long, dry hair yanked back into a ponytail, no make-up, cargo pants with a matching tank top and a serene expression that would have me punching out in my dreams for months to come.

I sat and waited for the comfy mats to be rolled out and the music to start but instead Brooke instigated a cringe-worthy quiz that was met with silences so long I wanted to hold my breath until I passed out. Eventually Lisa and I did as any mature adults would, and got one of the most mortifying fits of the giggles I've ever experienced. Out of the corner of my eye I could see her shoulders jiggling silently as a snort erupted from my nose, not-so-smoothly covered by a coughing fit.

The two of us twitched and sniggered our way through the next ten minutes until finally it was time to bring on the music. I've never been more grateful for the invitation to close my eyes, protecting me from the soul-searching gaze of this badly dressed flower child,

23

who, as the class progressed, I had a burning desire to kick right in the chakra. At least we knew what to expect here. The music was plinky plonky and our 'spirit guide' suggested we visit a relaxing place in our heads – perhaps a field or a deserted island – where we could be alone with no cares or interruptions.

For some reason, my brain was unable to maintain this picture of bliss, and before I knew it, some kid had run into my field and kicked a football at my head, while his Rottweiler lifted its chunky little leg to mark my new shoes as its territory. This isn't the first time I've struggled to make my brain do what I want. When I was ten, my gymnastics coach told us to practise our routines in our heads, so that when it came to performing them, they'd be perfect. Unfortunately, my snide little organ tended to send me flying off the corner of the mat, dropping on my head or, in one particularly extreme case the night before a competition, landing badly from a back flip and breaking my leg.

And it wasn't only visualisation where I was involved that fell victim to my unconscious mind's dark sense of humour. Even my sheep won't jump the fence. That's right, those imaginary sheep that behave perfectly in the sane minds of just about everyone else in the world turn into quivering wrecks in my head, running up to what is a fence of perfectly average height, and refusing to jump over it.

I opened my eyes with a sigh, but Brooke's encouraging nod made them snap back shut like crocodile clips. I sat for the remaining 40 minutes silently stewing over my lack of enthusiasm in the flat-hunting department and visualizing, without much effort, myself making friends with Mad Alice, the bag lady down the street, and having to carry her worldly possessions around in exchange for a spot in her matted sleeping bag under the bridge.

As the session came to an end and everyone else 'woke up' from their relaxation looking serene, rejuvenated and ready to face their future, I'd stared mine a little too closely in the face, breathed in its stale breath and recoiled at its huge, oily pores. I needed alcoholic refreshment pronto. Why I found myself handing over £10 to the grubby guru for the pleasure was beyond me. What I really wanted to do was shove those homemade beads where the sun doesn't shine.

We escaped back into the world of black auras and bad karma and took up our corner table in the Ploughman's Arms – one of the grimmest old men's pubs in the area, but also the nearest. It was £3.50 a pint, which was considerably cheaper than the bars down the road that didn't have nearly the 'character' – holes in the seats, stains on the carpet and what we would later discover were fleas.

I stared at the bottom of my glass, feeling robbed of the life-changing experience I'd pinned my hopes on that morning and wondered what the hell the point was. I was bored out of my mind at work, I was single, soon to be homeless and seemingly incapable of even the most basic attempts at 'self-help'.

So far the one saving grace had been that my parents were on holiday, so I hadn't had to own up to my latest disappointment – or be regaled by stories about other people's daughters who were doing significantly better in life. Always a pleasure. Unfortunately their 'cruise of a lifetime' came to an abrupt end in a few days, with an overnight stay in Southampton, and I was going to have to face the music. It was pretty unlikely I'd have hunted down a new man by then, and I still wasn't ready to face the quiver in my mother's voice as she waxed lyrical about grandchildren and dying alone.

At this point Lisa had wandered back from the bar with a property magazine and convinced me it was time to shop for an exciting new lifestyle. By the time we'd hit the back cover and not one flat in the area had come anywhere near my price range she mentioned the dreaded word: flatshare. Immediately my head (helpful as ever) filled with images of hairy German men making porn movies in the lounge and obsessive-compulsive weirdoes wearing marigolds in the shower…

I'd house-shared at uni, obviously, but somehow the antics that seemed fun back then no longer filled me with the same kind of glee. Add together the constant rows about cleaning, rent, bills, whether it was appropriate to throw a house party the night before our finals, my housemate Neil playing drum and bass music at 4am, and the screeches from Jon's girlfriend as he tried to insert his entire ball sack into her mouth every time she went near his bedroom, and you've got yourself a situation I never wanted to revisit as an 'adult'.

I decided that even if I had to move well out of the area and insert myself into a moth-infested bedsit next door to a crack den, it was by far the better option for my brave new life. Little did I know at the time quite

26

how realistic that would be…

It turns out flat-hunting on a freezing cold January night is about as much fun as a second game of Monopoly. Lisa had agreed to accompany me to check out what were described in their ads (again, I must get the number of the ASA) as "stylish lofts" and "airy studios" within ten minutes walk of the Tube station. Whether they'd hired the Olympic power walking team (is there one?) or their designer imposter watches were a touch on the slow side, the two of us spent at least half an hour walking between appointments that, on paper, should have been right next door.

The one thing these hellish homesteads had in common is that the combined space of the bedroom, lounge, kitchen and bathroom was smaller than my childhood room. "Oh my God, did someone die in here?" barked Lisa as she walked through the doorway of the fourth place, which did suffer from an unfortunate aroma. The young, eager agent passed it off as coming from a waste pipe next door, which he assured us was being fixed, before strolling the perimeter of the room and terming it "micro-chic". He invited us to have a proper look around – I twirled on the spot, done – while he went and hovered hopefully in the street. Lisa had already jacked open the window and was fiddling desperately with her lighter.

I felt like collapsing on the sofa bed and weeping, but instead I grabbed for my disinfectant hand gel and started grooming myself like a cat after a visit from a particularly 'grabby' three-year-old. Lisa steered me out of the door, fag still in hand. "It's a dump," she announced to the agent, handing him back his business card and making a beeline for a bar at the end of the road. I reminded her that we still had three appointments to go and my dream place could be just around the corner. It was Thursday evening, after all, no time for fun. Instead she made a detour to the newsagent to purchase a mini bottle of wine, which she proceeded to down in the fifteen minutes it took us to get to the next flat.

"Now, this isn't a studio, per se…" said the agent – a fat man in a suit at least two sizes too small, who insisted on touching my arm every time he spoke. "It's more of a community." What I was visualizing was a hippy commune, but what we were faced with was more of a young offenders' institute. There were long narrow hallways painted blue with bright orange doorways, arranged around a "courtyard" which courted no decoration besides a single orange bench. I imagined the inmates being sent for "time out" down there when they played their music too loud or used someone else's milk. A man with a tiny but scary-as-hell dog shoved past with two friends in Kappa tracksuits and gold chains and Lisa turned around and walked straight back out. I followed apologetically as the agent shouted after us, "Take a look inside. You might be surprised."

Again, the kind of surprise I envisaged involved crack dens and dead bodies, so we picked up the pace and literally ran from the building to the relative safety of the main road. With a final look of disbelief Lisa marched me into the open arms of the nearest pub, where I finally admitted to her, myself, and the patient barmaid that my search was fruitless. I felt cheated by the property search TV shows I'd been glued to for the past two years, particularly by Kirsty and Phil, who I'd expected to give a more realistic view of the world. While they gallivanted off to the countryside to find a weekend retreat for a millionaire couple who'd tired of their glamorous London lifestyle, I was literally risking my life in dives and dens in areas that had been strategically omitted from the Time Out Guide. There had to be a better way. But, in the meantime, there had to be more wine...

CHAPTER THREE

Make Mine Irish

I awoke with a start, clawing at an imaginary shower curtain, from a dream in which Norman Bates was my new landlord. It had been creepy for a number of reasons, not least because, at one point, I'd climbed up to the main house with a bottle of wine to try and seduce the psycho in exchange for a discount on my rent. I was mildly hyperventilating at the thought – and because my duvet was pulled over my head – so I threw open the window and wandered to the kitchen to get a glass of water. There were no clean glasses, so I attempted to lap my beverage out of a bowl. I was about to give in and begin the arduous task of loading the dishwasher when I remembered I had a much more pressing problem to solve.

In precisely a week's time I was going to be homeless and there was only one thing for it. I would have to phone my mum. My parents had been back from their cruise for two days, but I'd managed to bombard them with enough cheerful texts to throw them off the scent, while I stealthily dodged phone calls like a pro. Now I'd break the news to them in one mega-blow – Ben left me and I have nowhere to live. I'd then weep a bit for good measure and my mum, terrified by stories of drug addicts and rabid dogs, would send enough money to house me in a comfortable flat for the rest of my life. Or so I thought…

Instead, when I rang, I got my dad. This called for a completely new tactic, but I was unprepared and not a little hungover, so the story came out without the crescendo of desperation I'd intended. "What did you do?" he asked accusingly. "Nothing!" I insisted. "Well, he didn't just walk out for no reason, love". I couldn't believe my own father was taking Ben's side! Wasn't he supposed to be terrifyingly overprotective of his sweet young daughter? Wasn't he supposed to tell me Ben was never good enough for me anyway, and ask for his new address so he could go round and have it out with him, man-to-man?

"Did you see that documentary about the slow lorises last weekend?" he asked, having lost interest in my life story already. "The what?" "The slow loris, love, like the one we saw in the zoo when you were 12. Apparently people think they're cute and buy them as pets, but they're vicious little fuckers, and they're warning against it." "Ted!" shouted my mum from the background. Her swear-o-meter had clearly gone off and she was finally heading to the phone to save me. "You don't want a slow loris do you?" asked my dad.

"Well, no, not if they're vicious little fuckers." "Jess!" shouted my mum from what sounded like the laundry room. Were they double-teaming me again? It was most disconcerting. "I was just telling Jess about the slow loris," explained Dad. "The what?" asked mum. "The slow loris. Nycticebus. They're those tiny critters we were watching…" This was getting ridiculous. "Mum, Ben left!" I wailed as loudly as possible down the phone. "Yes, apparently she's fucked it up," explained Dad, helpfully, before clicking off. "Hello?" shouted mum. "Hi, Mum." "Hello?" "Mum, can you hear me?" "Ted, I think she hung up!" "Press the red button," he said with what sounded like an entire pizza in his mouth.

By the time my mother had figured out the modern technology of her telephone I'd lost all interest in telling her anything about Ben. My masterplan had been ruined by my dad's 60-second rule regarding anything he hadn't learned down in the depths of the cable channels – which he felt it his civic duty to pass on to everyone he knew. Barmen, doctors, bus drivers – nobody was safe from the alarming quantity of useless knowledge stored up in my father's head. He was once taken into custody at the airport after regaling one of the security guards with the intricate details of terrorist bombs, which he'd learned about the previous weekend during a whopping four-hour special at 2am. Parents' evenings also fell victim to his deluge of information and lack of tact when he explained to my English teacher how it had been "proven" that children excel more in a home-schooled environment. A conversation that sent a chill to my very bones.

"Mum, he just left!" I wailed, determined to play the injured party to the bitter end. In any case, I was still slightly foggy about exactly what had happened... "Is he coming back?" she asked matter-of-factly. "No!" "OK, then what's the plan?" The plan? The *plan*? Ummm... to sit alone and grow old and eventually have my skin pecked off by one-eyed seagulls? "There is no plan!" I shrieked. "It's all over!"

Mum took a deep breath. "Jess, I'm going to say this now, even though it's not what you want to hear." I groaned in anticipation. "Do you think it's because of your cooking? Because I don't know a single man that would have put up with the kind of slop you offered on a nightly basis. No wonder the poor boy was so skinny!" Poor boy? Was everyone on his side, even when I'd eradicated blame from the information? "Do you remember Gemma from school?" Here we go... "Well, I ran into her mum the other day and we ended up going for coffee – you know, in that little place at the top of Debenhams? – anyway, apparently Gemma is a fantastic cook. She even went on a course in the South of France over the summer and when she got back her boyfriend proposed!" Only my mother could put those two facts together and presume to have found the secret to the perfect relationship. "I'm pretty sure it wasn't my cooking. Anyway, I'm not a housewife, Mum, I do have a career." "Mmmm." There was silence for a few seconds.

"Sweetheart, I think this is the perfect opportunity for you to have a good long think about what you need to change. You can't have this happen every time and end up an old maid. Mine and your father's retirement money will only stretch so far." Far enough for a cruise... "And I don't want to be sending food parcels for my single daughter when I'm in a home!"

Food parcels? If she meant the tins of corned beef, packets of UHT milk and boil-in-the-bag fish she so helpfully provided me with each month as though we were at war, I wanted to tell her she could keep them. None of this was going according to plan and I started to wonder just why my parents hated me so much. What had I ever done to deserve such a complete lack of indulgence? "I can't believe you're not being more sympathetic," I sniffled. "I wish I hadn't bothered to tell you." I could almost hear her raise an eyebrow. "To be honest, sweetheart, I imagine you've given yourself enough sympathy as it is. This is no time to fall apart, this is time for reflection and a new action plan. Or do you want to be ringing next year in alone as well?"

"I have to be out of my flat in a week." I said miserably. "Did you tell her about that monkey show, about how the female attracts the male? I recorded it actually," chimed in my father helpfully. "I'm going to be homeless!" "You can borrow the video." The video? "Dad, nobody uses videos anymore!" I shouted down the receiver, hoping to send the message via my mother. "Sweetheart, there's no need to shout. Have you even looked for a new flat?"

I recounted tales of cockroaches, drug dens and scary-looking brutes, essentially implying that if she allowed me to move into any of the above 'affordable' properties I would be robbed/raped/murdered and/or forced into prostitution. "Well, if you don't like any of those, you can just come and live back with us for a while," she said, as though that didn't make me want to slowly cut my head off with the blunt edge of a nail file. I like my parents as much as the next person, but we were talking about 'the foreseeable future' and let's face it, even Christmas can seem like a struggle, and that's with presents involved.

I shuffled around desperately for an excuse or an alternative plan, but with just six days to go until I'd be shacked up with Alice under the bridge, I figured there was absolutely no other option. "You can look for flats from here, or maybe even look at moving somewhere closer?" she suggested. So, here I was, suddenly on my way to becoming a full-time citizen of the glamorous metropolis known as Leighton Buzzard. This would be a good time for someone to invent takeaway wine, because I was all out of options, and all out of alcohol...

"What day do you have to be out?" "Saturday," I said forlornly, desperately wracking my brain for any alternative. "I'll send your brother round with the hatchback," she said. "You can stay in the garage." "What?!" "We've converted it, darling! It's like one of those flats that are all in one room, what do you kids call them?" "Studios?" I ventured, shuddering at the thought. We said our goodbyes and I sunk further into the ass indent. Not only was I moving in with my parents, but I was going to have to see my brother, too.

While most of my friends had been blessed with perfectly normal siblings, growing out of their annoying phases as they hit adulthood, my brother Andy – "officially" 5'11" but clearly shorter, messy brown hair, dopey blue eyes, likes recreating moments from Jackass

35

ten years too late, dislikes any form of appropriate behaviour – went through an annoying phase that turned out just to be his personality. He's a massive practical joker who gets off on embarrassing anyone he sets eyes on and every trip out of the house will normally involve him tripping me over, pulling up my skirt or farting loudly in public. He's officially the worst.

I wasn't looking forward to his dissection of exactly what went wrong in my relationship, because chances are they'd include my "fat ass" or "lack of effort in bed" – my brother particularly enjoys inappropriate conversations with his family. Like two Christmases ago, when we were munching through my mother's overcooked turkey and he compared the turkey's "cavity" to his ex-girlfriend's vagina. Or when he deemed it an appropriate time to casually mention he had a spliff, if anyone wanted a smoke, at my aunt's funeral. He even had the audacity as a teenager to come down from his bedroom one evening half dressed and ask if anyone had a spare condom, because his girlfriend Nancy "really wanted it" and he didn't want to grow up to be a chauvinist who only had sex when it suited him. While the excuse was novel, my mother is far from a feminist, so he was forced to rummage through the kitchen drawers in search of cling film. An image that still haunts me to this day.

I looked around the flat trying to figure out how long it would take to pack up my life and which corner shop to visit to beg for cardboard boxes. The one with the nice lady or the pervy man? I decided on pervy man, A) because he was more likely to give me the boxes and B) because I needed a pick-me-up, no matter how creepy. As I put on my coat I scoured the shelves, and noticed Ben had left his James Bond collection behind. I wondered how much it would go for on eBay...

Ten minutes later and mission accomplished. Feeling dirty but desirable I lined up the boxes along the wall in the lounge and opened one of the two-for-a-fiver bottles of wine I'd felt inclined to buy from the shop 'as a thank you'. I decided that, with little else on the agenda that evening except consuming said bottles, I might as well have a clear-out. My belongings would be split into four groups: items to keep, items to throw away, items to give to the poor, unsuspecting homeless and items to keep but hide from my mother. I started in the lounge because I was already there and so was the TV. You've Been Framed was just coming on and I could do with a laugh at other people's expense.

I hit the DVD section of the shelves first, which was almost bare already thanks to Ben's hit-and-run. I picked up the James Bond box set, trying to decide whether I should make a 'to sell' pile, and placed it in the centre of the lounge. Next was the Friends box set and a selection of bargain basement discs that seemed like a good idea at the time, but which I'd failed to stick with past the first ten minutes. I was still trying to prove wrong the assumption that if something was offered up as a bargain it was because nobody wanted it, and if nobody wanted it, it was because it was lame. Every item I'd ever purchased had proved this point, but somehow I was still holding out for that star buy. That pub conversation where I reveal the price of a scarf and everyone celebrates my savvy shopping skills with a, "Noooooo!"

I stopped to laugh at a fat man falling over on a treadmill then moved on to the books. Scanning the first few shelves, I landed mostly on titles I'd spotted on the bestseller list, purchased, then read the back properly and decided they sounded boring. That should be a late New Year's resolution: read more. Maybe join a book club? Although I wasn't entirely sure what people did in them. Did they sit in silence each week reading together? Did they read aloud? Did they talk about the book like in an English lesson? I wondered if there would be set topics and essay questions. Maybe I'd just stick to reading alone. Since that's how I'd be doing everything else from now on. My unhelpful brain rolled its eyes and told me to shut the fuck up.

After an hour of making piles and filling boxes I went to open the second bottle of wine – a rosé this time, in the interest of variety. After all, it was Saturday night. I'd turned down various invitations to leave the house and engage with the real world, and was surprisingly grateful for my stash of frozen lentil stew. It struck me as the kind of meal that would help me survive an oncoming apocalypse.

I spotted a rogue DVD behind the shelf and grabbed at it. It was The Joy Of Sex. The 'dirty movie' Ben had bought when I'd suggested we needed to spice things up in the bedroom. I'll never forget how mortified I was to come home to a blanket, candles and an instructional DVD playing while Ben paraded around in his boxers with a glass of wine...

I chucked the disc into the rubbish pile, only to

notice some keepers stowed away there. I rummaged through the box marked 'charity', to see that it had stuff to hide from my mother in it. Lavender candles I'd decided to introduce into a 'regifting pile' were surrounded by a group of broken necklaces I was determined to fix with the mini-pliers from a Christmas cracker. I took a deep breath. Chaos. Somewhere the system had gone awry and Cougar Town was just starting on TV, so I decided it was a situation that could be rectified in the morning. I grabbed the wine cooler from the kitchen, put my feet up on the coffee table (something Ben never let me do) and settled in for a Saturday night of watching skinny middle-aged women drink wine. While I'd been moping around I'd failed to remember the best thing about being alone. I could do whatever the hell I wanted.

"Say ahhhhh" I said to the wine bottle as I peered down its neck at 2am. Damn. Were these kiddie-sized or something? I was pretty sure when I started drinking bottles were a lot fuller than they are these days. It was like crisp packets, whose contents seemed to be shrinking with every purchase, making you wonder whether you were also paying for the air as part of your 30 grams. Was it 30 grams? I decided it was important to solve this cryptic puzzle immediately, so I grabbed my laptop and googled crisp packets. I learned that the average bag contains somewhere between 25 and 35 grams, and congratulated myself for being spot-on with my estimation. Then I decided to order some crisps, because I was hungry and hadn't eaten any for a while. After comparing the prices on various supermarket websites I ordered a packet of salt and vinegar Walkers, which would cost me 50p plus £4.99 for delivery. Then I hit eBay… and eventually fell asleep with my finger perched precariously over the bid button for a "refurbished" treadmill. I will never learn.

Sunday morning was harsh. If my liver hadn't been attached it would have packed up and followed Ben out of the door. The two bottles of wine/vinegar I'd consumed last night were not sitting well. But it wasn't just my vital organs that were silently screaming. Just about every muscle in my body had completely seized up. It took five painful minutes to extract my head from its unnatural position against the armrest of the sofa, but it would clearly take longer to move it from the in-need-of-a-neck-brace pose it had struck on my shoulder. I limped to the hall mirror and confirmed that I was, indeed, the Hunchback of Notre Dame.

I made it to the kitchen and, in the absence of bread, milk, cereal or anything mildly breakfast related, I grabbed a portion of Charlie's lasagne out of the freezer and shoved it in the microwave. Five minutes later it emerged charcoaled and chewy and I sat on the sofa – head still locked somewhere between coy and disabled – to enjoy my healthy meal.

A flick through the TV channels revealed nothing trashy enough for a Sunday, and I was still heading up an anti-TV chef campaign after my tart fiasco. Instead, I filled the hours of 12 until two more constructively with the new Pet Salon game on my phone. These were demanding customers, and once I opened the doors I was loath to join every other salon in the area by providing what I imagined to be half-hearted handling and puffy poodle perms.

Lisa called around 2.15pm – thankfully on my landline, or I'm not quite sure what I would have done – and demanded that I leave the house. "Get out of the fucking house," was her friendly greeting. "What?" Was this like some kind of warped version of that psycho in Scream? "What are you doing?" "Relaxing." "Come and relax in the pub. It's happy hour from three, and I intend to get very bloody happy." "Look, it's not a good time," I said helplessly. "Like a hundred people just came into the salon and there aren't even enough chairs for them to wait on, and my doggy manicurist moves about as quickly as Lurch..." "Who?" "Addams Family." "You're watching The Addams Family?" "No, I'm working really hard not to let down my customers and since I've been on the phone to you three have already walked, so if you'll excuse me..." "Listen to me. You. Are. A. Dick. But I'm willing to overlook that if you come to Mike's Bar at three. See you there." With that she hung up and the last of my angry customers walked out.

Entering Mike's Bar was like being beamed 10,000 miles across the world and rocking up to a surf shack. Both Mike and the bar in question were immediately in front of you as you came in off the street. He wore a Hawaiian shirt. The surf board-come-bar wore a sticky-looking gleam. "G'day," he said, doing something bizarre with his mouth to force his South African accent into something resembling Australian. I objected already. It wasn't a good day for a start. It was tipping it down with rain, I was gruesomely hungover with a headache even the codeine left over from my wisdom tooth extraction couldn't shift and I was the sole patron of a gaudily themed bar that had taken me 15 soaking minutes to walk to. "Wet outside, huh?" I looked this asshole in the eye and was selecting my weapon of choice from the beer mats, straws and small cocktail umbrellas in front of me when Lisa came bounding out of the toilets and grabbed for the menu that was least stuck to the bar.

After ordering cocktails that came in koala-shaped mugs, Lisa lead me to a back room, where we settled on tree stumps next to a camp fire – an ingenious heating method for a space lined with wood on all sides. I looked around casually for the emergency exit. "Now, don't shout," Lisa said ominously. "But I saw fit to provide entertainment." Dance troupes, dwarves and jesters competed for space in my slow–working brain until two hot men entered the building and headed our way.

They weren't just hot. They were drool-worthy specimens, the likes of which were unseen outside the pages of GQ. I would have been more than happy to follow these male Sirens to my death at sea, on land, in bed... "Oh my God, did you pay for them?" I asked, mortified. "Don't be a dick," said Lisa as she stood up to greet them. I wasn't entirely convinced whether that was a yes or a no. I knew male bankers hired 'escorts' all the time, but Lisa? She didn't need any help in that department. "This is Tom from my building, and this is?" "Stuart," replied Stuart – 6'2", blue eyes, brown hair, likes big dumb dogs, dislikes circusfolk.

It turned out Stuart was visiting from Ireland and staying with "Tom from Lisa's building" for the next few weeks while he looked for a "London pad". His accent made me want to weep. It was just sing-song enough to be completely enchanting but there was a real raw, sexual edge that made me shiver. If Lisa was trying to help me get over Ben, it was working. I would certainly be willing to whet my whistle with this hottie and work my way back to the land of the sexually satisfied from there.

We spent the afternoon drinking and laughing – Stuart had a geeky sense of humour that I was finding unusually charming. I flicked my hair around so much that at one point my neck snapped back into hunchback pose. Luckily Stuart had learned some dodgy massage techniques in Thailand and immediately offered his services. I asked whether it would work better if he accompanied me back to my flat and I lost the clothes, but instead he pulled up a stump behind me and got to work on my 'tension'. I clung tightly onto my koala's tail, and concentrated every muscle on keeping my breathing regular and my moans of pleasure at bay.

Later, he walked me back to my flat and kissed me on the cheek, before refusing five invitations in a row to come in. I stopped at six – that would have just looked desperate – and was partly relieved because the flat was a mess and I still officially hadn't shaved my legs since last year. We swapped numbers and he promised to text during the week to let me know how his flat hunt was going. Lisa and I had shared my horror stories with him and at one point he'd looked about set to board the plane back to Dublin. But we assured him that a lifestyle of hanging out with awesome people like us would be totally worth paying through the teeth for what would surely be considered a slum in his green-gabled home country.

I sat next to my phone for every waking hour of the next three days, taking it to the toilet with me, into meetings at work, sleeping with it under my pillow... It was pretty pathetic stuff. I'd forgotten just how much waiting around was involved in the dating scene. Particularly with someone you're not even dating (did a kiss on the cheek mean anything, or was it an Irish thing? I made a note to Google it later).

Although I'd been expecting a text, I hadn't expected the random parcels that kept greeting me when I got home from work. The old lady in the flat next door smiled when she brought me my first two, but by the time a set of weights arrived on Wednesday she made it clear she wasn't my personal postal worker. It was the sorting office for me from now on. It seemed my drunken eBaying had consequences, and while I'd rarely won an auction in the past, my wine-happy mega-bids were proving successful. I now had a dairy-free cookbook (even though I love milk, cheese, butter – in fact, any bovine-related treats), a pair of winter boots two sizes too big, a red lacy negligee that looked like something out of the Moulin Rouge (which went straight in the bin – it turns out I'm surprisingly uncomfortable with other people's used sex clothes when sober) and a small plastic unicorn, which I may have mistaken for a My Little Pony at point of purchase. For someone who could barely afford a new bra, these were not particularly savvy buys, and I wondered if I could be bothered to re-list them and try to palm them off on some other drunken loser (it's been statistically proven that 37 per cent of eBay shoppers were drunk/high and/or out of their mind at the point of purchase. OK, that's a lie, but it can't be far off).

By Wednesday evening I still hadn't heard from Stuart and I was about to take it out on a bottle of wine, when my phone vibrated in my pocket. Pleasant. "House hunting a bust. Drinks Friday? Stuart." So, eloquence wasn't his forte, but I couldn't wait to see what was. I suggested a pool bar, which was not the classiest date, but it did allow for a lot of bending over and potential Ghost-style moments from behind. I rummaged through my wardrobe to see if I still had it. Yes – there it was. My 'lucky top' from uni. It was tight, red and made my average-sized ladies look enormous. At the right angle I could give him quite an indecent peek.

After failing to tuck my stomach into my skinny jeans, I spied my denim skirt lurking forlornly in the back of the wardrobe. It hadn't had an outing for a while, so essentially I was neglecting it, but even though I'd been out of the dating circuit for some time, I knew the rule was always legs or breasts – never both. So I apologetically slid the skirt aside in favour of some boot-cut jeans, which, before Christmas, had been too big. Never have I been so depressed to see an item of clothing fit perfectly.

Even though my potential date was two days away, I decided to set up a DIY spa in the living room, with a four-step plan to makeover my body. De-fuzzing was my prime concern at this stage, so I fished out my epilator – previously used once on my ankle hair, only

45

to be thrown aside as though it was a photo of my parents naked – and got to work. An hour later I'd managed the outside of my right leg. There was no way I was getting through this without some kind of anaesthetic, so I climbed back into my jeans and went to visit my leery friend at the shop. As I tried to explain that I needed the kind of alcohol that dogs carry in little barrels around their necks, he seemed less and less patient with his previous object of desire. He brought me everything from dog biscuits to sanitary towels before I climbed behind the cash register myself and picked up a bottle of whiskey. I wasn't sure whether this was the magical liquid canines preferred, but I just needed something to the dull the pain, and fast.

After pouring a glass and nearly choking to death, I decided whiskey must be the diet beverage I'd been searching for all my life, or at least for the past 30 minutes since my 'fat jeans' became my 'thin jeans'. Nothing that tastes that gross could also be bad for you – that was the rule. A few swigs later I'd stripped the hair from both legs and was wondering whether to attack my bikini line. Seeing as my vision was beginning to blur I deemed it irresponsible and potentially damaging to my sex life and unlikely future as a pushy mother. This relentless plucking was bordering on self-harm. In the meantime I needed to work my way through the basket of lotions and potions that had lain dormant in the bathroom for the past three years. I was pretty sure that combined together in the right order, these unwanted gifts (mostly from my concerned and hopeful mother) held the secret to eternal beauty. I separated them into parts of the body and got to work.

Looking hot was taking longer than I'd imagined and I was already pretty bored.

By the time I'd exfoliated, moisturised and tanned my left arm I'd completely lost interest. Getting laid was totally not worth wasting my entire evening when I could be watching TV. A new series of The Good Wife was starting and I was damn well going to give it the full attention it deserved. I figured I'd just carry on from where I left off tomorrow.

But by the time Thursday came around my beauty masterplan had gone out of the window along with my favourite vase (which met with an untimely death when I stuck my arm out a bit too excitedly to see if it was snowing – it wasn't). I had to get packing and fast, or come Saturday morning chances were my precious sibling would grab the nearest things, throw them into the car and drive away spouting some stupid philosophy like, "you should never own more than you can carry."

Eventually Friday arrived, cold, damp and uninspiring. Perfect for my first date in five years. Not wanting to take the piss at work and leave early just to slut it up, I faked a headache around 3pm, 'hung in there' until five, then rushed home to get the party started.

Half an hour later I looked in the mirror. The results were mixed. Yes, I had one brown arm and one white one, but surely under the dingy pool hall lighting nobody would notice? Other than that, I tilted my head in approval. I had done what my grandma would have referred to as 'making the best of yourself'. It's strange how content you can feel knowing this is as good as it gets...

By the time I reached the pool hall, Stuart was deep in conversation with the bartender. I casually sauntered over and leaned seductively over the bar. Nobody noticed. I brushed up against Stuart's arm, he scooched over. Eventually my, "Errr…" pulled the new BFFs from their reverie and I finally existed. We both ordered a beer and headed off into the darkest corner I could find before I attempted to sexily slip out of my M&S winter coat. Once I'd managed to wriggle my left arm out I immediately skulked further into the darkness. Was it possible it had become more tanned overnight? Maybe I was being paranoid.

Three lost games and four beers later I remembered I was supposed to be drinking low-calorie beverages and switched to whiskey and Diet Coke. This seemed to impress Stuart, who was living up to his Irish roots and was more than willing to take me on in an England verses Ireland drinking challenge. I purposely missed a few more shots (I'm secretly awesome at pool) but to no avail. Stuart cracked a few jokes and eventually suggested we go and sit at a non-pool table rather than get in the way of people who could actually play (those were almost his exact words).

Three, four, five? Who knows how many whiskies later the two of us were stumbling down the road, following the light of my mobile like it was the North Star. I'd put it onto sat nav and was relying on it to get us back to my place before one of us passed out and/or had to pee in the street. I caught sight of myself in a window – somehow my hair, which had been straightened to within an inch of its life just a few hours

48

earlier, was now curly on the left side and seemingly plastered against my face on the right. My carefully applied make-up was a bust too, and I realised I hadn't once retouched on my numerous visits to the toilets, which had mostly been taken up with peeing out ten drinks or, in fact, trying to vomit in an attempt to sober up.

When we finally got to my flat I was pretty sure I was going to wet myself with excitement. I hauled ass to the toilet to fix everything I could without being in there long enough that he would assume I was going to need air-freshener and/or was feeding my secret drug habit. Being a woman is hard. When I sauntered back out, attempting a sexy approach to my prey, I'd forgotten there were still some boxes in the middle of the lounge and flew head first over one marked "bits and bobs". While the alcohol soaked up the pain, it didn't keep my body entirely under control and my right boob popped out the front of my lucky red top. I gave a little 'huh' of surprise since it hadn't emerged the whole time I'd been bending over the pool table, and then had a confusing moment when I wasn't sure whether to bother putting it back in. It was obvious what was on the cards and far be it for me to get in the way of love.

I flicked my hair, cricked my neck and approached my target with a wily determination, made all the more impressive by the spinning walls around me. I was going to have to concentrate hard on the correct anatomical positions to make this work. I lumbered towards him on one shoe, guided by the sexual tension of my exposed right nipple. As I approached I called

49

out his name, noticed his eyes were closed, grasped for the arm of the sofa and passed out.

The next thing I knew, I was nestled in the fetal position on the floor, squinting into the desk lamp – which had joined me in my horizontal shame – and wondering what the hell that noise was. There it was again – a high-pitched buzzing that made my eyes vibrate inside my head. I eventually pulled myself onto my feet to find Stuart still sound asleep and snoring (black mark) on the sofa. I dragged my weary carcass to the window to see what the hell was going on.

That's when I saw it – Andy's car, parked a nonchalant metre from the curb and clearly uninhabited. I walked over to the door and pressed the button on the entry phone. "What the fuck are you doing? Let's go!" hollered my beloved sibling as he shoved hard against the door. "Just a minute!" I desperately scrabbled for an excuse to put him off for as long as possible. "The button's not working – give me two minutes and I'll come down and let you in." I ran around the flat throwing things in whatever boxes and bags I could find and shoved a jumper over the display-cabinet top, all the while serenaded by an incessant screech as my brother refused to take his finger off the button. When I was happy I looked mildly presentable and my piles of random belongings could pass as at least a vague effort to pack I headed to the sofa to find my gentleman caller gone. During all the commotion he must have scurried out, along with my only chance of fornication in weeks.

I strolled downstairs casually and opened the front door. Andy rolled his eyes and barged straight past me.

50

"I've totally got better things to do than try and break into my own sister's apartment," he said as he jumped up the stairs. I followed meekly behind him, feeling the failure of last night hit me square between the eyes in one hell of a hangover.

As he surveyed the damage in the lounge he reached into his back pocket and handed me a roll of bin bags. "Anything that's not packed within half an hour totally goes in the bin. Get picking favourites." My internal rant about his incessant use of the word 'totally', as though he were some kind of '90s surf dude, took a back seat to my desire to locate painkillers and I headed off toward the bathroom to rummage through the 'medicine cabinet' (dusty shelf with three-year old Lemsip, an empty bottle of insect repellent and two miniscule plasters).

"Hey, did I hear voices?" asked a bafflingly casual Stuart. "I just took your last paracetamol, hope that's OK." Not only was it not OK that my non-fuck buddy had robbed me of my only potential pain relief, it was incredibly not OK that he was about to get an Everybody Loves Raymond-style welcome into my family if I didn't think of something fast. Unfortunately the combination of beer, whiskey and sheer panic sloshing around in my system left me unable to function for a good 60 seconds, which turned out to be the exact amount of time it took my brother to re-emerge for the next box just as I was shoving Stuart out of the front door.

If this love boat wasn't sinking before, it was definitely taking on water now. Not only had I failed to receive the penetration I deserved last night, my second chance was fading quicker than the bargain tooth whitener I'd had shipped over from the States.

"So you just have sex with my sister then leave?" asked my brother, his social awareness as acute as ever. "No," said Stuart. "We didn't have sex." "Ahhh… that answers one question, at least." "What?" I was unwilling for this exchange to go on longer than it would take me to lead Stuart around my idiot sibling and get the hell out of the building. "I thought that was weird. He's way too hot for you." Then to Stuart. "Dude, you're like an eight and, let's face it, my sister's sliding further below average with each passing second." Again, there was no time to address the "dude", but enough to hear Stuart thank my brother for the compliment, the two of them to shake hands and Stuart to pick up a box as though nothing had happened and follow Andy down to the car.

I was slightly confused as to what had just occurred, but decided it was best to pack up my final things before the two of them drove off for some kind of bonding retreat in the countryside. I grabbed the last remaining items from my wardrobe and opened and closed every drawer in my bedroom, while dumb and dumber made fun of my packing and sighed at the sheer amount of crap I was attempting to take with me to my glamorous new life at casa mum and dad's.

Suddenly I heard a shout and a huge eruption of laughter. I ran into the living room in time to see my brother trying to restrain Stuart with a pair of purple furry handcuffs, while he attacked him with a matching feather duster. It seems I'd forgotten to tape up my 'things to hide from my mum' box and now my 'personal items' were being demolished, along with my dignity. "Supreme Self Confidence. What the hell is this?" squawked my brother rummaging through the box and lifting out a self-help CD. I ran towards him, going in for a tackle, but he swiped me aside and plunged his arm back into the lucky dip of horror.

I couldn't bring myself to look at Stuart, who was currently struggling to release himself from the iron grip of the purple furries. "Have you still got the key for these?" he asked, as though it was the most normal situation in the world. "Oh my God." Said my brother as he pulled out a questionable lacy number. He threw it back into the box, handed Stuart the keys to the handcuffs and said, "Come on, we've got 15 minutes then I'm out of this dump." Apparently Andy did have boundaries, and while sex toys wouldn't do it, his little sister's lingerie would.

I shuffled out after him carrying a box from the kitchen and attempting to kick him as I walked down the stairs. "You asshole." I hissed. "Oh, lighten up. It clearly wasn't going anywhere anyway. At least I've broken the ice for you – you should be thanking me."

After what felt like hours, the car was finally chockablock with a life's worth of crap. It seemed sad that everything I had to show for my longest-term relationship and, in fact, the past 29 years fitted snugly into the back of a rusty Honda Civic. I managed to look in the general direction of Stuart's face, but still not directly into his eyes as I thanked him for his help and shoved myself into the passenger seat, refusing to acknowledge the fact I'd just positioned myself on the remnants of my brother's journey snack, and we drove off into the sunset.

Well, we drove towards an ominous grey cloud, with my brother snickering like a schoolboy, but I'm trying to romanticise this as best I can.

CHAPTER FOUR

Criminal Behaviour

Waking up to the smell of damp and what I could only assume to be something in the region of dead mouse was not the most pleasant way to start the week. Monday morning had finally rolled around, I had been living in my parent's 'studio' garage for nearly 48 hours and I was scanning the room for a practical-looking cord with which to hang myself.

It appeared my sister Laura had also withdrawn from the outside world and had secretly been boarded in her comfy childhood room for the past six months. That made for two twenty-something kids failing at life within the same year. Now there's a sign of good parenting.

When my dad had initially described my bedroom as "no longer available to visitors" I'd imagined the customary gym or office. I'd also assumed he might feel at least mildly guilty about finally revealing Laura as the favourite child. But the first thing he did when I arrived was take me on a tour of his new 'jungle room'.

Again, it seems unfair I've been blessed with both a ridiculous brother and a slightly deranged father. It's cruel and unusual punishment that I should have to cling to my mother as the most normal thing in the family, bar a sister who is so normal just five minutes in her company induces a protective coma.

Dad's jungle room was one of the saddest things I've ever seen. On first impression it looked like a Homebase storage pen, but on closer inspection it was more like the bastard lovechild of a Natural History Museum exhibit and the soft toy section at Clinton Cards. Not only was every plant labelled and accompanied by a fact card, but koalas, monkeys, lemurs and various cuddly lizards were scattered haphazardly about the display with no respect for either scale (one lizard was bigger than a gibbon) or, in fact, geography. As I cast a disparaging eye over the mess I half expected to find a penguin cowering beneath the Areca Palm (or Chrysalidocarpus lutescens, according to my father's carefully laminated notes).

My spot in the garage was a welcome retreat, since nobody ever came out there. This is partly due to the fact that, although my family were very concerned for at least an hour, not one of them really wanted to hear me "whinge" about Ben. It could also be because you have to climb over a mountain of laundry to gain access to this particular penthouse suite. That suited me just fine, and thanks to my own "exterior access door", as my father termed it, I could come and go as I pleased without coming into contact with my lunatic family. It just so happened that door was also an 'original feature' (the sliding door that opens to let the car in). To avoid holding some kind of open day for the entire neighbourhood every time I left the house, I tended to lift the door half a foot off the ground and slip underneath it. A feat that may have proved less like a nursing home limbo had I bothered to stick to just one of my New Year's resolutions.

When I complained about the situation to my father he turned and walked straight back out of the room. Eventually he returned with a pencil sketch of an elaborate pulley system and said he might be able to fashion some kind of remote. As usual, he had entirely missed the point, so it was my turn to exit the arena – with no intention of a comeback.

After waiting outside the bathroom for half an hour while my mother hopefully worked her way through every product in the No 7 Protect & Perfect range, I showered and made my way back to the kitchen for breakfast. "Happy Valentine's Day!" she screamed, as she shoved my father in the ribs, and he, in turn, shoved a supermarket bunch of flowers in my general direction.

How the hell had I overlooked something like this? Even the cat was looking at me pitifully. I braced myself for a homemade card with one of my dad's unintelligible rhymes in it, but thankfully this seemed to be the end of the celebration for now. I smiled and put the flowers in the sink, while my mum got to work with the stems and eventually shoved them in an old pickle jar.

Luckily I'd booked the day off to unpack my

belongings into their musty new home, so I could at least avoid experiencing V Day in public. For once I was grateful my parents' social life far exceeded mine and I began to meticulously plan my day of pyjamas and tea while they were out gallivanting at a local National Trust gathering. I flicked through the TV guide (I'm fairly sure my family alone are keeping the Radio Times in business) and began to plan my day. This Morning, Location, Location, Location, Friends rerun, Friends rerun, Friends rerun...

Just then my sister Laura – 5'6", mousey blonde hair, grey eyes, likes staring into space, dislikes humour unrelated to Mr Bean – walked quietly into the kitchen. Damn. "Haven't you got a job to go to?" I asked, annoyed. "Haven't you got a boyfriend to take you out?" she replied, an impressive feat of wit coming from her. I went back to my reading and drinking tea out of the 'mega-mug', which my father got free from a sports website and was approximately the size of my head.

The two of us continued in silence for a good quarter of an hour until Laura sighed and said, "Look, if we're both in tonight, we might as well hang out together." "No date either?" I enquired. "Wayne is working late," she countered hotly.

Wayne – 5'8", ginger hair, green eyes, likes goldfish, dislikes "snazzy flavoured crisps" – is one of the funniest people I've ever met. The problem is, it's entirely unintentional. He works as a clerk at the local council (to this day I have no idea what that actually means) and has never left England. Not the UK, he's never left *England*. He, like my sister and I, still lives with his mother, only we can thoroughly detach our loserish situation from his because he never left in the first place. He will eat no meat other than chicken or beef, he's allergic to just about everything, he can barely walk down the street without a hit on his inhaler and, oh yeah, did I mention he was ginger? If anything, over the years I think he's caused my sister to become more dull. They never stray from the two local pubs, have fish and chips every Thursday, Indian on a Saturday and are relentlessly trying to gather the families together for a wholesome Sunday lunch. They've been dating for nearly three years and this has never once happened. It may have something to do with my maniac father. I'm continually encouraging Wayne to propose to my sister just to inject some permanent Tweedledumb and Tweedledumber comedy into our lives.

With no excuse ready I agreed to see V Day in with my sister in front of the TV, but gave strict instructions as to what we would not be watching. Unfortunately it hadn't even occurred to me that she was about to attack from an altogether different angle. She made me bake Valentine's treats.

Now, either Laura is even more clueless than I thought or the bitch is good. She smiled so sweetly as she pulled out the heart-shaped cookie cutters and got to work on the pink icing with red sprinkles. The majority of my mixture went straight from bowl to belly as I watched this strange species, wondering exactly what the hell she was trying to pull. Are you kidding me? I'm on the verge of personal meltdown and you want me to make heart-shaped love cookies?

There is nothing more depressing than baking on

Valentine's Day. Especially if you're single. It's only a matter of time before you get tired and emotional and gorge on three days' worth of calories in one sitting, leaving yourself even less attractive to the opposite sex than you started out. What the hell kind of plan was this for a chemically imbalanced singleton on the most depressing day of the year? Even people in relationships hate Valentine's Day. Either you sit and stare at your partner for two hours over dinner, realising at long last you have absolutely nothing to say to each other, or you're cooped up at home trying to look impressed with the tulip he's clearly picked out of someone's garden. Either way, it would likely be an anti-climax compared to the lies they told in movies. Not once had anyone led me to a secret garden adorned with fairy lights for a romantic picnic, not once had a guy chased me to a train station and declared his undying love for me, and not once had I had a Valentine's Day that was anything more than 'quite nice'.

I remembered two years ago when Selina texted us all with a photo of the roses her boyfriend sent her at work. I tried not to look disappointed with my comedy card and 'love token'. Another year a friend was taken to Claridge's for dinner. I was instructed to choose from the set menu at the local pub. Single or coupled, Valentine's Day was a cruel test sent to fuck with relationships on an annual basis.

This year, it was purely fucking with me. Once we'd tucked into our baked goods and Laura had gone to bed – since it was approaching 9.30pm – I headed to the spirit cabinet in an attempt to salvage the evening.

That was another good thing about my parents' advanced social schedule – they were always well stocked in the liquor department. I grabbed some bottles and headed to the fridge in search of mixers, and soon enough I'd lined up a selection of questionable-looking cocktails on the countertop.

After downing the first two in front of 'The Top 100 Love Songs Of All Time', I decided I needed a change of scenery and some proper music. Five minutes later I was enjoying my favourite '90s tape, Ragga Heat Reggae Beat, while having sex on the beach in the middle of the jungle room. It seemed like the nearest I was going to get to a holiday this year, so I settled in to design a few more cocktails and get my groove on with my new Loverman, Shabba Ranks.

I awoke bleary-eyed to blistering heat and the sound of tropical mating calls. Plants towered over me and monkeys swung from the trees. Whack. Said monkey hitting me in the face roused me from my relaxing reverie and focused my pupils on the figure standing over me, laughing. Sometime during the night my beloved father had changed the tape, turned up the heating (with surprisingly little thought for his precious plantlife) and decided to mess with me. I picked up the stuffed monkey from the floor, threw it back at what turned out to be his shin and attempted to stand up without knocking over any more glasses. "See, I knew you'd love the jungle room," he said, about as pleased with himself as I'd seen him since he figured out how to use Sky+.

I looked at my watch. 7am. Since it was now going to take me a painful hour-and-a-half to make it to work,

61

I figured I'd better make a start on sorting myself out. Two paracetamol, two asprin and two ibuprofen later – I'd recently read that you could take all three together, then almost immediately been corrected, but this last exchange had slipped my mind in my hungover state – I was dressed and ready to leave for another fun day in the office. I decided while I looked for flats it wouldn't hurt to peruse the job market at the same time. I'd been Account Assistant for nearly two years, and it was about time I stopped assisting and started doing already.

I spent lunchtime, and most of the rest of the day, surfing the internet for career inspiration. Did I even want to stay in marketing, or had I missed my calling elsewhere? I thought back to our career counsellor Mrs Butch (yes, that was her actual name, and yes, she was). Her first question had always been, "What are your favourite subjects?" Right now, mine were moping, The Vampire Diaries and alcohol, but I remembered a time when I also had an interest in shopping and comedy pictures of cats.

Just then, the head of brand development, Mark – 6'1", brown hair, brown eyes, likes inappropriate flirting, dislikes cheap suits – peered over my shoulder and raised an eyebrow. I clicked my mouse button until everything on my screen had minimised and we were both peering at my desktop picture of a sausage dog in a crash helmet, but it was clearly too late. "Follow me, Miss Lansdale," he said as he disappeared into a meeting room. Shit, shit, shit. Not only had I not discovered a new job, but I was about to lose my existing one. I really needed to get my shit together.

"Nice dress," he commented casually as he sat down at the head of a meeting table and I shuffled into the seat at the opposite end. "I won't bite." I scooched over a few more seats, not quite sure what was an appropriate distance for a major bollocking. "Look, it's no secret this company is struggling and anyone worth their salt is looking elsewhere at the moment." "Oh no, I was looking for a friend who's just moved to the city," I rambled. "She's only got one leg, so she can't get to a computer to search herself..." Thankfully he cut me off before I added some kind of degenerative disease to her ailments.

"Can you keep a secret?" he asked. I nodded my head, while the doubt in my eyebrows screamed no. "A few of us are branching out and starting our own company and we want you in." I looked at him, gobsmacked. "Everyone was pretty impressed with your work. Prior to last month, that is." I sat very still, looking at him through narrowed eyes. Was I about to become his secretary or were they looking for a particularly unenthusiastic post girl? Had people really noticed such a difference in me since New Year?

"We're meeting tomorrow night to finalise details. Come along and you can let me know your thoughts on Thursday. I think the bosses are getting suspicious, so we're going to need to move faster than we thought." I nodded my head enthusiastically. Finally something exciting was happening. After two years of trying to stick it to the man by stealing biros and plastic spoons, I needed a better outlet for my boredom and misplaced rage. If there was an office coup, I wanted in.

I walked to the train station with a spring in my

step, despite my late-onset hangover. It was a sneaky one that had appeared around 4pm, but I was trying to fight it off with good vibes, since the positive thinking towards my career this morning had reaped such impressive results.

I crawled under the garage door and headed straight for my clothes rail. Regardless of the fact it was in a pub, this was a meeting that could potentially change my life and I needed to A) wear something awesome, and B) not get drunk. As I perused my crumpled offerings and reached for a warm beer out of my sock drawer, neither of these were looking likely. I needed an outfit casual enough that the others (whoever they were) wouldn't know I'd made a special effort, while smart enough to show I was professional – and tight enough to impress Mark, who I'd decided was super-hot. Sure, his hair was shinier than mine, his teeth brighter than snow and his skin unusually even-toned, but in addition to his questionable metrosexuality, he was also incredibly cocky, which out of nowhere I was finding pretty damn attractive. I'd had two non-committal texts from Stuart since our 'date' and family meet-and-greet, neither of which had suggested us meeting up again, ever, so I needed to move on to a new target.

Wednesday went incredibly slowly, but it was livened up by the occasional conspiratorial wink from Mark and my mission to uncover the other traitors in the camp. There was Wendy, the PA to the boss. Out of everyone here she had the most depressing job, waiting on Mr. Phelps hand and foot. I actually saw her bent under his desk the other day cleaning a mark off his shoe while he was still wearing it. I was glad that's all she was doing, but I wasn't convinced it was much less offensive than my original assumption. Somehow she always demeaned herself with a smile on her face, though. Either she was an amazing actress or her childhood had a hell of a lot to answer for.

Then there was Sandra, the receptionist. Sandra was in her early 40s, with bright blonde hair that never moved. She wore only black and purple, but within her collection there was everything from sequined boob tubes to faux fur skirts. If there was anything going on in the building, she knew about it – from affairs to job interviews to whose kids had lice. She would certainly be aware of the oncoming revolution, but I couldn't decide if she'd be willing to risk her prime position next to the Coke machine by flying the roost.

Elsewhere there were John, Mike, Lee, Dev, Rod and Elliott, none of whom I'd taken much notice of over the past few years. They were neither hot nor important, so their existence slipped by the wayside into a regular exchange of nods and kitchen grumbles. My work buddy, Kiran – 5'6", jet-black bob, chocolate-brown eyes, likes singing the wrong lyrics to songs, dislikes clothes that require ironing – had been training in the Manchester offices since November, so I didn't have my usual partner in crime to help in the investigation. By this point we would have called at least three emergency toilet meetings and fashioned some kind of spying device and strategic line of questioning. All of which would have been discussed openly over the completely unsecure work email.

Since I'd been wrapped up in my own drama I'd

65

only really communicated via a few self-pitying texts and a drunken sad-face photo, while she attempted to encourage me north of Watford to express my grief in the new Vodka Revolution that had opened up there. I initially told her I would rather do an aerobics class in the nude in front of my entire junior school (something I'd recently experienced in a dream and was not keen to revisit), but since then her offer had begun to look more appealing. At least it would get me out of my garage sanctuary for a few nights.

I decided to drop her an email to see what she knew. "Guess where I am?" she shot back, clearly equally inundated with work. "The sexual health clinic?" I ventured sarcastically. "Scarily close!" she replied. It turned out she was back in London and currently waiting for her pap smear. The conversation descended into the finer points of smear test etiquette, after Kiran asked whether merely trimming was appropriate before said assault or whether she should have waxed, plucked and tidied the surrounding area ready for its close-up. Needless to say this was the moment Mark chose to stroll past and look over my shoulder again, facing a screenful of bush, chuff and pube jokes. He raised an eyebrow. "It's this kind of attention to detail that makes me look forward to having you ladies on board," he smirked into my ear, his warm breath blasting my neck and sending a shiver down my spine.

Do not get a crush on your potential new boss. Do not get a crush on your potential new boss. I silently repeated my new mantra for the next ten minutes until my phone rang and I was cajoled into actually doing some work. By the time 5.30pm came around I was desperate for a drink, having impressed myself with two solid hours of work and only three Facebook breaks. I grabbed my bag and headed to the toilets to fix myself up, then strutted towards the pub, which turned out to be a painfully trendy wine bar.

When I arrived, there were seven other people, few of whom I could recall seeing before. "Hey!" said Mark, getting up and moving along a seat for me. I sat down and was introduced to a potential new group of colleagues whose names I immediately forgot. Three were from another company, two were old uni friends of his and then there was me, Peter from accounts and Jody from my department (who is actually a boy – more on that later).

Champagne flowed, followed by tequila. At some point Kiran arrived, but I barely noticed since I was struggling to see straight. "You have access to all the databases, right?" asked Male Jody. I nodded, or allowed my head to loll then bob back up. "Great. Your mission, if you choose to accept it, is to get all the company's contacts loaded onto this C3PO memory stick by 3pm tomorrow. Do you think you can do that?" My head lulled again and before I knew it I appeared to be involved in some kind of Power Ranger high five.

Kiran shuffled round to sit next to me. "Oh my god. He so wants to touch you in a sex way!" she slurred into my ear a little too loudly. "What?" "Go for it. He's hot. He's available. He just bought two more bottles of champagne, so he's clearly loaded. What's not to like?" Kiran was right. What wasn't to like? Male

67

Jody was pretty sexy, in a scruffy, stubbly way, and he was showing me a lot of attention, which was pretty much all I needed to form a mild obsession these days.

Painfully aware that my first attempt to get back on my back had been a catastrophic failure, I criss-crossed the bar toward the toilets, Kiran in tow, and between us we did our best to turn me into the picture of drunken seduction. This involved her assaulting my facial features with some shockingly bright colours and me trying to restyle my hair under the hand-dryer. It wasn't a vast improvement, but it gave me the confidence to walk back out of the toilets and plonk myself down next to Male Jody, who immediately deemed it in his best interest to furnish me with further champagne.

As the bubbles fizzed pleasantly on my tongue, I was sure things were fizzling pretty nicely with Male Jody too. He'd turned around to give me his full attention, and even as everyone else dropped off one by one to go home, he didn't take his eyes off me. When Mark got up to leave it was just me, Drunk Kiran, Male Jody and two guys, whose names I still couldn't remember, left at the table. "Don't forget to keep this quiet until Friday guys," reminded Mark as he high-fived everyone who still had control over their hand-eye coordination. Not me. He patted me on the back like I was his grandmother.

What happened between then and Male Jody and I ending up alone in a separate pub is a touch on the hazy side. As we sat at a table, shouting over the loud music and daring each other to down shots of whiskey – me being under the assumption that I was now a pro – I wondered when it would be appropriate to make a move. Was this just intense work-flirting or could it lead to legitimate inter-colleague action?

"One more for the road?" asked Male Jody as he stood up and headed to the bar, returning with two cocktails. Had it been deemed home time already? I looked at my watch and realised I was five minutes away from missing my last train. Oh well, too late. He didn't seem too concerned so I assumed he had a place nearby. As I sipped my drink and nodded along to whatever he was saying, I imagined what his stylish bachelor pad would look like. After all, I was hardly going to invite him to my garage love shack in the Buzzard.

How would my parents react to a gentleman caller, I wondered? As long as he showed a vague interest in whatever crap my dad was spouting I'm sure he'd go down fine with him, and he was well-dressed and successful enough to impress even the most difficult of mothers. I cocked my head and looked at Male Jody again, this time trying to slot him into the category of potential boyfriend, rather than random work liaison.

He was tall, good-looking, attentive... Except for at this particular moment, when he was typing furiously on his phone – at least I knew he was well-coordinated. I, on the other hand, had nearly missed the table and placed my drink on the floor at least three times. "Great!" he said, and I snapped out of my unsteady reverie. "Do you fancy going on somewhere?" Yes, your flat, I thought as I tossed my hair seductively and nearly fell off my seat. "My girlfriend's just finished up with her friends and she's going to head this way." Your *what*? I nearly screamed over the music. "She's

69

hilarious – you two would really hit it off."

What? My brain was taking longer than usual to react to this sexual slap in the face. I continued to look at him in the same confused way I'd looked at my French teacher throughout our oral exam at school. Girlfriend? How the hell had I got this so wrong? And how the hell was I going to sleep anywhere other than a street corner this evening? I flipped back to game face as quickly as possible – looking back, there may have been somewhere around a ten-minute lapse – and made a clumsy yawning gesture, hitting a barman in the crotch as I did so. "I'm go home," I said decisively. "You two have sex on your own."

I got up to leave with some indication that my salutation had been less than above board, and patted Male Jody on the head as I walked by. When I reached the pavement I splashed into a huge puddle. Great. I was single, homeless (for the evening, at least) and caught in some kind of torrential rainstorm. There was only one thing for it. Someone else needed to sort me out. Without thinking, I dialed Check-List Charlie. She always knew what to do.

"Hello?" she rasped into the phone. "Hi!" I squealed. "What you doing?" "It's nearly one in the morning. I'm sleeping. What the hell are you doing?" Ten minutes into recounting the miniscule details of my disastrous night of no sex, Charlie interrupted me. "Can we talk about this tomorrow?" "Oh, well, that's if I'm still alive!" I said with the kind of dramatic intensity that deserved an award. "I missed my last train back to my parents' house, and now I have to sleep in the street," I added matter-of-factly. "Why don't you just

70

get a night bus?" she asked with a sigh. "Hold on."

After a few minutes of clicking on a keyboard and a barely audible grumble from Tom, her husband – "Hi, Tom!" I screamed into the handset. "It's the middle of the night, sort yourself out!" he yelled back – Charlie came back on the line with an action plan for me. "What road are you on?" I told her the name of the bar I'd just walked out of. "Stay still," she ordered. I took refuge in a doorway, even though I was already soaked through. "OK, turn left," she said patiently. I walked along the road, following her directions to bus stop E. "Wait for the number 317, which should be there in four minutes," she said. "It stops at the end of your parents' road." "How the hell..." I began, but Charlie cut me off with a firm, "Goodnight, Jess," and I was alone in the night once more.

At 3.17am I shuffled off the bus and meandered down the road to my parents' house. It turned out there was nothing more depressing than ending an embarrassing evening with a walk of shame into your family garage. I heaved the door up as far as I could, but it didn't budge far. I pulled again. It reluctantly gave an inch, and then another, making an ungodly screeching sound as it did so. "Shhhhh!" I hissed, shooting it a warning glance as I attempted to fold myself underneath. I still couldn't fit, so I tried sitting on the ground and pushing at it with my feet, muttering to myself like a madwoman. The light went on across the road. I froze. I saw the front door open, so I gave one last push and managed to roll underneath and slam the door shut behind me. Phew. I could do without explaining to the Wilkinsons why I was breaking into my own bedroom at nearly 3.30am on a weekday morning.

I took my shoes off and got into bed. I needed to salvage whatever sleep I could, so I could be as nonchalant as possible in front of Male Jody at work tomorrow. I was determined I was going to be a better person once we left for the new firm – which I didn't remember learning much about this evening – and I wasn't going to let another work crush get in the way. Anyway, Mark had been the initial target, and I hadn't yet racked up a complete sex fail on that one. All I needed now was blessed sleep...

What seemed like two seconds after closing my eyes, I awoke to a siren that made my whole body throb. Smoke alarm? Burglar alarm? That annoying noise when you leave the phone off the hook? I opened my eyes to see my room bathed in red light. Was this a dream? It seemed to be invading through the cracks in the garage door. My groggy head assured me I was in the throws of a champagne stupor and should probably try to go to sleep, even if I was in a dream... But, wait. Did going to sleep in a dream make you wake up in real life? Or did waking up in a dream make you wake up in real life? Or did it not make a blind bit of difference? Either way, going to sleep in my dream seemed a better option than sitting around waiting for whatever was about to happen. I closed my eyes again and tried to drift back off.

Then the voice of God spoke to me. "Jessica," it whispered. "Could you slowly and carefully make your way toward the kitchen door." What? I squinted into the beam of light that was flashing around my bedroom. Was this a joke? Were my parents punishing me for getting home late? I sat up slowly and tried to focus on the face at the door. My brain flickered into action: stranger danger. There was a stranger in the house and they were trying to kidnap me, albeit very calmly and politely. I opened my mouth to let out my best movie scream, but the kidnapper was gesturing desperately at their badge. "Jess, it's fine," said my mum's voice from behind him. I looked again at the police badge. Shit. Was I getting arrested?

As I scrambled around for my shoes I wracked my brain for memories of any illegal behaviour. Who had paid at the last bar? I'd left without giving the specifics much thought as soon as I found out Male Jody wasn't giving my specifics much thought. The policeman hissed, "Quickly," at me and I hurried into the kitchen to find my mum and sister waiting. No great surprise Laura was eager to catch a glimpse of my law-breaking shame.

The policeman reached out a hand and I thrust both of mine in front of me, ready for my cuffs. I'd seen the movies. It was better to go quietly. But, instead, he shoved me in the direction of the side door and the rest of my family followed. Suddenly I wondered whether going quietly was the best plan. Maybe I should Thelma & Louise it and run for the hills? I took a deep breath, ready to bolt, but there were two more policemen waiting outside. They ushered us quickly to a police van at the front of our house, where quite a crowd of people had gathered. Mr. Wilkinson was there – of course, elected head of the nosy neighbours.

73

"I can't believe they think he's in our house," hissed my mother to my father. "Who?" I asked. Did they think Male Jody was here too? Had he left a long line of unpaid bar bills throughout the city? "They think that man who did over Mrs. Redman's last week is in our house!" squawked my mother, somewhere between terror and joy over what an exciting story this was going to make at her next coffee morning. "I saw him break in!" said Mr. Wilkinson proudly. "He was trying to get in through the garage, but he was too big to fit under the door…"

As it dawned on me what had happened I was caught in a quandary between outrage that Mr. Wilkinson thought I was "too big" to fit under the door, and mortification that I had been caught trying to break into my own home. Either way I had sparked a neighbourhood-wide crimewatch and I couldn't see that trying to joke or flirt my way out of this was going to work. Either I was a criminal and in trouble with the police for wasting their time, and with my parents for being a mess, or I could just stand back, wait until they'd declared our house a safe zone and go the hell back to bed.

"Oh my god, we could have been killed!" I said to anyone who would listen. If I was going to play the role of potential victim I was going to give it my drama-GCSE best. By now most of the street had tiptoed outside to see what all the fuss was about. Nobody seemed scared, just excited that something was actually happening. That this was the only nightlife in the area reminded me just how desperately I needed to get back to civilization. Or somewhere with taxis and late-night bars, for a start.

Eventually our house was declared burglar-free and the neighbours were sent on their way under the instruction to lock all doors and windows carefully and ring the police if they saw anything suspicious – something I imagined would then happen at least half-hourly until daylight.

Needless to say I fell straight back to sleep, all too aware that the only danger to me was myself. My father, on the other hand, set up a computer in the lounge and another in my parents' room so he and my mother could Skype each other while they surveyed the local area from both a south-westerly and north-easterly perspective. My father was armed with a torch and what looked like a garlic press as he cowered behind the lounge curtain, keeping careful watch over his neighbours. Quite the hero.

CHAPTER FIVE

Back In Business

By the time my alarm went off I felt like I'd been asleep for a luxurious five minutes. My head was throbbing and I could still taste alcohol, but thankfully my run-in with the law had overshadowed my embarrassment earlier in the night. I stood motionless in the shower for what seemed like an hour, threw on what turned out to be my mum's shirt and headed off once more on my glamorous commute.

Today I just had to concentrate on keeping the new company a secret, which wasn't too much of a problem since I still didn't really know anything about it. In fact, all I knew was who was going – although I couldn't remember most of their names – and that we were going next week. Where were the offices? Who cared! How much would it pay? Not a clue. Somehow nothing seemed to matter other than getting the hell out of where I was and strutting in the direction of my successful new career.

As I gazed out of the window at the world rushing by I decided to give myself a six-month deadline. I needed a new job – done (with months to spare) – a new flat and a new man. My aborted attempts at the second two didn't bode well, but with a bit more effort I was confident I could pull myself back up to second place behind Check-List Charlie. This was just a glitch, and all I needed was a masterplan.

By lunchtime my motivation had slumped. I'd chosen a duff soup from the sandwich man and was trying to eke out my banana and Diet Coke into a satisfying meal. Lisa had texted to ask how the flat-hunt was going (although steered well clear of offering any further help), so I decided to bite the bullet and check out the freaks and geeks looking to add to their clans in the city.

By the end of lunch – or, as it turned out, around 3.30pm (flat-hunting was surprisingly time-consuming) – I was wondering why no-one had thought to provide a translation service for accommodation ads. It was impossible to decipher much from phrases like "virtual en-suite" and "classic brick style", and while some hopefuls sold themselves on their social skills – "two fun, friendly females looking for a like-minded woman in her 20s" – others merely threw in something like "very clean", which immediately brought me back to visions of asocial men in rubber gloves. It was like negotiating a dating website – the skill was in second-guessing what these people were hiding, or the minute your back was turned they'd be trying on your underwear while they watched you sleep.

77

I decided to make a few appointments for the weekend, so I could find out exactly how debased these weirdos were. My approach was slapdash. Since I no longer needed to be south of the river for Ben's work, and I had no idea where my new office would be, London was pretty much my oyster. That is, the parts of London that were within my budget: a number of run-down neighbourhoods with questionable access to public transport were my cracked, slightly soiled oyster. A further hour of clicking through listings failed to dig up any pearls. I took a deep breath and texted Lisa. I was in need of a familiar face (that didn't remind me of a serial killer). And a glass of wine.

It turned out Lisa had agreed to go to the launch of some new workout DVD because the current beefcake she was dating worked in sports PR. After she guaranteed I would not have to cross the threshold from the unhealthy to the healthy and actually enter a gym, I decided that a night of what Lisa assured me would be free drinks was just what I needed to regain the momentum for my property search.

Living with my parents hadn't been quite the disaster I'd anticipated so far, but I sensed that if I mooched around their studio garage much longer I was going to lose all connection with the real world. I had visions of finally giving up on my masterplan and instead focusing my half-hearted attentions on seducing my sister's useless sack of a boyfriend – just to tick ginger off my list.

I wasn't really dressed for a night out – in fact, I wasn't really dressed for any kind of public consumption – but my workmates had seen it all before so I'd made it through the day with my head held as high as I could be bothered to hold it (which was fairly low every time I passed Male Jody's desk). I dragged myself in the direction of the shops in search of a miracle, and settled on an oversized white shirt with gold buttons, changed into it, and stuffed my mother's static monstrosity into my bag as I made my way up Neal Street towards the bar.

There was a huge queue at the entrance so I joined at the back, eyeing up the long line of lovelies flashing their fake-tanned legs and flicking their bleached-blonde hair. I smoothed my hand down my own fluffy mane, wondering what ever happened to my portable straighteners, and whether they'd make much of an impact on my constantly expanding haystack anyway. I reminded myself that now I was single, bad hair days would need to be things of the past. Who knew when I'd meet Mr. Right? I couldn't risk losing him because I looked like Sideshow Bob.

The queue was moving about as fast as my father in a hardware store, so I dialled Lisa to see where she was. As expected, she was already in hobnobbing mode inside. She sauntered into the street in a backless black dress and a pair of four-inch heels, grabbed me, paraded past the wannabes and, with one dazzling smile at the bouncers, whisked me inside and up to the safety of the VIP area.

I always felt like I'd stepped onto a film set when I went to an event with Lisa. It was like every good-looking person in London had received a memo and gathered in a tiny room to gaze at each other and congratulate themselves on their impressive genes. I readjusted my shirt – which was a touch more see-through than I'd noticed in the shop – and followed Lisa up to the bar.

"You look like you need a drink," she said as she requested a bottle of champagne. I felt like I needed an injection of vodka straight to the vein, but I grabbed the sparkly glass thankfully and proceeded to down it in three manly gulps. "Nice," she commented, automatically refilling me. We turned back to the room, Lisa waving every five seconds at a parade of hot men. I smiled at the waiter and he gave me a crisp nod in response. I knew better than to try and attract any male attention within a five-metre radius of Lisa. She grabbed my hand and led me to a table in the far corner, a waiter sweeping up our bottle and following us diligently. Although he was dressed in the standard black trousers and white shirt, he might as well have been wearing his boxers and a bow-tie for the salacious looks he was receiving from just about every over-forty-pretending-to-be-twenty woman in the room.

"Where's Saa... Siii..," "Steve," snapped Lisa, outraged that I didn't have her new man's name tattooed on my brain, what with them dating for a whole week-and-a-half. "He's over with the talent." I peered a few metres away to a table inhabited by big, beefy men in tight T-shirts and even tighter jeans. "They're from the workout DVD?" I asked. "It's a strip-club workout," she said matter-of-factly as the man she'd pointed out as Steve swooped in to whisper into a fellow beefcake's ear. He rested his hand on his knee as he did so, but Lisa didn't seem to notice. I was about to drop the h-bomb, when she asked how my

80

flat-hunt was going. Touché. How could I comment on her situation when I was still living at my parents'? I'd swap that for a gay boyfriend any day.

I admitted I technically hadn't looked inside any since January, but assured Lisa that I was carefully researching the market on a daily basis. She rolled her eyes. A woman tottered over to our table purring, "Dahhhhhhhhling," into Lisa's ear in a way I thought had gone out of fashion in the '90s. She turned to look me up and down, then slapped the smile back on her face and zoomed in for an air kiss. I went for a second and was left hanging, but she'd already moved on, having managed to introduce herself, ask my name and turn away before I could open my mouth, all within the time it took our waiter to force the cork out of our second bottle.

The wall behind us was floor-to-ceiling glass overlooking the main party downstairs. Topless men walked around on stilts with a giant vodka bottle on a tray, stopping occasionally to point a tiny hose at anyone with a casual attitude to alcoholism, or in fact, hygiene. I looked back at Lisa twitching in her seat. "Do you need to 'work the room'?" I teased. "Piss off." But within five minutes she'd made a beeline for the CEO of the PR firm, and I was left holding her bag like the sickly friend at a theme park. I lifted my glass in the direction of the waiter, struggling to keep it still while he poured a top-up. As my eyes met his crotch long before his face (purely due to my sitting position) it took me a good few seconds to notice it was a different guy. This one was equally handsome, but with short blond hair and what looked like the end of a tattoo peeking out of his collar. I gazed at him from my seat for what may have been an inappropriate amount of time before I realised he'd stopped pouring. But, as I went to take a sip of my wine in a coquettish fashion, I noticed his hand was still over mine. Had he placed it there to steady my drunken wavering? Probably. Had he snatched it away the second his job was done? No...

"Where's your friend?" he asked coolly. Still not removing his hand from my now sweating counterpart. OK, so he was only enquiring after the hot friend. "Oh, she's just over there," I said, pointing haphazardly. "Don't worry," I added with a grumble. His full lips broke into a smile and he squatted down like an adult to an upset child. "I only ask because I'm allowed to stay with you if you're on your own. Company policy. No guest left behind, or something like that..." He cocked his head to the side, as though willing me to say something clever and flirtatious in response. "I'm not on my own, I just don't know anyone." I blurted out. What a loser. That didn't even make sense. I wanted him to know that it wasn't like nobody wanted to talk to me, it was just that nobody knew I was there. More like nobody had noticed me. Except for Hot Waiter Number Two...

He folded himself casually into Lisa's chair and swept his tray onto the table. I looked over at the bar, wondering if he was going to get in trouble. "I told you," he said smiling. "Company policy." "So you're paid to keep people company?" I snarked. "There's a name for that." The minute it left my mouth I knew my attempt at a bold, sexy challenge had misfired. I just sounded like a bitch. No wonder hot men never spoke

82

to me. "I get the picture," he said, hands in the air in a familiar pose of surrender. Before I could decide how to switch tactics, he was up and gone, along with my chance of another refill. Great. No champagne, no sex. That's some smooth flirting, right there.

I went back to watching the fun downstairs. And it did look fun. I wanted to leave the VIP cage and embrace the land where people wore real smiles and half-price shoes. Where they waved their hands in the air like they just didn't care... I nodded along to the only Word Up lyrics I knew and looked around for Lisa. She was still deep in conversation with the CEO – a man whose plastic surgery was masquerading as 45 and whose tight suit claimed to be bulging with muscle, rather than relocated cheek fat. His top button was undone to the point of indecency, wiry grey chest hair threatening to reach out and fondle his swarm of beauties with his next obnoxious guffaw. Lisa turned to me and mimed a gag. I got up and stomped towards her, my black trainers revealed in all their unladylike glory under the weird fluorescent lighting. She rushed over. "You're not leaving, are you? I still haven't introduced you to Steve!" I held up my empty glass. "Where's the guy?" she asked, grabbing for the nearest bottle to replenish my mood. "Come on – meet Steve then we'll head downstairs and dance."

Up close, Steve looked even more like the beefcake strippers than he had from across the room. In typical rugby player fashion, his neck was as thick as his head and every muscle in his body looked about ready to burst. In fairness, he was acting the perfect gent, moving round to make room for us both, even though it meant him being squashed up to the perma-tanned hunk next to him... He asked lots of questions and actually listened to the answers, which seemed a rare talent in this room. Elsewhere all I could see for miles were women wearing the kind of expression you saw on a three-year-old pageant queen, their smiles eerily vacant and their gestures forcefully relaxed, as their eyes darted around the room in search of someone more attractive and/or successful than the person they were currently schmoozing.

An hour later we were still at the talent table, getting increasingly talented at downing cocktails as the guys exchanged stories about being 'on tour' and their first stripping jobs. William, who will henceforth be referred to as Beefcake Bill, had studied to be a doctor before having a change of heart in his final year when he watched some dodgy Canadian B-movie about a group of strippers bonding. Finally Beefcake Bill admitted to his parents that he was both gay and, in fact, built for an altogether different kind of service industry. The others had similar stories. It seemed none of them had been encouraged to pursue their naked ambition by their careers counsellor – instead one had been a mechanic, another a hairdresser and one used to write slogans for nappies, which all sounded hilarious after one or two (or seven) drinks.

As I tossed my head back shampoo ad-style following another of Mike's increasingly X-rated slogans about getting wet, a waiter's arm brushed past me as it collected the empties from the table. "Sorry," he muttered as I looked around nonchalantly. It was him. Hot Waiter Number Two. "About before..." I started with what I hoped was a dazzling smile. "Don't worry," he said, his face a mask of indifference. "I get it," this time raising his eyebrows in the direction of my chunk of hunks on the opposite side of the table. Did he think I wasn't interested because he wasn't a beefcake? Did he think I was one of those girls that threw myself at celebrities and random DVD strippers?

Before I could convince myself that I didn't care what Hot Waiter Number Two thought, he'd disappeared back through the crowd and Lisa grabbed my arm with a questioning look. "What was that?" she asked looking way too excited. "Nothing, just crossed wires." I said huffily. "He is soooo into you," squeaked Beefcake Bill, jumping up and sliding into the seat beside me. "Tell me all!"

I recounted my fleeting romance, second-by-painful-second, as Beefcake Bill nodded along, looking as concerned as if I was telling him my New Year trauma. "So, go and talk to him," he shouted, my frizz fluttering in his sickly cocktail breeze. "I think he's made it pretty clear he thinks I'm a dick," I responded, sinking further into my chair and spilling a drop of champagne on my top. "Excuse me!" Bill bellowed towards the bar, raising his arms to get attention. "Spillage!" "It's fine!" I grimaced back at him, but not before my waiter had appeared with a cloth. "She's spilt it down her top," explained Bill, a wicked glint in his eye. "I fear she may be too intoxicated to clean it herself…" I grabbed the cloth out of Hot Waiter Number Two's hand and dabbed manically at my stain. "It's fine," I said, not making eye contact and flinging the cloth back in his direction.

"What the hell was that?" both Bill and I screamed at the same time. "How am I supposed to help you, if you won't help yourself?!" he demanded. "If you were anyone else, I'd give up," he said, dramatically flinging his cocktail umbrella over the side of his big gay drink. Before I could chime in with the facts that A) he barely knew me, so he was welcome to give up, and B) I never asked for help in the first place, he was gripping both of my hands and staring into my eyes. Was this guy part-time hypnotist as well as failed-doctor? I tried to wiggle away, but, like a dog being tamed by the dreaded whisperer, I found myself quite calmly staring back.

"Stop waiting for him to seduce you, and go and get him," he said matter-of-factly. "You're going about this sooooo wrong. You can get anyone you want if you go at it right. I'm going to train you for the next half an hour, then you're going to go and get that man." Cue montage of intense discussion and snippets of advice from Bill and his beefcake friends, Lisa chiming in every few minutes with a cheer or an attempt to undo my top button. Finally, Steve 'jujed' up my hair with his failsafe spray and they declared me ready to "go get some action."

As I twirled in my chair towards the bar, ready to make my approach, Hot Waiter Number Two walked out of the door. I started to reach for my drink in surrender, but Steve had bolted after him, turning to give a thumbs-up to Lisa before he darted out of the club. "Where has he gone?" I demanded. "He's going to trail Hot Waiter Number Two. He'll call once he knows his location." I wasn't entirely sure how they'd jammed this plan into place in the split second it took for me to turn my chair, but I found myself surprisingly OK with the fact that my man mission had already resorted to mild stalking, and within a few minutes we got the call and the signal to meet Steve in a late-night bar around the corner. I looked at my watch anxiously to avoid a repeat of last night's homecoming.

"Don't worry," Lisa mind-read. "If you don't get any action you can just stay with me. Text your mum now and say you're not coming home." It seemed like the perfect crime, so I did as I was told and we headed outside, Lisa pausing to fix me up before we made our beeline for my new potential penetrator. We walked casually into the bar, its music as loud as its floor was sticky, and took a seat in a booth near the toilets. "Why are we by the toilets?" I sulked, wrinkling my nose dramatically. "Because, sooner or later he'll have to walk past," replied Lisa, as though she undertook this kind of covert operation on a daily basis.

"Target located," said Steve, as he wandered over with three green-tinted drinks. I had no idea what they were and I didn't care. "Don't let us down. Just go in with the line we discussed and lock him in," said Lisa seriously. I wasn't convinced my training had thoroughly prepared me for this first mission, but, even without appropriate uniform or, indeed, any memory of tactics, I accepted and moved towards my target. I slinked over to the bar, ready to squeeze casually onto the stool next to Hot Waiter Number Two. He seemed to be drinking alone. I wasn't sure whether that was a bonus or a black mark. He didn't notice my sensual lady walk, but I did get his attention on my third attempt at mounting the stool. At this point I'd given up on a sideways slide and was full-on straddling the fucker in a typically elegant move. As the legs tottered precariously his hand shot out to grab my arm before I toppled off backwards, no doubt destined for the emergency room.

Heeding Lisa's warning about being too easily flustered, I calmly said thank you and launched into my attack. "So," I said, leaning what I hoped was sexily on the bar and twirling my hair around my finger – in reality this involved missing the bar twice with my elbow and practically resting my face on it before getting my finger tangled up in my frizz – "if you're off work now, does that mean you won't sit with me?" I fluttered my eyelashes, pouted my lips and made an attempt at Lisa's wry smile, which seemed to have the men going wild. "Was that a line?" asked Hot Waiter Number Two, looking amused. "Yes," I relented with a sigh, downing the rest of my drink – still green, even under the less ambient bar lights. "Wow, that's almost as bad as mine!" he laughed, locking his brown eyes on me in a way that made me fear for my balance. I relented, and smiled back. Somehow, my flirting seemed to have worked, even if it hadn't featured the Samantha Jones-style dialogue I'd envisioned.

Hot Waiter Number Two, aka Paul – 6'2", blue eyes, blond hair, likes Indiana Jones, dislikes blue icing on cookies – was also aka a lawyer. OK, so he was studying to be a lawyer, but it shifted him from one-night stand to boyfriend-potential within the space of a few seconds. It also turned out he was mildly entertaining, and between that and his super-straight teeth, he was definitely a good option to get me back in the game.

The bell rang for last orders and he glanced at his watch. Damn. He'd better not be about to run out on me, or worse, invite his girlfriend to bond with us. Just then Lisa and Steve came over, all, "Oh, hey, fancy seeing you here," and Steve invited us back to his flat for further drinks. It seemed like a good in-between stage, so we both agreed. It turned out Steve's flat wasn't far from Paul's, so we could all still operate under the pretence that he would be going home to his own bed, alone, at the end of the evening. Which, if our mission was fully accomplished, he would not.

Steve's flat was ridiculous. Firstly, it was huge, or by London standards enormous. It had carpets so white I stopped to take my shoes off before I'd even left the hallway. "Don't worry," he said, with a sweep of his muscle-arm. But I was already on my ass tugging desperately at my trainers as the other three watched thoughtfully. They carried on into the lounge, leaving me to finally relent and undo my laces, before running in after them like their annoying little sister. The lounge had three huge leather sofas and the biggest TV I'd ever seen built into the wall. Elsewhere, everything was super-minimalist, with various white objects opening to reveal snacks, seats and even an ice-cold wine cooler. I thoroughly approved.

The coffee table opened into a sunken fridge, from which Steve produced four beers. The views across the river were impressive, and, had it not been raining, I imagined us enjoying them from his sizeable terrace. It was a far cry from mine and Ben's shabby one-bed in Brixton, or, indeed, my Leighton Buzzard family estate.

I had no idea how a guy working in PR had so much money, and immediately wondered if that was the new direction I should have taken my career in. I remembered for a split second that tomorrow was the day we'd be handing in our notice en masse, and wondered whether this evening had been the best use of my time. I still didn't know where my new office would be, I still didn't know anything about my job, pay, contract or, in fact, the name of the new company. I was just starting to wonder whether I'd really lost it and made the whole thing up, when Paul jolted me back to reality by resting his hand on my knee. Bingo.

I turned around and smiled, trying to ignore the fact Lisa and Steve were staring bug-eyed at us like we were in the zoo. Lisa stretched out her arms in a big, dramatic yawn. "Well, I need my beauty sleep," she said getting up and wandering towards the hallway. I couldn't believe she was kicking us out already. "Yeah – you guys make yourselves comfortable. That sofa pulls out into a futon. Shout if you need anything," Steve added, the perfect host. Completely oblivious to the ass-clenching level of embarrassment his presumption had just caused.

Hot Waiter Number Two noticed my squirm and cracked open two more beers. "Let's just finish these and head off. I wasn't expecting anything…" "Me either!" I barked, as though the idea was ludicrous. We sipped in silence for a few minutes before he pounced, both of us carefully sliding our bottles across the table, so as not to spill on the gleaming carpets, as we attempted a graceful shift into 'recline'.

Now, it may have been a while, and any experience

I'd had over the past few years had very much been 'relationship sex' – right boob, left boob, pants off, let's go... – but there was no denying Paul was one talented guy. I woke up the next morning stiff and sore, but knowing that if the side effects had been printed on Paul's back, I'd still have taken the full dose. I looked at him sleeping peacefully. No snoring, no dribbling – which was more than could be said for me, as I scrubbed furiously at a small patch of slobber on the sofa arm. I cocked my head as I considered whether allowing him to pleasure me once a week was enough, or whether I should book him in more often. Finally I had found sexual success, so the next mission was to repeat it. As soon as possible...

I heard a clink and a "Shit!" from the kitchen, so, gathering up my clothes, I peeked around the corner to find Lisa trying to shovel coffee beans back into a long tube. Her arm shot out to grab mine like a lizard catching a fly, pulled me into the kitchen and slammed the door shut. "So...?" she demanded. I smiled coyly as I gestured to the coffee pot. I pulled Paul's shirt around me, trying to look as nonchalant as possible, but five seconds later we were high-fiving my sexual success.

With Hot Waiter Number Two still fast asleep on the sofa I took a shower in Steve's ridiculously big bathroom – it was about the size of my parents' lounge, with double sinks, a shower big enough for a football team (which I imagined may have been accommodated, or at least a large number of strippers), and the softest towels I'd ever felt in my life. When I finally stepped back into the real world, Lisa offered me the pick of her side of the wardrobe, which was impressively full given they hadn't yet celebrated a fortnight's anniversary. I grabbed a black jumper – daring as ever – and watched, confused, as she pulled on a curve-killing trouser suit. "Steve likes me in a trouser suit," she winked conspiratorially. "He likes the power." As I pondered again how to break it to her that her PR man wasn't interested in what she was selling, I found myself lost for the appropriate words and lacking in solid evidence, so I just sipped my coffee politely and had the conversation in my head.

It was 8.45am, which Lisa and I deemed an appropriate time to wake Sleeping Beauty from his slumber. "Shall I just poke him?" I whispered. Lisa suggested I wake him in an entirely different way, but I'd just brushed my teeth and felt it was borderline sexual assault, given we'd known each other less than 24 hours. Instead I poked him casually in the arm until he eventually rolled over. "Oh my god, I'm so lazy. I bet it's lunchtime," he said with a smile. I explained that the rest of us had real jobs and had to be in work in half an hour, so we swapped numbers and he walked me past the kitchen, past the bedroom with Lisa's head poking out, and to the front door. He kissed me on the cheek, which seemed chaste after last night's antics, but I was grateful to avoid the morning breath and we agreed to check our diaries and arrange a drink for the following week.

I tried to walk to the Tube with a spring in my step, but it seemed I'd pulled a muscle in my left leg, so the result was more a lopsided skip. I made it to work with a record five minutes to spare, so I headed to the coffee bar to try and sober myself up. After two espresso shots, I turned and bumped into Mark. He looked suave and cocky as usual and gave me a wink as he leaned across me to order a cappuccino. "I'm glad I caught you," he said with a Christian Grey smoulder, ordering, paying and taking his coffee one-handed all the while resting his other hand on my back. "Come with me, Miss Lansdale."

Once again I found myself in a meeting room with Mark, this time seated side by side. He'd arranged to speak to the bosses that afternoon and we were all to hand in our notice immediately after. He was convinced they'd let us go straight away, given that we were leaving to set up a competing company, and advised me to organise the files on my computer this morning, and get together anything else I needed before lunch. Suddenly this seemed like a really big deal, and I berated myself for not taking it more seriously. It hadn't occurred to me that we might be asked to leave the premises as soon as the bosses found out, or that they could immediately freeze our emails.

I rushed back to my desk, deleting various files and embarrassing messages. In the end, I figured it was easier to pull out what I needed then just delete my entire inbox. While I was hardly the bearer of state secrets, an average email between myself and Kiran was bound to include sordid sexual stories, gossip about Ella from HR's boob job and/or details of our latest steal from the stationery cupboard.

By the time 12.30pm rolled around I'd been so busy trying to get my shit together at work that I hadn't once looked at my phone. I'd heard it vibrate under my desk, but figured it would just be my bank, and any news of my impending bankruptcy could wait a few more hours. I whisked it out of my bag and my suspicions were confirmed by the unknown caller ID. But when I opened the text, it was from Paul.

Hold the phone (which I was), the man who had popped my newly single cherry was actually staying in contact. With all the drama of the past week, I hadn't for a second imagined that this thing with Hot Waiter Number Two was going anywhere. But, here he was, sending a jokey text before he'd even made it home. I allowed myself a smug grin for the fact that my skills had been officially sanctioned, and tossed my phone back into my bag. He could wait.

Five minutes later I snatched at my mobile and feverishly typed a response. I couldn't believe I'd been willing to play games and put my future sex life at risk. Like my job, this was no laughing matter and I needed to take it seriously. I responded with what I hoped was casual and friendly but also a touch illicit, so there was no confusion as to my intentions. I was a girl with needs and he was there to fulfill them. Preferably within the next seven days, so there was no time for messing around.

I turned my attention back to my computer, where I was typing out my resignation letter. I'd never resigned from anywhere before so I wasn't entirely sure what to write, but I slipped in the word "tender" because I'd heard it on TV, and sat back fairly happy with the result. The next 15 minutes were spent guarding the printer like a lioness on the Serengeti, collecting page after page of spreadsheets and thrusting them into the hands of anyone who came within a five-metre radius. Had I actually pressed print? If I left my station to check, no doubt my resignation would shoot out just in time for the boss to walk past, ruining the whole game plan for my fellow rebels.

Eventually it came out, and I noticed I'd spelled my own name wrong, but I didn't even care. My palms were sweating and I just wanted to get the rest of the afternoon over with. I sat back down at my desk, jittery and in no mood to eat lunch. Why hadn't I been stressing about this all week like any normal person? Why had I left it to the last minute to squeeze all my anxiety into one never-ending morning?

Soon enough Mark approached my desk, whispered, "It's time," into my ear, and gestured for me to follow him up to the fourth floor. I stumbled along behind him, our march gradually joined by the other deserters as though we were about to burst into a flash mob dance at any second. Male Jody took up the rear, and I realised I hadn't given him a second thought since I was brutally rebuffed by the girlfriend card earlier that week. Clearly, I was getting good at rejection, which boded well for my single lifestyle.

We walked into the meeting room to find it already populated by half the floor. I looked at Mark questioningly and he turned to Mr. Phelps. "I know you wanted to speak with me, Mark, but we need to make an announcement first." He gestured for us all to be seated. Had the management found out? Were they about to sack us? My head was spinning, and I was pretty sure my ass was sweating, but I managed to hold eye contact with Mark long enough to deduce his was probably sweating more – being the commander of the coup and all.

The next fifteen minutes were a blur. Mr. Phelps got straight to the point and told us the company was folding. The office wouldn't be open come Monday because all their assets were being seized by the liquidation company. We all stared at him open-mouthed until he eventually left the room. Ella from HR (and her new boobs) assured us she would be around next week should we have any queries and she'd be in her office for the rest of the afternoon. As she got up to make her escape, around 20 lost souls followed her. I sat nailed to my seat, completely gobsmacked. Had Mark known about this? Why else had he encouraged us to remove all our stuff from our computers? I had a C-3PO memory stick in my bag filled with the company contacts and was now feeling like the biggest traitor.

I walked back down to the office to find people milling around like zombies, looking through desk drawers, searching for bags and boxes. Had Mark kept us all in the dark? I was trapped between being thankful that I had a job to go to, and outraged that he could know something like this and not tell any of us. Or did the others know? Is that why we all blindly signed up to new jobs we still knew nothing about? I tried to think back to the 'meeting' in the pub, but recalled very little apart from its sexless conclusion.

My phone buzzed again. It was Kiran. "Did you hear?" I started to text then decided to call, and rushed into the toilets. Thankfully it wasn't the school-style stalls, where you could hear everything through the gaps above and below the door. Instead they were big

96

wooden doors that closed heavily, cutting you off from all human contact while you went about your business. Something that wasn't such a bonus when I got locked in last year and nobody noticed for four long, lonely hours. Ron from maintenance had to come and remove the door from its hinges, by which time quite a crowd of colleagues – both male and female – had set up camp to watch the drama unfold. I was applauded when I finally made it back to my desk, and had spent the next few days weighing up the potential embarrassment of getting locked in again against peeing in a precarious position with my foot on the unlocked door.

Kiran, having taken what she referred to as a 'duvet day' – something she assured me was practically a legal requirement these days – had just had 'the call' from Ella explaining the situation. After exchanging a number of conspiracy theories about what was actually going on behind the scenes, I finally hung up, flushed – might as well kill two birds – and headed to Kiran's desk to grab anything useful and remove anything incriminating before the 'authorities' stepped in. I tried to ignore the fact that the birthday present I'd given her last year was still in the bottom drawer.

CHAPTER SIX

Moving On

"It's a new dawn, it's a new day…" Nina Simone rang out – or more rattled out – of the cheap radio alarm my father had reanimated from the '80s. As usual, her music was the overture to my sorry excuse for a life, only this time it was a new day. Today was the day I would leave my garage cocoon as a confident career woman, striding into a bold new world of success and happiness. I would dress well, act confident and walk at the pace of a Benny Hill sketch to make myself look busier and more important than everyone else.

I'd learned this last technique from my ex-colleague Sally, who had started at the company, impressed, been promoted, and then headhunted all within six months. I attributed her success (in what was her first-ever job) purely to her remarkable speed and desire to tell everyone what she was doing *all* the time. She didn't send an email without reporting back to a million people who didn't care and would always rush *everywhere*. Her fastest lap of the office was 47 seconds, which had included a stop at the water cooler. The girl gave the impression she was doing a ridiculous amount at work, and the more I watched what she did in-between bursts of activity – tweeting, texting, reading a magazine on her iPad – the more I realised she was a career genius. 'Fake it until you make it' was unwise in many situations – particularly sexual ones – but at work, it would be my new mantra.

I quickly showered and dressed in my new power outfit of a black shift dress, kitten heels and black blazer (in my head all successful women dressed like Sandra Bullock in The Proposal). Once I'd extracted myself from the grip of my mother's excited preening, I sashayed elegantly/precariously out of the door. Five minutes later I was on the bus, sat next to a man with roving eyes and halitosis, but nothing was going to kill my high as I headed off for a date with my glamorous destiny.

I arrived at the building almost 15 minutes early – this really was a new me – and called Mark from reception. A few minutes later the lift pinged and out strolled the new boss, who looked to have invested in a new working wardrobe himself. I couldn't put my finger on exactly what was different, but against my better judgment I knew I still wanted to put my finger on him. The bastard was looking hotter than ever.

We zoomed up ten floors in silence and stepped out into a huge room that looked something like the inside of a factory – concrete floors, exposed brick walls and plastic coverings strewn haphazardly about.

He lead me to a bank of desks in the centre and instructed me to sit – again, no treat – and explained that the office was still in "transition." We'd have to put up with workmen coming in and out all week, while they put the "finishing touches" on the place. From what I could see, the beginning touches were hardly underway, but I smiled to myself as I imagined the next week as one long Diet Coke break, with Kiran and I lazing back in our chairs perving on the topless hunks drilling holes in various walls. Then Jody walked in, bringing me crashing back to reality. He strolled around the desk, did one of those complicated 'hood-style handshakes with Mark – neither of whom came close to pulling it off – and was directed to park himself in the seat next to mine. Great, being reminded of my flirting failure on a daily basis was just what I needed. My mood dipped even lower when Kiran arrived and was directed around the other side of the desks. I couldn't even sit next to my friend!?

Determined to stay positive, and professional, I started setting up my workspace. While everyone else was linking up their computer equipment, I was pulling my never-ending office supplies out of my bag like Mary Poppins. I was especially excited about the new sparkly black pen I'd purchased at the weekend from Ryman's, and found it particularly pleasing when lined up next to a matching hole punch and stapler. I'd stopped at the set square and compass – I didn't want to look like a geek.

The office was buzzing and I soon got back into the spirit of things. The day was mostly made up of mini meetings where we decided on everything from hours to the contents of vending machines. Mark was going all-out to make it look like we were all in it together, but something about the two glass offices at the end of the room, where he had set up a comfy-looking, leather-clad suite overlooking our 'Marketing Hub', wasn't quite playing ball. We were handed business cards referring to each of us as "Marketing Associate", which meant absolutely nothing but kept everyone on an even par, except, of course, Mark, whose own nametag said "Director". As far as I was concerned, Associate was still better than Assistant, so that was fine by me, although Director could prove problematic when it came to not throwing myself at his beautifully buffed feet.

The day went by quickly and I even spoke to the non-important, non-hotties who had slipped under the radar at the original pub meeting. I waited for some kind of sense of impending doom, but none came. At 5pm we all headed to the pub – a routine I could happily accommodate – and I managed to leave a solid six on the slosh scale (a term of measurement invented by Selina back at uni – one being mildly flirtatious, ten being unconscious).

Back home, after being grilled by my dad, who showed very little faith that this was an actual job, I headed into the garage to fire up my laptop. I was in the zone, and nothing would stop me getting my life together. I'd got a new job, a kind of promotion, and a man (or potential long-term penetrator) and I needed a bachelorette pad to invite him back to ASAP. OK, so there would probably have to be a few bachelorette buddies in there too, but I'd been sleeping in my parents' garage long enough. I needed to keep the timeframe to a minimum so it could legitimately be excluded from my life CV.

I skipped past the ads with more than two flatmates (I wasn't looking for a dorm room), the ones with no photos (what were they hiding?), and the ones with too many photos (one barbecue picture was enough, 30 was pushing it), and landed on one that seemed safe, sane and a hell of a lot closer to work than Leighton Buzzard. I emailed the girl in the ad, trying to hit a happy medium between friendly and desperate, then clicked on my inbox every five seconds for the next half an hour, clearly crossing over to the wrong side.

Once I headed to bed I slept fitfully and dreamed I was sharing a flat with Carrie from the movie, who wasn't a bad flatmate, but every time I took a shower, blood came out. I eventually told her I was leaving and she stretched up a giant hand and dragged me down from my bed into the ground, which was the point at which I finally woke, wishing more than ever that my brain could at least pretend to be on my side.

When I arrived at work the next day, the office was vastly improved. Although beanbags and a pool table seemed to have taken precedence over the meeting room and kitchenette, I was happy to spend lunchtime leaning provocatively in the interest of making an effort at work. A lot of our old clients had come with us in the move, so we were busier than ever, and I was determined to begin my sure-fire ascent to the top just as soon as I'd located my David Hasselhoff mug...

It was 4.45pm before I finally checked my personal

email – potentially a world record – and thankfully the flatshare girl, Denise, had emailed back. I couldn't cope with non-sexual rejection as well as the rejection I was sure I was suddenly getting from Paul, who hadn't been in touch since Friday. Clearly what had seemed like a good idea in the afterglow had lost its appeal over the weekend. Denise invited me to come and see the flat the following day and I agreed. Both she and her other flatmate, Leanne, would be in to vet me. I texted Lisa to ask if she'd help me practise some potential interview questions, she called me a loser, then I headed home via the stationery shop, where I purchased a black sparkly ruler to add to my ensemble.

When I arrived at my potential new home the following evening I was relieved to see it seemed pretty normal. No rabid dogs, no Kappa tracksuits and no weird smells. I already wanted to know where to sign. As soon as I walked into the living room Denise – 5'9", ash-blonde hair, hazel eyes, likes leapoard-print slippers (by the look of it), dislikes 'restrictive' cocktail menus – smiled, gestured to two bottles of wine, and asked, "Red or white?" I was definitely going to fit in here. I went for white and we sat down. Leanne – 5'5", long 'strawberry blonde' hair, blue eyes, likes showing off her belly button ring, dislikes penguins in large groups (childhood issue) – flew in about two minutes later with her hair wrapped in a towel, apologising that she'd just got out of the shower. "My legs were like a forest," she explained, eyes wide with disgust. Since I knew that situation well, I was convinced we were the perfect match.

"We just wanted to have a chat and then we'll

show you around," said Denise. Suddenly my palms were sweaty. I loved them, but what if I didn't perform in my interview? What if I said I stayed up until midnight when they went to bed at 10pm? What if I said I ate meat and they were vegetarians? What if I admitted I had an irrational hatred of guinea pigs and they had a whole colony at the end of the garden? I took a big breath and an even bigger sip of wine. Never had I been so desperate for someone to like me.

The questions started about jobs. I said I worked in marketing and didn't go into much detail – mostly because I still wasn't entirely sure what my new role was. Denise was a journalist and Leanne worked for a charity. I looked closely for signs of excessive dogooderism, but as she chipped at her bright red nail polish and poured herself a second glass of wine, I was reassured she wasn't entirely a lost cause. Then we moved on to tidiness and social lives, all three of us equally laid-back about the topics. Then Leanne asked what my hobbies were, a question I hadn't thought about since I was about 12. I looked around the room for inspiration and saw a book on art. "I love art," I lied, going into great detail about how I loved to sketch al fresco in the summer. I noticed a photo of Denise on a bike and added that I loved to cycle. Never has anything been less true. I hate cycling with a passion. I haven't touched a bike since I fell off during a particularly tricky bend on a 'romantic' weekend in the Lake District with Ben.

After a quick mooch around the flat, my eyes peeled for last-minute signs of personality clash, I went home to await the phone call. I received a text five minutes later to say I'd got the room – apparently there were so many freaks on the hunt they were keen to lock me in as soon as possible. New job, new flat, now I could focus my undivided attention on securing the hot new man. I thought about breaking the cardinal rule and texting Paul. After all, maybe he'd been away at the weekend and the battery had gone dead on his phone. Maybe his flat was so high up that he couldn't get a signal. Maybe he'd been mugged and lost my number, and had spent the weekend hanging around the bars where we met hoping to bump into the love of his life just one more time... I decided against it, willing him to just bloody get in touch already. Why did I have to do all the stressing in this relationship?

I arrived home and informed my parents that my stay with them would be coming to an end in exactly three days' time. Both failed to look even mildly bothered by the fact their youngest was flying the roost for a second time. My mother's only concern was that my brother was away at the weekend and my father would have to move my stuff in his ridiculous new Range Rover. Why he needed a four-wheel drive to get to B&Q and back was beyond me, but even though he had to jump about a mile to get into the front seat, it seemed to make him feel manly. It was better than the usual mid-life-crisis-mobile. At least he stood very little chance of picking up hotties outside Tesco in his obnoxious gas-guzzler.

As I returned to the safe zone of the garage, I decided to text Irish Stuart to share my success in the flat-hunting arena. He had been there at the start of my moving adventure, so it seemed like a safe way to get in touch without actually looking like I was interested. He texted back straight away saying he'd found somewhere, too, and was moving in within the next couple of weeks. We'd both gone for North London, so he suggested we explore the pubs together once we'd settled in. He even offered to lend his moving services again, but I was determined to block the last experience from my mind, so I politely declined, wishing desperately he could block it from his. I wondered whether my furry handcuffs had left a mark…

Since my first text had yielded such good results, I decided to drop Paul a line while I was at it. I was clearly on a roll. Again, my flat-hunting success was the perfect friendly shield to hide my desperate, wanton need, and he texted back ten minutes later saying he couldn't wait to check it out, and that he hoped it would be somewhat more comfy than Steve's sofa. I wasn't great at reading between the lines, but I was pretty sure that meant I would be pleasured again in the near future by Hot Waiter Number Two. I congratulated myself on having two men on the go at once. It was like being the heroine in a Jackie Collins novel. Although, so far, there had been no murder, kidnap or sunshine. And very little sex.

At work the next day the new successful me was still out to impress and I spent the morning flirting with Male Jody. I figured that at least I should secure myself first dibs in case his relationship was on the rocks. The afternoon was taken up with meetings, but I threw a few furtive glances in the direction of Mark, which were rewarded by an inappropriate comment about my legs. I was truly on fire.

When I walked into my parents' kitchen on Saturday morning, up and packed and ready to skedaddle out of my suburban black hole, I found my dad with his head in his hands at the kitchen table. Finally someone in my family was giving my departure the attention it deserved. The poor man looked devastated. I started to tell him it would all be fine, that I would still visit at least twice a year to collect my birthday and Christmas presents. But he shook his head, that wasn't it. Apparently there had been some kind of foreign insect outbreak in the jungle room and at least half of his faux-forest had been heartlessly munched to the stalk.

My mum came clomping into the kitchen in a pair of walking boots and announced that my father was too distraught to drive. She would be my moving man for the day. This alarmed me for a number of reasons. Firstly, my mother is 5' 4" and about as strong as a toddler. Secondly, and most significantly, she would try to make friends with my new flatmates and settle herself in for a girly night on the sofa before I'd even unpacked a box. Just as I was trying to magic up an alternative plan, my sister walked into the kitchen. With Wayne.

Letting Laura feel smug for the day because her boyfriend had to help her pathetic single sister seemed like a small price to pay in exchange for someone who would get in, get the job done, then get out. Much like I imagined their sex life (which I wished I hadn't). I disguised my new plan under the veil of supporting my father and his horticultural tragedy. Clearly my mother should be with him during this trying time, and my

107

asocial sibling could be relied upon to steer well clear of my potential new BFFs.

As I predicted, the move took two hours flat, and Laura didn't even come up to say goodbye. Instead, she waited in the car while Wayne dutifully dragged the last of the boxes up the stairs. I thanked him, and, in lieu of any normal social relationship after three years of knowing each other, shook his hand. Within five minutes of Tweedledum and Dumber leaving the building I was sitting on the sofa, glass in hand, testing out Denise's new margarita recipe. She was stretching her mixological talents to the extreme on account of my arrival, so I thought it rude not to try her concoctions. By the time we reached batch number seven I could have written a biography of her sexual history. The girl hadn't had a dry spell of longer than a week for three years, and I decided to make her my new sex guru.

As Denise handed me my hundredth 'margarita' (by this point they were mostly rum and blackcurrant squash) we sat down to mooch through the men on a dating website Leanne had used last year. Denise had hacked into her account and we'd made contact with quite a few half-decent specimens already. Denise even set up a series of dates for the coming weeks. "We need to hunt as a pack," she assured me. "We'll figure out who goes on which date nearer the time." I casually mentioned that I had two men on the go already, expecting her to be impressed. "That leaves room for another five," she said matter-of-factly. "One for each day of the week." I wondered whether I would need to do some kind of pelvic floor exercises if I was to adhere to such a demanding schedule, but I decided that wasn't a first-night query.

Eventually Denise started snoring with her glass held above her head, so I took it and put it in what seemed like a perfectly safe place in the middle of the living room carpet and headed to my room to unpack. After trying to hack through the gaffer tape on my boxes with a pair of tweezers I found in the hallway, I gave up and passed out on top of my unmade bed. Looked like my new life wasn't going to be that much of a change...

CHAPTER SEVEN

Foreign Affair

The first time I noticed our 80-year-old neighbour Ronald staring through my bedroom window was the morning of April 12th. A morning when I had chosen to sleep in a weird pair of silk pantaloons. And nothing else. I was on the 'detached' side of the flat, practically within touching distance of the house next door, so at first I thought there was just an old-man ghost in my room. I tend to think old people are sweet and I like to give them the benefit of the doubt, so I waved casually. But when I realised he was still in the land of the living, I grabbed for a baggy sweatshirt and retreated to a 'safe zone' in the far corner of the room.

Since then Ronald has greeted me every morning with his slow, sad tortoise wave, and every morning I've waved back, trying not to think about how long he's been standing there. When he's not playing Rear Window, Ronald spends the majority of his time in a strangely modern La-Z-Boy out on his front porch, stroking what I have an increasing suspicion may be a stuffed cat.

On this particular Sunday morning Ronald had deemed it an appropriate time to bring out his summer wardrobe, and when I opened my curtains I shielded my eyes not only from the dazzling morning sunshine, but from Ronald's Hawaiian shirt and bright green Bermuda shorts. Maybe he thought he'd retired to Florida, rather than a narrow street in sunny Finchley. I treated him to his morning wave, then wandered into the lounge to see if anyone else was around, picked up a couple of empty bottles and headed into the kitchen. I prepared a nutritious breakfast of toast and tea and sat down on the sofa ready to start the day. As I waited for my five-year-old laptop to drag itself out of hibernation, I flicked through the TV channels and settled on Animals Do The Funniest Things. It was one of the few programme titles I wholeheartedly agreed with.

A message popped up to say my friend Matt was waiting to engage in a Skype conversation from Hong Kong. I hadn't heard much from him since he'd found himself a Hongkonger girlfriend. I'd imagined her as a coquettish Geisha, like in the movies, but he'd immediately called me a racist and reminded me I was thinking of Japan. I quickly lost interest in his un-exotic tryst. After all, my own trysting was more important than foreign affairs.

By the time I'd washed my face, teased my hair into less of a post-electric chair style and thrown on a bra under my top (so as not to offend him with a nipple slip), Matt was looking pretty bored. He'd split up with

111

Queen Kong and was announcing his imminent arrival back in the UK. Matt had lasted an impressive six months out there and had racked up an even more impressive eight jobs. He was finally ready to admit defeat and settle for the same rainy existence the rest of us had accepted the moment we left uni.

He was moving back to London next month, so I would have a ready-made drinking buddy who might help shed some light on the male psyche. My Irish adventure was proving slow-moving, and while I'd been out with Stuart a couple of times since I'd moved, his Hangover-style humour was starting to grate almost as much as his underwear-on technique. Paul had become a reliable fuck buddy, but I was avoiding spending too much time with him outside of the bedroom since I'd discovered he was a touch on the clingy side. Denise thought the situation was perfect (even if she was keen for me to throw a few more balls into the court). "Talk all you like with Irish, but you need Waiter's skills too," she reminded me one morning as I struggled to get Paul out of the flat without so much as a cup of tea. What happened to the good old days, when men snuck out before you woke up? I was starting to realise I was more of a traditionalist than I'd thought.

Denise had been testing out various men from Leanne's dating website and lining up 'meetings' with random guys like some kind of volunteer madam. The 'clients' didn't seem to question when Denise or I turned up in place of Leanne, but then, these specimens hadn't been chosen for their sharp wit. I'd been sent out with a supposed film producer earlier in the week, but an hour of staring at his square-shaped, slug-trail beard had me crying off after two drinks with a fake migraine. Leanne had been sent out last night to meet a guy who claimed to be a doctor and hadn't yet returned. Considering Denise was still asleep and I was calmly sat on the sofa, I realised we were showing surprisingly little interest in our flatmate's potential abduction. At this very moment she was probably being subjected to crazy medical experiments like in some schlocky horror film.

I sent Leanne a text, and, having played my part in her potential safe return, settled in to check out holidays online. Lisa and I were planning a girls' trip abroad so that we could drink wine in the sunshine instead of in the rain. She'd finally picked up on some of Steve's 'effeminate' behaviour and sent him packing, and the minute he'd packed he'd disappeared on a lads' holiday with his personal trainer. First things first, we needed a guest list. Although Charlie, Selina, Lisa and I had been friends for years, we hadn't all been in the same room since Charlie's wedding (where there had been a tense situation after she discovered Selina in the coat cupboard 'getting to know' her brother).

In this instance Lisa had used me as pathetic bait, saying I needed to get away and perve on some foreign men. Charlie agreed as long as there were cultural activities nearby. Selina agreed as long as there was a swim-up bar. I'd just started to shortlist some potentials when Leanne texted back. "In Clapham. Sore. Back later." At least I knew her evening had gone well and that Doctor Mike had given her a thorough once-over.

I went back to flicking through hotels online, gradually filtering out anything that said "family friendly" or was lacking a mini bar. I got three emails from Charlie with expensive-looking town-centre B&Bs and about a hundred from Selina that looked like 18-30s holidays. I wasn't sure which seemed worse, so I demanded Lisa come over immediately so that we could agree on an alternative and gang up on them.

By the time Lisa arrived, just after lunch, Denise had emerged looking like she'd consumed a lake of tequila. Five minutes and four cups of coffee later, the flat smelled like a greasy spoon café. Denise came into the lounge to take our breakfast orders, which we reeled off with little concern for the fact it was approaching mid-afternoon. Lisa and I agreed it would be our last food indulgence before we began work on our bikini bodies. There's nothing like a girls' holiday to bring out a bit of unhealthy competition. I decided to find a fat friend before next year's break, so I could actually eat in the lead-up to my bikini-fest.

Denise peered over my shoulder at the string of whitewashed faux temples and casually mentioned her mother had a villa in Crete and we might as well just go there. Halfway through my protest of, "We couldn't possibly…" Lisa had demanded to see it online. I shot her a look that she stealthily ducked, before clapping eyes on what looked like the home of a Hollywood star. In the two seconds it took me to try and formulate a polite way of asking whether Denise's family were secretly filthy rich, Lisa had invited her on holiday with us. By the end of the day Leanne was on board and the six of us had booked a week in Villa del Fancypants.

Over the next three weeks, Denise, Leanne and I flirted with what we considered a fail-safe regime of diet and exercise. We only ate two slices of pizza each when we ordered takeaway, we went for runs three times a week (that lasted on average between five and ten minutes) and carefully studied the Kama Sutra to see which positions would burn the most calories. By the time the holiday rolled around I'd lost a whopping pound and a half. I stood in my bedroom (away from the window) trying to squeeze into my sixth-form bikini. It had been skulking in my drawer for ten judgmental years, a constant reminder that I would never fit into a size 8 again. I looked in the mirror just as the stitching burst on the bottoms and they slid, defeated, to the floor.

I finished packing and headed into the lounge for a glass of wine. Denise was curled up with a tub of ice-cream, while Leanne was tucking into the box of chocolates she'd bought for her parents' anniversary. I threw my bikini in the bin. "No luck?" asked Denise, shovelling more Ben & Jerry's down her throat. It turned out she'd only lost one pound and Leanne had actually gained a half. I felt slightly better knowing I was the biggest loser at our sad little fat camp, and went to bed happy after only three glasses of wine.

We arrived at the airport the next morning at 5.30am. The ticket said to be there by 7, but Charlie had demanded we plan for various potential apocalypses and now we were tired, grumpy and suffering from a unanimous bad hair day. It turned out our check-in desk didn't open for another hour, so we glared at Charlie as she issued us with our travel documents and headed off for some airport shopping.

I decided to torture myself further in the bikini

arena, while Charlie headed to the book shop to scan the bestsellers, Selina to Boots to compare the value of various condoms, and Leanne to a bakery to salivate over some calorific muffins, while Denise had already set up camp on a bench, using her carry-on as a pillow. The last I saw of Lisa she was peering through the window of a closed bar.

I wandered around the bikini shop in an early-morning daze, and decided to give myself a pre-holiday pick-me-up by trying on bikinis a size too big. I took a selection (a few of which were the dreaded 'support' range) into the changing rooms, only to emerge five minutes later hot, sweaty and clutching the one item I'd managed to squeeze my ginormous ass into; it was green with yellow spots. I was in no position to bring fashion into the equation, so I purchased said reptilian number, and returned to our hub, where Lisa and Denise were fast asleep, both dribbling elegantly onto their own hair.

Charlie was engrossed in Ulysses, though I was partly grateful and partly disturbed to see her sneak an occasional look at the companion guide, which was almost as long. Why anyone would read a book that required another book to decipher it was beyond me, and why someone would take up precious luggage weight with them was a mystery all unto itself. Leanne was thoroughly mourning the failure of her diet with a Krispy Kreme, and Selina had gone AWOL.

They announced our check-in desk open, Selina returned weighed down by Boots bags, and we sullenly gathered our selection of purple, leopard print and Louis Vuitton luggage (me, Selina and Lisa respectively)

116

and headed to what was already a tedious-looking queue. Selina jabbed me in the ribs and waved coyly at a group of guys in the line next to us. "There's seven of them," she said with a wink. "One for each of you and two for me." I didn't like to break it to her that, according to the board, they were on their way to Ibiza, and therefore it was a little long-distance for a holiday romance.

We finally made it onto the plane, where Charlie helpfully provided eye-masks and earplugs, and we all settled down for a snoring competition that was a far cry from the shot-fuelled journeys of our early twenties. I started to lament the sad disappearance of our youth, but failed to keep my eyes open long enough to care.

Exactly 15 minutes before we were due to land, Charlie woke us up one-by-one so we could 'freshen up'. I looked at my reflection in the window, figured I was fighting a losing battle and immediately went back to sleep. As we disembarked, I realised I was the only one who didn't look like I was ready for my close-up. Everyone had removed hidden layers, made use of quick-fix hair secrets they'd read in magazines and finished the look with a pair of giant shades. I had packed my sunglasses in my check-in luggage and was sweltering in my jeans and comfy sweatshirt.

By the time we arrived at the villa, it was almost lunchtime. Luckily Denise's parents' gardener had gathered us a selection of "fruit from the orchard" and left out some bread and the all-important wine. We flung our luggage aside and took our last supper out to the Olympic-sized pool. Once we'd digested (with the help of the wine and a sticky old bottle of local spirits

Selina discovered in the lounge cupboard) we scurried off to bagsy the best rooms and prepare to showcase our swimwear collections.

We nonchalantly eyed each other's figures to decide where we stood in the pecking order (I settled on 'average', then stopped looking in case I went down any further) as we sipped what tasted like pure alcohol decorated with a slice of lime and a small cocktail umbrella. Even though we had no 'staff', we'd found the keys to the cabana bar, which was somewhat better stocked than the lounge cupboard. Despite our European location, Denise and Selina had cranked up the Caribbean tunes, and were busting some mixologist moves while they knocked up a selection of concoctions that looked a lot like our uni 'Punch Of Death'.

Within a couple of hours, the pool area looked like something from Girls Gone Wild, and Lisa, Selina and Leanne had thrown caution to the wind – and their bikini tops into the pool. While I was aware "we've all got them" (thanks, Selina), I wasn't quite ready to part with my newly acquired citrus treat, and headed to a shady corner, where Charlie was enjoying a virgin margarita. She'd moved from her seat only once since we'd arrived, to provide the girls with "nipple cream" of a high enough factor to avoid potential chafing. Selina and Leanne eventually retired to the roof terrace, because it was "closer to the sun", and I sat back to get involved in my annual Jackie Collins marathon.

That evening we headed into the local town, sporting sunburn of various degrees. Luckily, Charlie's cream had avoided issues in any intimate areas, but those of us who had gone tops-on had to dress cleverly around our strap marks. My green and yellow ensemble had branded me with big juicy halterneck lines that were impossible to work around. After flicking through my selection of strapless and spaghetti-strap dresses, I attempted to accessorise with a summer scarf, before Selina ripped it from my throat and offered me a tight halterneck top. Then Denise helpfully paired it with a sequin tube skirt, the likes of which I hadn't seen since I was 18. I felt like a dick, but it was nothing a few margaritas wouldn't cure, and 15 minutes later I headed confidently but unsteadily out of the door.

It was only a five-minute walk beyond a pocket of matching whitewashed hotels into town. Denise marched us past a selection of perfectly acceptable-looking bars, before settling on the aptly named El Greco and ushering us inside. What had looked like someone's house from the street opened up into a huge indoor garden with fairy lights. I'm a great believer that everywhere looks better with fairy lights.

The waiters were dressed as Greek warriors (or whatever the guys were in that really long Brad Pitt movie) and the cocktail list went on for 20 pages. My kind of bar. We took a seat next to a fountain of a woman spurting water into a man's mouth and immediately spotted a table of guys to our right. After a vote that was taken more seriously than the general election, we ordered three different pitchers of cocktails and one mixed mezze platter, then turned to take a vote on who got which guy.

From what I could see they weren't your typical Brits abroad. Between their Oxbridge fashions, their non-aggressive demeanor and what looked like pink cocktails, they seemed to offer a higher class of penetration than I'd expected. There was not a football shirt or gold chain in sight. I had my eye on one with shoulder-length brown hair and casual stubble. I'd never had sex with a man with long hair before, unless you counted Pete back in sixth form, right at the stage when his Hugh Grant quiff had parted into lacklustre curtains.

I looked at Selina, wondering why she was still at the table, and not sitting in one of their laps, when our drinks arrived. The barman was hot, and gave me a wink, but I'd seen too many news stories about women running away with Lothario foreigners who took their money, used them for a visa or gave them the clap, to fall for that old pony. We tested out the cocktails one at a time, before attempting to mix them into a rainbow concoction that turned out more like a blocked drain.

Eventually some, what I assume to be local, music came on and we had our excuse to instigate the co-ed entertainment. We tottered onto the dance floor as I wrestled with the bottom hem of my top, which kept riding up to reveal several inches of my bright pink stomach. Denise tried to yank it up into a crop top, but luckily Charlie was on hand with safety pins to put me out of my misery. After a good half an hour of posing and talking, the menfolk finally made their approach.

The posh totty congregated on the opposite side of the dance floor, and we spent ten minutes whispering and throwing seductive glances like we were at the school disco. Finally, our trusty maneater Selina decided to cut the crap and get some action. She strutted straight into the middle of the group and, within seconds, had forcibly dragged them into no man's land in the centre of the dance floor. Our clumsy courting then took on the form of a giant circle and there was only one thing to do. Someone had to go in. I pictured myself stepping out alone like Jennifer Garner in 13 Going On 30, but instead I gave Lisa a shove and started clapping.

Luckily she was savvy enough to fall back on a few crowd-pleasing stripper moves, and she soon had the boys following suit. It seemed they were better at communicating through the medium of dance than they were at communicating like normal human beings, so we jammed for a good hour until Leanne decided to, as she put it, "touch herself up" in the ladies. Realising our impressive moves didn't entirely outweigh our melting make-up, we all scurried in after her, leaving the men to hold our drinks in case they thought about making an early exit.

Now that we'd seen their auditions, we divided up the night's entertainment fairly, leaving Charlie to babysit the three rejects. She was thrilled. But instead of complaining she reminded us of the dangers of date rape and suggested we get back to our drinks pronto in case our Lotharios preferred their women unconscious.

Once again my manhunt seemed to be just that, dissolving into a sleek operation as we exited the toilet area and walked north-west towards our targets. 'My' guy was at the bar, which suited me, so I quickly downed the remainder of my drink, and sauntered over for 'operation refill and get felt up'. His name was Evan, which was ridiculous, but close up he was even hotter than I'd thought so I was willing to overlook it. For the rest of the evening I referred to him as Bob. He was perusing the cocktail menu, so in the interest of making him entirely pliable to my needs I suggested we share a pitcher for the sake of good value. He agreed.

After cracking a few jokes that had worked very well for me in the past, I realised what Bob made up for in looks, he was sorely lacking in sense of humour. We engaged in pointless chitchat for what felt like hours, but nearly got to second base when he reached over to 'fix' my halterneck strap, so I assumed I'd get my reward. If I got my way, I was hoping for one hell of a stubble rash by the end of the night. The boys were staying in a hotel on the way back to our villa, so it seemed like a good time to make an exit en masse and see the sites of the inside of his bedroom. But having two keys between six girls was proving problematic. Charlie wanted to go home, Selina and Leanne wanted to go clubbing and Lisa and Denise wanted to stick around for one more drink.

I broke away from the pack, keyless, and suggested we go for a walk. We didn't get much exercise in the five minutes it took to hit his complex, but I was saving my energy for more athletic endeavours. We got to his hotel and headed straight to the bedroom, discarding our clothes in what may have been world-record time.

But I needn't have congratulated myself, because the entire experience was over in equally record time. Bob's initial mount and final grunt were around 90 seconds apart. Are you kidding me? That pitcher wasn't looking like such a good idea now. I rolled over, willing to give him a second chance, but the fucker was fast asleep. At this point I decided to cut my losses. His bed was comfortable and he wasn't snoring, so at least I could make the most of a bad situation and get some sleep. Maybe he would be less of a bitter disappointment in the cold light of day.

A few hours later the room was spinning and I was as hot as the sun. I stumbled out of bed, pulling the entire sheet with me and hauled myself into the bathroom. I splashed my face with water for a few minutes, before submerging half my throbbing head in the sink. I was struggling to tell the walls from the floor, so I lay down on the nearest wall and put my face against the cold porcelain tiles. Time warped, and I became aware I'd been lying there for a while. I was fairly sure I wasn't going to throw up, so I felt my way back to the bedroom door and half stepped, half fell through. When my hand hit the floor it was cold and rough. My brain whispered that we were actually outside, just in time for my ears to hear the front door slam shut behind me.

I got up unsteadily, now with a bloody knee to add to my woes, and turned the handle. Only it didn't turn. I wrestled with it for a good ten minutes, before my brain raised its eyebrow and called me a dick. I started banging on the door and shouting for Bob, only nobody came, and I couldn't remember Bob's real name. I banged and shouted for what seemed like an eternity, before slumping in the doorway, my sheet falling open around me. Just then the front door opened and another man, Not-Bob, peered out.

Many men would be happy to find a naked woman on their doorstep – it's not the kind of thing the traditional stork offers – but Not-Bob looked unamused. "It's OK," I said, attempting to form the sheet into some kind of toga, "I'm with Bob." "Who's Bob?" asked Not-Bob, who I didn't recognize from the bar. I started to relay my story to him, but, after assuring me he didn't want any trouble, he tried to shut the door in my face. I wedged my naked foot in the gap, like some crazy person or debt collector, not stopping to think that what looked like a strong gesture in the movies was likely to break my trotter.

Hopping in the doorway, I eventually convinced him to go into the bedroom, where he would find a pair of black heels, a sequin skirt and a black top, and then "he'd be sorry." A minute later he reluctantly swung the door open and gestured for me to sort my shit out quickly and get the hell out. Bob, the useless twat, was still fast asleep as I got dressed, gathered my belongings and tottered out of the building on my crumpled foot.

I looked around at the stairs, which seemed like the Escheresque final scene of Labyrinth, and randomly chose my path home. After stumbling past hundreds of doorways, and climbing up every time I thought I was going down, I eventually made it back to the dirty, gritty earth. I noticed a security guard next to the exit gate with what was probably a torch, but at the time I was fairly sure was a gun. I needed to avoid this bastard at all costs, so I tiptoed, back against the scratchy whitewashed walls, in a full circle to find an alternative exit. It was no use, I was going to have to go over the wall. It didn't look so high, but my perception was not at its best.

I peered back at my nemesis and saw him raise his

gun in the direction of a rustle in the bushes. This was my only chance of escape. I ran as fast as I could in a zigzag towards a dip in the wall, and launched myself onto it. I imagined an episode of Total Wipeout as I pulled myself into a straddle over the top. I was pulling my skirt down and wondering how to apply for the show, when a bright light hit me square between the eyes. The guard shouted something I didn't understand and headed towards me, refusing to pull the spotlight from my shameful face. I battled with my right leg to try and get it over to the other side, but the tube skirt had suddenly run out of give.

As I was deciding whether pulling my skirt up and flashing my ladyparts (I hadn't been able to locate my underwear) or getting caught were preferable, two big rough hands had lifted me down from the wall. I tried to scream and lash out, but my nemesis put up his hands in that familiar sign of submission. He rummaged in his pocket and I saw that his gun was indeed a torch, and his handcuffs were in fact plasters, one of which he applied carefully to my knee before pushing me gently in the direction of the gate.

I felt an overwhelming desire to hug my evening's saviour, but as I went in for the close encounter, he'd already headed back to his post. According to my watch it was 4am. I looked around me, trying to decide which way to walk to get back to the villa, and headed uphill. Eventually I spotted the gate and slipped through, past Selina and her takeaway from the bar sleeping on a sunbed, into the kitchen where I drank half my bodyweight directly from the tap, then up to my room, where I passed out, half-clothed, on my bed. Again.

The next morning we were unanimously hungover. Even Charlie was worse for wear. I discovered her in her corner with a cold compress when I ambled downstairs, nearly tripping over Leanne as she dragged a mattress out into the sun so she could sleep and tan at once. Soon we were all by the pool, where we lay two-to-a-bed for the entire day, sipping pathetically from water bottles and forgetting to top up our suncream. The next few days took on a similar itinerary of drunken night in town followed by hungover day by the pool, but any further potential for holiday romance was blighted by a coach party of 'slightly' younger girls (Denise's outraged words). By Thursday we couldn't take it any longer. Even Selina agreed we were too old for this shit, and we spent the night playing what started out as poker and ended up as snap.

Our flight home was equally mild and middle-aged, as we all (except for Lisa, who blamed acclimatisation for our lack of endurance) reflected on our inability to take the pace as we gingerly approached our fourth decade.

CHAPTER EIGHT

Client Liaison

I was awoken by a loud buzzing in my ear. After swatting at an imaginary fly, I eventually opened my eyes to see Leanne's five-year-old nephew Leon wielding a vibrator like a lightsaber. I closed my eyes hoping the vision would go away, but when he hit me on the head with it I was forced to take him out with a pillow. Firstly, it was 9am on Saturday morning. Secondly, it wasn't my vibrator. Assuming through hopeful logic that it wasn't Leon's either, I was fairly sure I had one of my flatmates' love cooties in my hair, and it was not the way I wished to start the weekend.

He'd dropped the offending article when he fell, and ran out crying to his mother. Since my actions had been in self-defence, I wasn't too worried, and I crawled out of bed to shut my door. But just then Leanne's sister appeared in the doorway, apologising for Leon's intrusion – a conversation that became increasingly awkward as she spied the plastic weapon by the side of my bed. The whole, "It's not mine, I was holding it for a friend," was not going to fly. Luckily she scurried out of the room pretty quickly, closing the door behind her, so I curled up and went back to sleep.

When I woke again at midday, the flat seemed quiet, so I ventured into the lounge. Denise was sitting watching The Kardashians, which we both claimed to hate, but tuned into at least once a day when nobody else was looking. She went into the kitchen to "put on a brew", while I decided to do some detective work surrounding the sex-toy invasion. With my hand inside a dirty sock, I picked it up and headed back to Suspect 1.

"Oh my God," screeched Denise immediately, grabbing for the vibrator. "I thought I'd left this at my mum's." Case solved. It turned out she'd even agreed to see her mother twice in one month so she could plan an emergency retrieval operation. She headed off to put it away and phone her mum to cancel their plans for lunch the following day. "It better be clean!" I yelled. "It touched my head!" "What were you doing with it on your head?" One of the Kardashians was hooked up to a lie detector, so I momentarily lost track of the conversation, and by the time Denise came back we'd both lost interest.

I opened my laptop to do a bit of online shopping. I'd spied a pair of leopard-print shoes the previous weekend and was keeping my eye on the voucher websites to see if I could get them at a discount steal. The annoying bing-bong of a Skype alert came up, and I switched Matt on before I remembered that I'd barely bothered to wash the sleep dribble off my cheek. "You look well," he said sarcastically, as I ducked out of view of the camera. "I've seen it all before," he reminded me. And yes, he'd turned up at my house early many a time at uni to find me slumped in a heap in my dressing gown, last night's make-up down my face, eating cereal out of the box. And I wondered why he'd never set me up with his friends.

"What do you want?" I asked. "I'm now officially a Londoner, and I need you to take me out and celebrate tonight. Don't try and pretend you've got a date, because we both know how unlikely that is. I can see you." I couldn't be bothered to argue, so I told him I'd see him at 8pm at The Eagle, which was approximately five minutes from my flat and an hour from his. That seemed fair. I also said I would bring Denise. She'd given up on Leanne's dating site and had seemingly also given up on men. She'd only had two dates in the past two weeks, which was like a life-threatening drought for her.

After three calls from Matt demanding to know where we were, we casually sauntered into the pub at 8.45pm. We grabbed a bottle of wine that was on special offer at the bar and joined him at a table by the toilets. "Nice spot," acknowledged Denise, and I made the introductions. "I think I saw you naked a few months back," said Matt conversationally. I'd neglected to inform Denise of this infringement of her privacy, after she'd walked past my room sans clothes and was caught red-cheeked on Skype-cam.

"So, what's your new place like?" I asked, changing the subject. "It's in a new build down by the river. It's

129

got a pool in the bottom and my balcony overlooks the Thames. It's pretty cool." "Are you fucking *kidding* me?" Denise and I screeched in unison. "Of course I am, what am I, Mark Zuckerberg?" "I thought you hated Facebook?" "It's in the middle of Hackney in an ex-council building and my A4-sized window overlooks a pub car park, happy?" "Very," I said, sitting back. Nobody liked to see a newbie move to London and bypass the requisite five years of damp, peeling wallpaper and the odd couple of rats to move straight into a life of luxury. That kind of suffering was the only thing keeping the twenty-somethings together in this city.

"So, where are you working?" asked Denise. "At an ad agency in Covent Garden." We failed to feign interest while pouring our second glass of wine, so Matt added that it was the company that made the Ribena commercials. Sitting with somebody who knew the actual Ribena berries seemed a bit more glamorous, but we still waited patiently for another brand name to cement the deal. "They're making the new Mini ad at the moment, too." "Do you get to drive one?" asked Denise, which, granted, was a pretty ridiculous question. Matt tilted his head to the side and eventually shrugged his shoulders and said yes.

It turned out this was all Denise needed to target him as a potential sex buddy. So I spent the rest of the evening watching her pull some pretty aggressive moves, while Matt tried to wriggle out of her clutches. I don't know what he was so worried about. She was way hotter than him, and he needed a good British bonk after months in foreign climes and almost exclusively

130

foreign vaginas.

I went to the bar and got another bargain-bucket bottle of wine. I never actually saw them open it, and it smelled pretty weird, but at £10 I couldn't complain. I'd taken an executive decision on Matt's behalf that he would swap to wine at this point in the evening, and, to his credit, even when he nearly choked on the vin de vinegar, he didn't complain. He was too busy trying to reclaim his personal space from Denise's grabby hands. When she went to the toilet he asked if she was his welcome home gift. "She's just bored and horny," I replied. "Well, flattering as that is…" Matt started to put his coat on. "Oh relax, I'll tell her you've got some crazy foreign STD, and she'll run a mile. Maybe we need to think ahead and bring her someone to entertain her next time…"

It turned out Denise had solved the problem herself during the three-metre walk between our table and the bathroom. She emerged talking to some bulky blond guy whose head/neck combo was even more Hulk-like than Lisa's gay ex. He sat down with us, and we watched as Denise straightened her posture like a praying mantis ready to pounce, thrusting her ample breasts as close to his face as was probably legal in a public place.

"She's fucking terrifying," whispered Matt as he watched her like some weird mating programme on National Geographic. She was being particularly sexually aggressive tonight, which, as a woman, I supported, but as a human I found equally scary. After a few minutes of gawping at what would no doubt turn into a live sex show, Matt and I sat back and reminisced about uni days, which seemed to include a suspicious amount of stories involving us accidentally seeing each other naked.

I needed to pee, but I didn't want to leave Matt to watch the show alone. Then I desperately needed to pee and I no longer gave a shit, so I headed off to stand in the queue for the ladies. I'd hit prime time at 11pm, so I settled against the wall and nodded my head to the music as I crossed my legs and sighed knowingly at the girl next to me. She wasn't interested in making friends. When I finally emerged, I briefly considered going back to fix my hair, then figured it was home time anyway and Matt didn't care, so I headed back out through the saloon-style door.

As I negotiated the corner I bumped head-first into a guy who turned out to be Stuart. We both mumbled our apologies and rubbed our heads before finally recognising each other. It was too late to adjust my hair, so I went for a casual flick and banged my head on the wall. Stuart didn't even crack a smile, so I figued he must be stone-cold sober. His eyes were darting around the room. I allowed myself a smug smirk as they rested on Matt. "Don't worry, just a close friend from uni," I said casually. Maybe eliciting a bit of jealousy would finally get him to move this thing forward. Stuart laughed nervously as my eyes landed on a young brunette who was watching us closely from the exit. "Friend from uni," he said, equally casually. OK. Was he trying to make me jealous now? We both stood in silence for a few seconds. I wondered whether to ask them to join us – maybe getting close with his friends would help get me closer to his bedroom.

The bell for last orders rang and Matt started putting on his coat. I'd better be quick. "Do you want to…" I started, just as Stuart said, "Well, good to see you. I'll give you a call tomorrow." He headed back in her direction, and started collecting up their belongings. She slid her hand into his and kissed him. Full on the lips. This was no uni friend. Stuart's eyes immediately darted back to me. He whispered something to her and she headed towards the door as he made his way back to our corner.

I was trying to decide how I felt about him having two women on the go. I had two men on the go. Fair was fair. But I was never great at sharing. He bustled over to my table. "That's not what it looks like," he said. "I've just been trying to find a way to…" "Let her down gently?" I finished for him. I was disappointed he couldn't come up with a more original response. He picked up my hand. "I'm going to break up with her tonight," he said. I tried to look like I cared.

Just then a man bumped into him and spilled his drink down Stuart's coat. "Dude!" exclaimed Stuart, gesturing. Wait… Something sounded a little too familiar. "Have you seen Andy since you met him at my flat?" I ventured. "Yeah. We went for a drink when he was down last weekend."

So, not only was this asshole seeing another woman behind my back, he was also seeing my brother. I was willing to accept one, but certainly not the other. I didn't need a non-fuck buddy who reminded me of a sibling, and I certainly didn't want to wake up in six months' time to someone farting and sticking my head under the duvet. I was officially done.

133

I calmly suggested Stuart stayed away from both me and my family, and headed out of the door. Then I had to hover until Matt took the hint and gathered up my things. In the meantime, my exit was ruined by Stuart walking past me on his way out, linking arms with the other woman and strolling happily off down the road. Bastard.

Eventually Matt came out with coat, bag, Denise and the Hulk in tow, rolled his eyes at my latest dating drama, pointed us in the direction of our flat and went off to catch the Tube home. I got in and watched reruns of The Kardashians I'd already seen that morning, while I tried to drown out the noise coming from Denise's bedroom. I finished off the vodka in the kitchen cupboard, sat and drunk texted Charlie for a while, then got up to go to bed. I was halfway into my new silk nightie (just because you're sleeping alone, doesn't mean you can't feel glamorous) when my phone rang. It was Paul (we'd stopped calling him Hot Waiter Number Two when I accidentally said it to his face while drunk. Three times).

"Come over," he said. "What? It's 1am," I replied, poised with a make-up wipe nearly touching my face. Could I be bothered with a booty call? I was in two minds. One reminded me that I hadn't had any action since the holiday (and that barely counted as more than a wedgie) and that I'd just terminated my only other option. The other reminded me that it was raining outside. Paul's moves hadn't faltered since that first night, but were they worth changing and facing the elements for? No. Were they worth staying up for an extra hour waiting for him to arrive here? Just. After my pub encounter I was keen to prove I was a reasonable woman.

"You come here. Legs close at 2am, so you'd better be quick," I said and hung up. Either it was super-sexy or super-offensive, but I wasn't too bothered either way. I decided to call a halt on the make-up removal just in case, and headed back to the lounge. I flicked down the channels for something trashy to keep me company until my company arrived.

Paul was on my doorstep 15 minutes later – I was getting better at this than I'd thought. I demanded he remove his wet shoes and coat, then marched him straight to the bedroom. I stood and waited patiently as he struggled with his clothes, refusing to lift a finger to remove either mine or his. I was pretty tired at this point, and if this was going to work he was going to need to take control and have very little expectation beyond a quick missionary moment. He pulled my negligee over my head, which caused an alarming amount of static for something I'd understood to be pure silk.

Paul made a steady start on the fornication, while I lay back wondering whether those leopard-print shoes had come on sale yet. Right breast, left breast, neck kiss. Right breast, left breast, nipple lick. This was taking forever. I glanced at the clock and set myself a challenge to get the whole thing over within ten minutes. Seven-and-a-half minutes later, mission accomplished. I rolled over and went to sleep.

The mission to get Paul out of the door the following morning was a little less successful. It seemed our arrangement now included breakfast and

135

conversation, which all felt a bit much before 9am. Regardless, I managed to make it to the office with minutes to spare. Work had been going pretty well since the move to the new company, and I was now heading up my first campaign. It was with a smaller-than-average client, with a smaller-than-average budget, but it was a start, and I was determined to impress everyone with my inner businesswoman.

Mark had been out and about a lot, "drumming up new business", which seemed to mean spending most of his time in the pub and/or on holiday while the rest of us worked our asses off for about a tenth of his wage. Luckily for him, he was as hot and charming as ever, and now that he was back in the office almost full-time my brooding anger against the establishment never lasted longer than my 15-minute pool break.

On this particular Monday morning I was dutifully researching campaign ideas on the internet (stealing from other people's hard work) when Mark slid round the back of my chair. "Working hard, I see," he breathed down my neck. I struggled not to give a sex shudder and concentrated on moving far enough down my Google answers to mask my search term of "impressive marketing campaigns". It seemed on a par with a pilot Googling "how to fly" just before taking off.

"Lunch tomorrow?" he asked casually. I nodded blankly as he walked away. We hadn't had much to do with each other since the initial social flurry, but there hadn't been a lot of time for work drinks, with most people putting in ten-hour days (I was putting in an average of eight, and I considered myself hugely overworked). I'd been out for a few beers with Male Jody and his girlfriend, which were fun until around 9pm, when she hit a rosé rage and I slipped out unnoticed and legged it back to my sane(ish) single friends.

Kiran and I sat too far away from each other to talk, but we still messaged each other at least once every ten minutes, so I was up-to-date with all her love, lunch and, in fact toilet issues. She'd recently taken a shine to the sandwich guy who brought the lunch trolley around the office. This crush had gone on for weeks before she finally slipped him her number along with her payment last Tuesday. Since then they'd met up twice, but Kiran had told him someone in the office knew her ex-boyfriend, who was a cage-fighter, so she'd managed to keep her guilty secret just that, for now.

I messaged her with a simple "OMG", then teased her with snippets of the Mark situation (was there one, or was I just bored and looking for drama? The second seemed more likely) until we could head to the pub at half five. When the clock hit 5.29pm, we both ran for the lift. "What happened?" she hissed. "Mark asked me out!" I said, for some reason without moving my lips, even though the lift doors were already shut. "What?" "Well, he asked me out for lunch," I said. She opened her mouth, but the doors opened at the floor below and a group of women from Gorge.com (presumably a beauty company or some kind of overeaters anonymous) got in. We listened in on them clucking about some hot guy in their office, raising our eyebrows and failing to see the irony, before pushing our way out on the ground floor and heading to the dodgy sports bar at the side of the building. Again, it was raining, which brought out my lazy side, so a jug of vodka and Red Bull and a greasy burger within three steps of the front door would work just fine for our spontaneous girls' night.

"This is so exciting," said Kiran, as we sat down as far from the big screen as possible. "It's not a sex thing," I said, simultaneously asking myself whether it could be. "No, I couldn't get a Mark," I concluded. "Of course you could. Men like Mark are looking to slum it with someone beneath them." "Thanks." "No, I mean, there's that whole sexy power thing between boss and employee." I rolled my eyes. But I was ready to go for a higher echelon of prey than I'd been getting my claws stuck into so far. I needed a real man, albeit one that clearly waxed his eyebrows.

"I bet you could get him to move us closer together if you slept with him," Kiran said matter-of-factly. I felt like she was low-balling me. Surely if you were looking to get something out of sleeping with the boss you should really aim higher than an alteration in the seating plan. We both sat, thoughtful, imagining what an older man might add to our lifestyles, as we watched the 21-year-old barman walk past. I berated myself for being such an old perv, and then excused myself to order another drink from him.

We got straight back to the subject of Mark, who we agreed was perfect boyfriend material. We listed the pros and cons for dating the boss, ignored all the cons, then decided to head back to Kiran's, where I could borrow a sexy businesswoman costume from her sister. She actually *was* a sexy businesswoman, although neither of us really knew what she did. She was just fabulous and successful all day long, like something out of Sex And The City (which we still held responsible for lying to us about every aspect of adulthood).

"See, it's good that Jess is taking her career seriously," she said pointedly, as we ransacked her officewear collection. "She's trying to fuck the boss," Kiran retorted, making bug eyes at her. Good to know I wasn't the only one who acted like a 14-year-old around my family.

Assuming fashion was the answer as usual, we settled on a red pencil dress. The style said business, but the tight fit and colour screamed pleasure. I wondered whether to tie my hair up, then casually take it down at lunch, like a sexy secretary. Was that what I was going for? I was confused.

I slept fitfully, with dreams of Mark and Ben duelling in the courtyard of my childhood She-Ra castle. It didn't fill me with confidence that Mark was spending more time admiring his reflection in his sword, like a DreamWorks Prince Charming, than attempting much of an attack, and Ben actually got on a horse and rode away after some other fair maiden halfway through. My princess sat and watched from the window eating cake and drinking wine.

I was rudely awoken at 5.30am by a call from my mother. "What's wrong?" I asked through my sleep-fog. "Nothing, I just thought I'd get you before you head off for work." "Mum, that's hours away." "Oh, well, now that you're up…" I struggled into a sitting position and reached for my bottle of water. I couldn't see any pills that might dull the pain of this early-morning attack, so I sank back against the pillow and closed my eyes. My mother had been twittering away about my birthday plans. There didn't seem to be any actual questions involved, or at least I assumed there weren't since she hadn't stopped for breath for about five minutes.

"Don't worry, your father and I will sort everything out. We've got a guest list and we'll have it in the back garden. I know it's not very warm, but Jenny down the road knows somewhere where I can hire a heated marquee. All you have to do is turn up."

"OK," I said with a sigh. If my parents wanted to gather a gaggle of relatives I hadn't seen since I was 12 and force me to discuss how much I'd grown in exchange for a few book tokens and animal-themed ornaments (my extended family were stuck in the 1980s when it came to gifting) then I'd suck it up and give them a day next month. Especially if it meant I could get the hell off the phone and go back to sleep now. I still had a few weeks to sort out my *real* birthday – one that involved friends, alcohol and at least one person throwing up (most likely me).

I reawoke around 8am, which didn't give me as long as I'd planned to convert myself from exhausted underling to alluring colleague/potential sex partner. Hopefully the dress would do all the work and I wouldn't have to bother. After Mark's lack of effort in my dream, I was feeling less keen to throw myself at his finely pedicured feet. Once I was ready I looked in the mirror. It wasn't bad, although I felt like the lady from the Special K advert, and it was an unwelcome reminder that I'd gained a few pounds. Next week I vowed to conform to the bowl for breakfast/bowl for lunch diet, so that I'd be lollipop-head skinny by the time my birthday rolled around.

I walked into work to catch Kiran emerging casually from the stationery cupboard, followed a few seconds later by the sandwich guy, who suddenly seemed to be offering refreshment around the clock. When I turned on my computer a message was already waiting for me. "Got any plasters?" I'd had one in my bag for approximately five years that was around the size of my thumbnail. "What for?" Apparently the sandwich guy was no slouch in the bedroom (storeroom) and had thrown her up against a shelf of pencils, which were safely stored lead-out. Kiran now had a series of puncture holes across her lower back and one on her right ass cheek. "I'm actually bleeding," she half complained, half showed off.

It wasn't the coolest sex injury ever, but at least it showed willing. My sex life with Paul had become very 'pre-watershed' and was now exclusively confined to the bedroom. It seemed I was doomed to a lifetime of sensible sex, even though I'd escaped the original monotony of long-term servicing earlier in the year. I looked back with rose-coloured glasses at my teenage years, when any sexual encounters had taken place in parks, train stations, people's gardens – in fact, almost exclusively outside, bar the few luxurious invitations to do it in the back or, if said young man was blessed with reclining seats, the front of the car.

As I recalled one particular encounter in the park by the duck pond, Mark brushed past the back of my chair and dropped a piece of paper on my desk. He was talking on his mobile, so there was no greeting or instruction, but he did half stroke my shoulder/half nearly slap me in the face as he did so. I looked down. It was a menu for the wine bar round the corner, where we usually took clients. I was partly impressed that we were going to such a suave place for lunch, but slightly put off that we'd be dining in what was very much a company restaurant. It wasn't the kind of place you snuck off to for a lunchtime flirt. "1.30pm" was scrawled in the top right corner. That gave me an hour. I read through a few emails, marking them one-by-one as "deal with later" and awaited further instructions. When it reached 1.25pm and none came, I legged it out of the door and down to the bar, failing to so much as reapply my lipstick on the way.

When I walked in, Mark was already sitting at a table in the far corner. A private area, I noticed, slightly masked from the rest of the room. I headed over nonchalantly. He looked up, smiled, said, "You're three minutes late," then instructed me to sit next to him on his leather sofa. Now, I'm no expert, but this seemed like good body language. I turned my knees towards him so that they were practically touching and casually leaned my left elbow on the table, getting all up-close and personal. As I did so, I managed to knock my cutlery onto the floor. I bent down (as smoothly as possible in my Kardashian-fit dress) to pick it up and saw Mark's legs stand up, followed by another pair of legs approaching the table.

"Mark," said the man's voice attached to the legs. "Brendan," Mark replied, like they were old friends. I struggled to get to my feet, while keeping my knees together, resulting in a kind of fat kid stuck in a sack manoeuvre, as he held out his hand to me, saying, "You must be Jess. It's nice to finally meet you." The voice sounded familiar. Brendan – 6'1", brown hair, brown eyes, likes courtroom dramas, dislikes ham (due to his close relationship with his brother's micro-pig). The person interrupting my non-date with the boss was, in fact, my new client. I was currently under the table in a tight red dress. The first impression might have been OK had I been living inside a late-night movie channel.

We all sat down to peruse the menu. Suddenly I was very aware of the need to down-sex the situation, so I scoured for anything that didn't involve slurping or doing intricate things with my fingers. I settled on the most boring thing on the menu – chicken, chips and peas. The boys both went for giant slabs of man meat – each upping the weight of their steak (apparently Brendan didn't know any cows) as they eyed each other in front of the waiter. For the first time ever I put on my jacket to try and dowdy-down my look, while they, though engaged in perfectly polite conversation, seemed on the verge of slapping their penises out on the table. I wished they'd just do it already so we could get this lunch over with.

I felt like a complete idiot for misreading the Mark situation. I was like a dog on heat, trying to mount anything that came within wagging distance and it was getting a touch pathetic. On top of that, I was totally unprepared to talk to Brendan. I'd pretty much ignored my emails all morning, so most of what they were talking about was going completely over my head. Instead of the successful new me I was acting like a horny version of the old me and I needed to get my act together fast if this meal was going to be anything other than a complete disaster. I threw in a few ideas stolen from the internet, and tried to eat my chicken while causing as little drama as possible. I vowed to make up for it by calling Brendan tomorrow full of confidence and career-woman charm. Right now, I was just concentrating on nodding in the right places and not dropping my peas on the floor.

When the lunch finally came to a blissful end, Brendan invited us to a party his company were having on Friday, to celebrate their 20-year anniversary. It was going to be a big black-tie do in Knightsbridge, but he'd reserved room for two suckers from our company with nothing better to do. Mark immediately agreed for both of us. Not great. On the bright side, it would finally give me an excuse to wear my university ball gown again. If I'd have told my five-year-old self that, as an adult, I only dressed as a princess every five years, she would probably go ahead and jump from the window of Barbie's dream house and put an end to it there and then.

"Looking good, Lansdale," said Male Jody with a wink as I walked back into the office feeling like a fool. At least my misguided effort had had an effect on someone, albeit someone who had clearly had a few too many beers at lunchtime. In fact, most of the men in the office had looked up at his comment, and I slunk back to my chair part smug and part horrified at being the centre of so much attention (OK, so my feminist side was struggling to make her point and I was really 90 per cent smug).

A huge bouquet of flowers was waiting on my desk, much to the intrigue of my colleagues. A few months ago I might have primped and preened around them to show off how desirable I was, and as little as 20 minutes ago I might have thought they were from Mark. But, right now, I just wanted them off my desk and Male Jody's right eye to return to his computer screen. My first thought was they'd been delivered to the wrong place, but I decided I was going to have to keep them anyway because I couldn't stand any more humiliation today. I half breathed a sigh of relief and half rolled my eyes when I saw the card was from Paul. This was the latest in a line of boyfriend behaviours he'd been trying out and it was starting to alarm me. In lieu of anywhere to put them, I took the flowers into the toilets, filled a sink up with water and dumped them in. I spent the next hour trying to compose a grateful yet off-putting email to my floral fornicator. I ended up with, "Thanks for the flowers. Jess." It was winning.

When I ran into Mark by the mini fridge later, he congratulated me on a good lunch meeting. "The dress seemed to have the desired effect," he winked. At least he thought I'd sold my conscience for the sake of the company, rather than his personal enjoyment. And he clearly approved. My inner feminist started to speak up again, but I took a quick sip of water to keep her gagged until Mark walked away.

I'd mostly been emailing Kiran since lunch, and when I returned to my actual work emails, Brendan had sent me three in a row. The first saying, "Great to finally meet you. Really looking forward to working with you. Red is my favourite colour." The second said,

"Delete that previous email. Too many lunchtime beers. I very much valued your ideas and I look forward to hearing more over the coming months." Finally, the third email said, "Really hope I didn't offend with my first email. Wipe that from the record. I actually hate red. It reminds me of Elmo. Elmo is terrifying."

I stared at them for a while. In my fluster I'd failed to take in much about Brendan, other than the fact that he was my first-ever client and I thought I was making a complete hash of our first-ever meeting. On reflection, he'd been friendly, funny and not bad-looking. My brain sighed at what was about to come, reminding me that having a crush on my boss, a half crush on a coupled-up colleague and a crush on my new client wasn't the most productive way to enter the successful new phase of my marketing career. I tried to reason, as quickly as possible before I did something stupid, that I had barely noticed Brendan's raw sexual magnitude at lunch, and therefore it wasn't worth throwing myself into yet another potentially mortifying situation over. I tried to hammer home the fact that this campaign was a test and I needed to squeeze my legs shut long enough to pass. But my fingers had already rushed across the keyboard in response. I felt like an idiot for misconstruing the Mark situation, and I needed an emergency pick-me-up. "Great to meet you too, and very much looking forward to seeing you and meeting your colleagues on Friday. PS. If, on reflection, you're so disgusted by red, can I ask what colours you find more pleasing?" Send.

I started to message Kiran to bring her up-to-date

with my about-turn, when a message flashed up from Mark. "Again, good work in the meeting. Clearly being wined and dined suits you. Thanks for the invite, by the way. I'll see what I can do." I looked up towards his office with a quizzical expression on my face. What? Had I accidentally sent him an email meant for Kiran, and invited him to the pub? The advance mortification kicked in as I flicked back through my messages, but everything seemed above board. I messaged Kiran. "Oh my god!" she typed. "You invited Mark to your birthday?" "No," I replied. I hadn't even decided where to go yet, let alone weighed up whether to mix work friends with real life. "I got an invite from your dad this morning," she said, as my jaw dropped so far a trail of drool came out.

My father was inviting *real* people to my family party? How did he even get my work number? I was pretty sure he didn't have any idea of the name of the company, let alone the specifics within. This was an unprecedented disaster and I needed to crisis-manage the hell out of it straight away. I dialled my dad's number, hoping he'd only managed to get hold of Kiran and Mark. After all, randomly phoning my work and repeating a few names he'd heard me say didn't necessarily imply a widespread outbreak. I was pretty sure I hadn't mentioned anybody else from the office. In fact, I was pretty sure he thought I worked in telesales.

My mother picked up on around the hundredth ring. Apparently the answering machine I bought them for Christmas would cut in at 101. "Mum, you have to get a hold of your husband!" I exploded. "What is he

147

doing calling my work?" "Oh, calm down. He didn't call anyone. He just sent a text. It was very polite." "But how does he have their mobile numbers? Our mobile numbers aren't on our website, are they?" I said in alarm, desperately Googling the company to see if mine was out there in the cables, or the clouds, or wherever the hell the internet was saved, available to any stalker or slasher who cared to write it down. "No, it's from your address book," she said with a laugh. "I told you we had a guest list organised for the party." "But I haven't had an address book since I was about 15!" I shouted, judging this as an appropriate time to take my family slanging match into the soundproof toilet cubicles. "It's all on your father's computer," she said. "Isn't he clever managing to get them onto our mobile from there? I have no idea what he did."

The realisation came gradually, mostly because, if it were true, this was about the worst thing that could ever happen, *ever*. I'd once charged my phone from my father's laptop while I was living at home and it had seemingly backed up all my contacts on his machine. Goddamn modern technology! If he'd invited Mark, who the hell else had he invited? "How many people has he texted?" I asked, as calmly as humanly possible, but pretty sure that I was breaking out in stress spots as I spoke. "Ummm…" my mum said, finally realising this wasn't the exciting birthday treat she'd intended. "How many did you have on there?" Oh. Dear. God. "He texted everyone?" I asked, already knowing the answer. "Yes, love, but don't worry. Only 60 per cent of people usually come, and the marquee I've ordered is very spacious."

I put down the phone, and tried to take in the scale of the disaster. Every single person in my phone book. I scrolled down the names and groaned for about 15 minutes. Everyone from ex-boyfriends to our local pizza place (listed under Marco, which I assumed my sleuth of a father would mistake for an actual person) would have been hit with this mortifying mega-blow. It was bad enough that I had now officially invited people I barely knew to my birthday party, like the class geek trying their luck with the popular kids. It was worse that the invitation had come from my father, who no doubt would have added at least one embarrassing flourish, and that the whole sorry experience was going to take place in a tent in my mother's back garden in the middle of Leighton Buzzard. Just when I thought my cool, single, city-gal lifestyle was taking off, my family had stamped their badly dressed foot down to remind me where I came from.

I needed to move forward with my damage control and fast. Should I come clean and try to explain my family to everyone? "Sorry, my father is a moron, and actually you're not invited to my birthday and never would be." That didn't scream tactical social move. Did I just send a text in a few days saying that unfortunately it was cancelled, then make sure it was just me and my family at the party, so nobody would ever find out? Or did I just stay quiet, assuming that anyone who didn't want to go (which was surely everybody) wouldn't, and therefore no further embarrassment need come of this situation? I decided to keep schtum for now, and try to grimace through any further mention, maybe hammering home the large family contingent in an attempt to make the party sound at least half as lame as it was destined to be. Nobody would turn up anyway. I looked up at the trendy exposed ceiling beam and prayed to IKEA that that was true.

In the meantime, I demanded Kiran join me in the ladies and show me the offending text. I opened the stall door and pulled her in, grabbing her phone out of her hand. "I hope you haven't gone yet," she said, wrinkling up her nose." "I'm not in here to pee, I'm in here to kill myself," I said as I opened the message. My relief at the perfectly normal phrasing of the invite was momentary. When I got to the bottom the scale of the drama hit me square in the face. There I was, aged five, naked in a paddling pool. My father had (badly) Photoshopped a birthday hat onto my head, which was actually bigger than my body. I let out a groan at his terrible Photoshop skills – I'd spent a long weekend trying to teach him the basics last summer, and not only had he not remembered a thing I'd told him, he was also turning my teachings against me in the most outrageous manner. I had one question: What the hell did I ever do to him?

I tried to recall the relaxation teachings from my self-help mission earlier in the year, but, as I sat on the lid of the toilet in silence for nearly half an hour, it only resulted in me hyperventilating in as calm a fashion as possible. At some point, Kiran let herself out and returned to her desk. I now had to choose between humiliation and death in private. She may as well have left me with a razor blade.

Why had my father chosen this year to act like such a lunatic? As it was, it hadn't exactly been filled with happy "Dear Diary" moments. Not only had he invited my boss, on whom I had an unshakeable sex crush, to a family party in the middle of nowhere, he'd also invited Paul, who would no doubt see it as a major step forward in our relationship. And then there was Gary, the handyman from down the road, the Asda delivery guy, whose number I saved into my phone when he got lost on the way to our flat, and my hairdresser Graham.

I figured the afternoon lost and phoned back, attempting to explain to my mother that just because these people were in my phone under their first names did not mean they were my best friends, and they needed to cancel the party immediately, or I would be forced to shoot myself in the face. "I thought there were rather a lot of people on the guest list," she laughed. "I said to your father, Jess can't possibly have that many friends." While I took offence at the final part, it was also true. I could count on two hands the number of friends I would invite out on my birthday, and on one finger the number I would hit with a family event.

As usual, my mother failed to grasp the gravity of the situation and told me not to worry, that plenty of people would turn up. I sighed, and hung up, realising she would never understand that this was what I was worried about. At the exact time I needed to cement the new me with some kind of suave cocktail event that would make me known far and wide as a successful catch, I would be attempting to hide in the corner of a stuffy old marquee, while my family attacked friends, colleagues and providers of local services with evidence of my past. With every embarrassment, mistake and failure I'd been running from ever since I left home.

I lollopped back to my desk, sexy red dress slightly hiked up on one side, but caring very little. I sat down, took a deep breath, and decided while my social life was falling apart, I should at least make sure my career was on the up. I opened my emails to another two responses from Brendan. His favourite colour was blue. My dress for Friday night was blue. It all seemed much too obvious, but it was the only dress I had and I was overdrawn, maxed out on my credit card and far from in a position to purchase a new one to wear at a one-off work event. I decided it must be fate, and if God was forcing me to flirt with my client, I was going to try and do the Christian thing and listen. The only saving grace was that I hadn't yet put Brendan's details in my phone, so at least he hadn't been invited to the Lansdale family circus.

I pulled Kiran aside for another after-work SOS, but we decided the more effort I put into a situation, the more it seemed to go wrong, so she said I needed to set myself a new challenge. Enough with the 'Man Plan', as she put it. From now on, I was not going to attempt to seduce a single guy for the rest of my life. Instead, I was going to casually stand aside and wait for them to flock to me. We decided that work men were off the table anyway. I needed to keep the four key areas of my life – work, friends, sex, family – completely separate (apart from her, she added quickly – although I assumed this didn't mean she was open to a potential fling. Things were enough of a mess without throwing bisexuality into the ring). This didn't solve the family birthday fiasco, but Kiran assured me we could deal with that nearer the time. She offered to perform arson on the marquee the night before, but said I should definitely check whether it was covered by insurance, as she was only willing to commit "victimless crimes".

With our new sensible outlook in mind, I made it home by 9.30pm and only four glasses of wine. I walked into the lounge to find Leanne and a random man eating dinner at the table. I said my hellos, grabbed a bottle of wine and scurried back towards my bedroom. I saw Denise's light was on, so I barged in there and sat down on her bed. She was reading a magazine and cursing the fact that Leanne had secretly been on five dates with this man and not deemed it appropriate to tell us she was practically half-way towards marriage. She left the room and re-emerged with two mugs, and we cracked the wine open to bitch about the poor guy's shirt.

Sometime during our communal man-hunt Leanne had found a prize and kept it well and truly to herself. We felt betrayed in the way that only single women can when their friends desert them for a life of coupled-up bliss. How dare she drop out on us and not even have the good grace to tell us it was over? We ordered a pizza. I explained Kiran's suggestion that I shouldn't throw myself at my new client. Denise sighed. We both wondered what was happening to the world. We discussed it with the pizza boy. We took another bottle of wine out of the fridge. We asked Leanne's bloke what his intentions were. We returned to Denise's bedroom. We wrote the chorus to a song. We went to bed.

Friday rolled around and I was determined not to treat it as a potential sexual encounter. I tried to recall the months I'd gone without either having or thinking about sex while I'd been shacked up in coupleville. Instead, I would be steely and professional. I would not care whether my dress looked hot. I would not care that I had a medium/large spot on my chin. I would not flirt. And I would not drink more than four glasses of wine, which, since the party started at 6pm and finished at midnight, meant one every hour-and-a-half. Maybe I would have one an hour to start with then cut back later on…

I dragged my long, blue dress out of the wardrobe. My enforced lack of interest in the event meant I hadn't so much as tried it on to make sure it still fitted. It didn't. I went into Denise's room in search of safety pins, since the zip wouldn't close all the way up, but Leanne caught me in the hallway, took one look a my pathetic size 12 girl in a size 8 situation and went rummaging through her drawers for support pants. We decided it might be necessary to wear two pairs at once, since both offered "mild support". Together we hoped they would provide something more in the region of "strong support" and that it would be worth the chronic VPL that was occurring as a result.

Leanne offered to curl my hair, but I stuck to the plan and said I was just going to tie it up. She compromised and fashioned it into some kind of bun. I decided to keep the make-up minimal, settling for exactly the same cosmetics I used during the day, but just more of them.

The result was OK. But I reminded myself that was exactly what I was going for. Leanne asked one final time if I was sure I didn't want to spend a few more minutes in front of the mirror. I walked back to my bedroom and grabbed my bag as the taxi beeped its horn. Ronald gave me the thumbs up through the window, and I took that compliment and ran. It didn't matter that he was about 100 years old. It didn't matter that he could barely see five metres in front of him.

By the time the taxi stopped I practically jumped out. I was of the belief that show tunes should only be indulged in theatres, old people's homes and within a week of Christmas Day. I'd listened to what sounded like the am-dram recording of The Sound Of Music for the entire journey, and while it was one of my favourite children's films, Nazi invasion aside – my mother had strategically fast-forwarded to the point where I believed the children had gone on to be theatre stars with very formal bodyguards – I did not need the amateur version of Climb Every Mountain to be my inspirational song for the night.

However, I immediately found myself calling on the tune as I climbed a ridiculous number of steps to the venue. I assumed the party would be in some stuffy function room, with big, round conference tables pushed into corners to make room for a small, potentially career-damaging dance foor. After I'd been in the lift for around ten minutes, what I actually walked out into was a huge penthouse floor. Every surface was shiny and reflective, and glittering lights were dancing to the music, making it difficult to tell the doors from the floor-to-ceiling windows. I made a note not to walk into any glass, which is something I really shouldn't have to do, and set off on a confident power-stride to the bar.

After listening to the first few orders I ascertained it was a free bar, which would make sticking to my four wines particularly difficult. I ordered a cocktail instead, assuming it might last longer. I was wrong. My Woo Woo lasted all of five minutes, during which time I hadn't even left the bar area. I'd been taking in my surroundings, and desperately trying to tell one suited-and-booted male from another in the dim, club-like lighting. I noticed a few people heading out onto a terrace, so I grabbed my second drink and wandered in the direction of the floor-to-ceiling window that I had also seen act as a door. I was concentrating so hard on remembering which one it was, I barely noticed Brendan shout my name.

He gestured for me to join a group of five nearly identical-looking men, and I headed over with what I hoped was the purposeful walk of a successful and only averagely horny businesswoman. I wondered whether he noticed I was wearing a blue dress and whether or not he thought it was for him. I remembered I was taking a night off from thinking about things like that and smiled as I approached the group. Brendan made the introductions and asked if I was heading out onto the terrace. I said I was, and he gestured for me to lead the way.

Shit. I had completely forgotten which glass wall lead to the outside world, and which lead to my utter humiliation. Again, it was like Labyrinth, but without even the annoying door knockers to give me a clue. I tried to dawdle and see if I could spot anyone else heading outside, but no such luck. Just as I'd targeted a screen and was holding my breath, hoping it would swing open rather than make me want to jump the 30 storeys back down, the wall three panels over swung into the room and Mark came strolling through. I tried to manoeuvre subtly in his direction, the five men following behind me like a flock of geese. Brendan introduced Mark to the group, and we all headed to the terrace, pride and nasal cartilage intact.

The view was pretty spectacular. I slowly drained my drink as I wandered from ledge to ledge, looking out over the sparkling lights of London from three different angles. Like most people around me, I was secretly trying to see if I could find my flat, even though it was a good few miles from the city centre. Mark came up behind me. "Can you see it then?" "What?" "Your flat?" I took a sheepish swig of my drink. "No." We both continued to gaze out until Brendan came over. "I thought you lived north," he said casually. "I do." "Well, you're looking east." He held me by the sides of the arms and guided me like his confused old grandma to the adjacent ledge.

"See, that's Alexandra Palace," he pointed, "and, can you see that big chunk of green?" I nodded obediently. "That's Hampstead Heath." I was enjoying my guided tour, but even with my layered underwear situation it was getting pretty chilly and I feared the ample padding in my bra was not enough to disguise it. We headed back inside and sat at a table by a glass window/wall/door so we could still see out. Brendan didn't seem bothered about schmoozing, but I guess

157

you shouldn't have to when it's your own party. People should come to you like they do with the queen. I looked out of the window and saw the Bride Of Frankenstein staring back. Apparently my casual hairstyle hadn't stood up well against the wind.

I manoeuvered not-so-casually in the direction of the toilet to fix it, and wondered why more bathrooms didn't just have stalls where you could sort out your hair and make-up, because that's what 90 per cent of women were doing in there, and it just got in the way of those who actually needed to pee. Luckily, it was still early and most of the women hadn't made their entrances yet, so the toilets were empty bar the lady with the soap. And towels. And sweets. And perfume. This situation was out of my comfort zone. I smiled at her and locked myself in a cubicle.

Did I have to tip if I picked up my own soap and dried my hands on my dress? Was leaving a pound enough? What if I wanted to use some perfume? Was it a pound a pop? Should I give her £5 and then just go for it and use everything? Should I strike up conversation? Offer to bring her a drink? She looked bored out of her mind. Did everyone worry like this when they met with a toilet attendant? I rifled through my bag. I only had a £10 note. I could tell her I was going to get some change, then ask at the bar, where they weren't taking money, so probably didn't have any. I could just apologise and say I didn't have any change. Then wipe my hands on my dress and get the hell out of there. That would defeat the object of going in in the first place though. I needed to stand next to her to get a good look at my hair in the mirror.

I sat on the lid for a few minutes wondering what to do. Then stood up, pulled at the toilet roll, flushed some down the toilet for good measure and emerged from the stall. I hadn't expected free drinks, so my £10 would be well spent in the toilets instead. I would treat it like an all-inclusive holiday, hoping that if I gave her the £10 now, she would be nice to me for the rest of the evening (she wasn't).

I wandered over to the mirror, washed my hands, gracefully accepted her offer of soap, a towel and hand cream, then tipped my make-up out on the side, scrabbling around to find my mini hairbrush. I started yanking at various bits and trying to force them back into place, but my mop was not cooperating and when I glanced at the attendant, she was grimacing in my direction. I figured I was fighting a losing battle, as usual, and moved on to the perfume. I was determined to get my money's worth, so I carefully sniffed at each bottle to see which I liked. They all smelled pretty much the same – like the stuff my dad used to give my mum at Christmas in tiny sample bottles. I decided on the first one I'd allowed to pollute my nasal passages and sprayed it directly into my face. Neither of us said anything, and I reached for my eye-make up, ready for when my eyes stopped watering. I realised at this point I had probably been in the toilets for around a quarter of an hour, and that both the attendant and Brendan probably thought I was a freak and/or experiencing extreme digestive issues.

I quickly stuffed everything back into my bag, dramatically pulled out my £10 note and put it in her tray with a smug smile. She barely looked at me in return and immediately went back to staring at the wall. Money well spent.

As I approached the table where I'd left Brendan about three years earlier, I noticed he and Mark were deep in conversation. I tried to mime 'drink' at them, but with my bag in my hand I have a feeling it came out more like 'blow job', to which Mark raised an eyebrow and nodded enthusiastically, so I headed to the bar and decided to pick up two beers anyway. For myself I made the executive decision to move on to champagne. After all, how could anything bad come out of something that looked like sherbet fizz?

I returned to the table and sat down opposite Mark and Brendan and handed them their beers. They were discussing some intricate details of the campaign, but I was still sober enough to partake in the conversation, so I jumped in, guns blazing and, for once, didn't make a muppet of myself. Here I was with other professionals, in a glamorous setting, and I actually felt like I belonged. I felt like I wanted to get my phone out and take a selfie of this momentous occasion where I actually had my shit together. I accepted a few more champagnes and the three of us were laughing and joking together like old friends. I imagined Mark pulling me into his office on Monday morning, congratulating me on my fabulous partying skills and immediately promoting me to his number two. Then the champagne hit me and I giggled to myself over the phrase "number two" and decided I'd better get my eye back on the ball.

Mark came and sat next to me and whispered something in my ear that I didn't really hear, so I nodded in agreement. He reached into his pocket and handed me a little bit of folded up paper and gave me a wink. I went to hold it up to the light to get a good look, but he snatched my hand back down and shoved it towards my bag with a questioning look on his face. My alcohol fog was still relatively thin, so it only took me a few further minutes of confusion before I realised he'd just handed me drugs. Brendan was watching me out of the corner of his eye. Clearly I had accidentally said yes, and it would be making too much of a big deal to now take it back out of my bag and say no, so I did what any good teenager would do and pretended to be cool.

I got up and walked to the toilets again, suddenly more worried that I hadn't come bearing gifts for the attendant (would she accept cocaine?) than the fact I was currently in possession of Class A narcotics. I would just stand in front of the mirror for a few minutes than head back out, giving the occasional sniff for good measure. I'd seen the movie Blow, I knew the deal. But then, would Mark expect some to be missing when he took it back? How much? I wandered into a cubicle and carefully opened up the little paper gift. The movies always showed big piles of the stuff, this was only a little sprinkling. Maybe he'd expect me to take it all?

OK, so I had no idea how to fake this, but I knew a person who did. I took a picture with my phone then texted Lisa, asking how much I should leave. She texted back, saying just get rid of half, or stop being such a loser and just try it. I carefully brushed half into the toilet and wrapped the remainder back up. At this point, I was so desperate to get back to the party and out of this situation that I walked straight past the attendant and outside, failing to even wash my hands, which is really disgusting (luckily I had my sanitizing hand gel, which I lathered on as I walked).

By the time I got back to the table, Mark was there alone. "Where's Brendan?" I asked. "He's no fun," replied Mark with a roll of the eyes, as he guided me back out onto the terrace. It turned out he was pretty hot and sweaty, and because of my fake drug habit, I now had to join him outside in the freezing cold, with all the other coked-up bores wittering on about themselves and sucking their teeth. I gave a sigh and gazed back inside, where I saw Brendan watching me. He immediately looked away. Great. I'd impressed my boss, but disgusted my client. It was a no-win situation.

Mark pulled my arm. "Don't worry," he said, a little too close for comfort. "I told him to back off." He winked conspiratorially and grabbed my hand to pull me down to an outdoor sofa. "Anyway, I pay your wages, so I have first dibs." Looking into his dilated pupils I could tell he still thought he was being suave, and no doubt expected me to fall at his feet. Suddenly what had previously come across as charm seemed super-sleazy. He'd crossed a finely tweezed line between sexy and sex pest and I made my excuses to head inside for another drink. At one point I might have been desperate for his sweaty palms all over me, but right now, I just wanted to talk to someone without having to pull my dress up to hide the half millimetre of cleavage that was clearly holding his attention.

Mark was officially off the list, and I thought I was officially off Brendan's list, so I looked around for a woman to speak to who wouldn't cause me any bother. Nobody seemed forthcoming. Somewhere around 11pm, what had been a perfectly legitimate schmoozathon had turned into something more like a uni party where everyone was just there to hook up. I sat at the bar and ordered another champagne, figuring I'd leave after this if I couldn't find any female networkees. Brendan came up next to me and raised his eyebrows. I turned back to the bar. I wasn't in the mood to expend my energy on a lost cause. He hopped up on the stool next to me.

"You didn't take it, did you?" he stated, as he picked up a cherry and plonked it into my champagne. We watched it bob around in the top, looking out of place and in need of escape. Exactly how I felt now. "Can I say something wholly unprofessional?" he asked. Finally, a comment about the dress. I was starting to think he hadn't even noticed. "Your boss is a wanker," he said matter-of-factly. I laughed despite the disappointing lack of sexual harassment. "Do you know, he actually warned me off you? I think he wants you all to himself," he said with a visual shudder. "Yeah. Pen, ink, office nib..." I said, trying to remember the saying about not shagging your boss.

"Well, if that's your motto I'm perfectly safe in saying I like the dress," he said, smiling. "You are indeed," I said, relieved. At least he'd noticed, which was nice. But I was done trying to mix sex with my career. If I was going to do that I would be getting paid a hell of a lot more. "I've got a taxi coming in half an hour," he said. "It's on the company, so I'll get it to drop you off first. No funny business," he said, hands raised in a familiar pose of surrender. I realised it was actually nice speaking to him without Mark's overbearing presence. I didn't need to be dragged around as the token female employee by my boss, who was, against all odds, apparently trying to get me into bed.

We waited in reception for the taxi, and Brendan was the perfect gentleman, going a good 20 miles out of his way to drop me off, and handing me a lollipop he'd swiped from the toilets as I tried to make an elegant exit, before giving up and hiking my skirt over my knee with a smile. Maybe I didn't need to be the super-confident career-woman after all. I'd managed to get on much better with my client just by being my unglamorous self. It was probably best to tone done the Jessness come Monday, but I was grateful for the least disastrous end to the evening possible. I would just have to deal with Mark after the weekend. He was, after all, a massive drug-addict perv. And that definitely wasn't on my list of things to do before I turned 30.

CHAPTER NINE

It's My Party

As my birthday approached I was plagued by nightmares (and not just the usual teeth-falling-out stress dreams). On this particular morning, I had dreamt that I'd been turned away from my local pub for failing to show valid ID to prove I was under the age of 80. Then I'd glanced in a shop window to see hair sprouting from my face in huge grey tufts, and had finally arrived home (to my parents' house) to find a delivery of adult nappies waiting patiently outside the garage door. I was officially freaking out.

I was turning 30, and I still had a hell of a lot of things on my list to achieve. I needed to write my first book, or at least get an idea for my first book. I needed to try a wine that cost more than £10 a bottle. I needed to have sex with someone with a pierced tongue and feet larger than a size 12. I was running out of time.

I'd spent the past few days trying to retract my

father's invitation for what was going to be the most humiliating experience of my life. My mother was hoping for a full house (or full tent, as it were), but I'd been texting as many people as humanly possible to apologise for a last-minute cancellation. Things were getting even worse in the parent department (most recently my mother had suggested installing a 'pole' on the dance floor because it was "what everyone is doing in the village"). Since I'd managed not to cause any of my own dramas over the past week, or certainly fewer than usual, I was damned well determined that my parents weren't going to drag me down as I made the transition from messed-up twenty-something to sensible grown-up.

Thankfully my father's jungle room had finally died a death, after the heating broke down for two weeks and killed off the last survivors of the foreign insect outbreak. There were very few weird things left for him to show my friends (without stepping into some pretty undesirable territory). My mother was in full organization mode. She was ringing me at least five times a day to discuss catering and music options. After she'd given up ballet, she'd taken up wedding planning for a few years before meeting my father and settling on arranging coffee mornings as her full-time job.

I'd begged a number of my most annoying friends, which was almost all of them, to cancel their attendance. They had all flatly refused, a particularly sadistic few calling my mother directly. They were very much looking forward to watching my social downfall while sucking up to various family members and drinking what they were assuming would be "good wine". My mother had recently joined the Virgin Wine Club, and had started sending me a bottle a month from their selection. Denise had tried to order another bottle with our next Tesco delivery, only to discover it was worth a whopping £8.99. By far the most expensive bottle ever consumed. This had led to the urban myth that my parents were in some way sophisticated. Which they are not.

Luckily nobody from work other than Kiran seemed to be attending. Unless you counted the sandwich guy, who was coming as her guest. But just to make sure nobody felt inclined to turn up at the last minute, I planned a Thursday night drinking session to tick the workmate box. Mark seemed particularly keen. I, however, was not.

I was on the verge of having my birthday celebrations back under control when I got a text message from Paul asking if I was free that night so he could give me my birthday present. He had been constantly trying to develop our fuck-buddy relationship into something more serious, and it was stressing me out. I was clearly going to need to set him free, but it seemed like an unwise choice until I had back-up plans firmly in place.

My guilt got the better of me, and I agreed. After all, who was I to deny anyone the joy of giving me a present? He'd offered to cook at his flat, so I turned up in my jeans and a jumper expecting we'd eat a Bolognese, wash it down with some wine, and then hit the bedroom. But when I arrived, the table was set with candles and obscene amounts of cutlery. Clearly this prelude was going to take some time – there were three different forks.

This was exactly the kind of evening I might get jealous over, but here, in person, it seemed ridiculous. What was the point of wining and dining me when we'd been happily booty-calling for months? Shouldn't Paul be acting like a man by now? Shouldn't he stop calling altogether, rather than start acting like a creepy obsessive? I sighed and sat down as instructed, since there was a treat waiting in the form of a glass of wine and a big, flat present.

Paul sat down looking so excited I wanted to slap him. Why was something that should be romantic so horrifically awkward? Why was he turning into such a nightmare? I took a good gulp of wine and started to rip at the paper as he watched on, all eager. There's nothing worse than being scrutinized while you're opening a present. I prepared my grateful smile as I pulled out a stack of paper. What the hell was this?

It looked like a nursery project. The poor misguided fool had cut out pictures and stuck them onto small pieces of cardboard, which he'd then tried to shape into hearts. Not only was he horribly untalented, he was also 32. Too old to be presenting arts and crafts to an adult. I'd clearly failed to mask my disdain, so I quickly snapped into a rigid smile as I planned my escape route. Maybe I'd eat the first course then feign illness, or claim an allergy to one of the ingredients and say I needed to go home and take my medication.

"Turn over to the next page," he said excitedly. Clearly he still had no idea of his faux pas. I turned to the next piece of scraggly A4 card to be faced with what looked like a threat from a horror movie. Using letters cut out from magazines and newspapers, Paul had painstakingly taken the time, as all good stalkers do, to write a poem. I skimmed over the gory specifics, but the final line implied he was going to kidnap me. OK, so it was probably more in the realm of weekend away, but my survival instinct had kicked in and I was officially done here.

He explained he had a long weekend in Venice planned, but that he hadn't confirmed the final booking because he wanted to check with me on dates. I racked my conscience to see what the least offensive way out of this was. He hadn't actually booked, so saying no at this point would be perfectly OK. It would mean an end to our arrangement, but maybe it was just the get-out clause I needed. In the meantime, I just needed to decide whether it was kinder to tell him after dinner – which actually smelled pretty good – or just rip the plaster off quickly and leave the room within the next two minutes. As hungry as I was, I was desperate to get the hell out of there, and as Paul reached for my hand across the table, I jumped out of my seat, downed my wine, shouted something about periods and ran for the door.

So, I hadn't entirely solved the problem, but I was pretty sure my carefully coded message would have hit home. This was not what I signed up for, and as I approached 30, I no longer had time to invest in relationships that were creepy and increasingly ridiculous – particularly not ones that involved homemade stalker presents. I made a promise to my guilty conscience that I would sit down and explain nicely that it wasn't working – in an open, healthy,

169

friendly text.

I got home and recounted my nightmare evening over the phone to Selina, and eventually via three-way with Matt and Charlie. Selina thought I'd done exactly the right thing. I puffed up with pride, before Charlie guilt-bombed me and asked whether I'd tried to call Paul to make sure he was OK. Matt just said I needed to sort my shit out and stop hanging around with random losers. All very helpful, but I was going to ignore everyone except Selina.

I did, however, spend a good four minutes constructing the best "It's not you, it's me" message I could. I figured if I wanted better dating karma, I needed to put better energy out there. This wasn't great, admittedly, but the text must have pushed me back up by a few points. If karma is measured in points. Which I don't think it is...

All I knew was that this latest fiasco had left me pretty much 100 per cent single in time for my 30th year. I headed into the lounge, where Leanne and Denise were tucking into a low-fat pizza. I pulled up a cushion and grabbed a slice just as Leanne photobombed me with her boyfriend's genitals. The general consensus was hairy but well-sized and Denise headed to the kitchen to put on a low-fat garlic bread. We'd forgiven Leanne for finding happiness with someone who turned out to be relatively normal, and had now gifted her with the position of relationship guru.

I looked at Denise, who, despite her keenness to slut it around when I'd first moved in, hadn't been on a date in weeks. Leanne had found a steady, happy relationship and actually felt the need to hide it from her crazy single friends. Even Lisa, who had phone numbers thrust in her general direction every time she left the house, had remained stoically quiet on the man front since the issue with the gay PR. And when I'd spoken to Selina last week she'd bored me with details of her latest trip to IKEA. Not so much as a mention of a hot warehouse guy and only one illicit joke about Swedish meatballs. What the hell was happening to us? And where the hell were all the decent men?

On the morning of my 30th birthday, I awoke feeling old. It may have been the 15 whisky and Diet Cokes I'd consumed the previous night (I was heading towards middle age and I needed to watch my weight), or that my cracked make-up had rested in crevices I'd never noticed before, but either way, I was not feeling ready to face the day/year/afternoon of horror in my parents' garden. I picked up my phone to see what time it was. Maybe I still had time to get up, take my make-up off, put my night cream on and have it work as quickly as possible while I snoozed. The 12 missed calls from my mother suggested not.

As I crawled out of bed I heard shushing in the lounge, so I decided to take a shower before I emerged to whatever shenanigans Denise and Leanne had ready for me. Selfish? Yes. But it was my birthday, and I wasn't about to walk straight into the centre of a celebratory attack without washing off at least the top layer of my hangover. I spent a good half an hour in there using all the lotions and potions my mother had sent me over the past few weeks (the same magic anti-ageing miracles she used herself). I officially wanted to

171

hang myself with the shower cord.

When I finally made my appearance in the lounge Denise and Leanne were already munching on my birthday cake. There was still enough left for a candle, so they sang happy birthday with one eye on a cookery show and I was handed a slice and a mug of cold tea. "What time are we headed to the Buzzard?" asked Leanne as she casually pulled a wax strip off her leg, then took a huge sip of what smelled suspiciously like an Irish coffee.

"Can I remind you that you were officially uninvited by the guest of honour?" I said in a last-ditch attempt to keep my family humiliation to myself. "It's fine, I'll just call your mum," said Denise, as she picked up her mobile and faked pressing buttons like a parent to a child when they threatened to call the scarier parent – or, in Selina's case, the "children's prison", which was actually the sorting office around the corner. Her mother had a lot to answer for. These days that would pass as actual child abuse, and may be one of the many reasons Selina ended up in actual prison (well, a police cell) on her 18th birthday.

The official start time was 6.30pm, but my mother had demanded I arrive by six to "get the party started". I had no idea why she thought she could pull these things off, but at some point I would need to stage an intervention. My brother's addiction to the word "dude" was one of the most annoying things ever, but it was a small issue on a very long list of reasons to disown him. My mother, however, was a different story. She had recently used the following phrases in day-to-day conversation: "I'm all over it like butter on bread",

172

"As if", "Bring it on." She had also used the phrase "the bomb" on the phone to Denise. It was officially out of control and I needed to lock it down. It was too late to save the party, but I made a note to speak to her about how ridiculous she was becoming.

I wandered back into my room and opened my wardrobe. I knew my mother would expect me to wear a dress, but most of mine were too slutty for parental consumption. I spotted a long-sleeved black one and threw it on with some black tights. The result was more funeral than birthday, but I wasn't convinced that by the end of the night, it wouldn't be wholly appropriate.

Once Denise and Leanne were ready – they seemed to have dressed as Stepford daughters in pastels and pearls – we set out on our trek, picking up Lisa on the way. She immediately handed us each a mini bottle of wine to "get the party started". I told her my mother had used that exact phrase just days ago and she stopped speaking for almost five minutes.

Finally the train pulled into Leighton Buzzard and I saw my father, who was wearing a suit for the first time in around 100 years, waving frantically from the car park. I put my hand up briefly to signal we'd seen him and encourage him to get the hell back in the car, but he continued to gesticulate like a deranged monkey until we were less than a metre in front of him.

Even though he'd never met Denise or Leanne before, he gave them both a massive hug. And then a kiss. On the lips. I took a deep breath and reminded myself that this was just the beginning of the evening to come, and if I was going to worry about my father face-raping my friends, I might as well head back into the

173

station and jump off the bridge right now. While the wine had mildly calmed my nerves, I needed something a little stronger if I was going to make it through my party without crying. Right now I definitely wanted to.

As we pulled onto our road, I could already see the marquee. It looked as though it was filling our entire garden and spilling into the neighbours'. My mother had rented a smaller one to go out the front, seemingly for the sole purpose of getting from the road to the house. She had also accessorized the remainder of the house with flashing fairy lights. It looked like a ten-year-old had been let loose in an events catalogue and pretty much circled everything.

We scrambled out of my father's gas guzzler, which smelled strongly of eau de McDonald's, and headed through a door of hanging fairy lights into what he referred to as the "welcome walk". Inside, the walls were decorated with pictures of my face. If it had been cute baby photos that would be one thing, but my parents had deemed it appropriate to seek out the most hideous of teenage hair disasters and line them up in a social house of horrors. One was my official school portrait aged 13, where I was smiling widely with big metal braces and a perm tighter than Orphan Annie's. The rest got steadily worse from there.

I tried to usher the girls through as quickly as possible, but they were taking photos on their phones, no doubt sharing my humiliation on social media, so I huffed past them and into the house. It looked like my parents had found it vacant and decided to squat inside. They'd removed the furniture – all except the drinks cabinet, which had grown a small attached side-bar since I'd last been round – and covered the entire room in plastic sheets. My Aunt Mary was behind the bar, very carefully measuring shots from what looked like an antique cocktail book.

I tried to dodge her and make it to the garden unscathed by her famously suicide-inducing comments, but she spotted me, carefully put down her apparatus, and stalked slowly in my direction. "Jess!" she said, holding my shoulders and pulling me in just close enough for three air kisses. She'd recently been to Paris and come back even more annoying than when she left. "Hi, Aunt Mary," I said in the sing-song voice with which I'd communicated to my extended family since childhood.

I tried to release myself from her cast-iron grip and make it into the open air of what would turn out to be a horrendously stuffy marquee, but she held fast, her bony fingers stuck in deep. I wondered if she was trying to cause the amputation of my right arm as my birthday present, but she suddenly released the pressure and said she'd just had the perfect idea for my gift. I said not to worry, this party was more than enough. But she ran to her handbag and scrawled an IOU note. I assumed it was more for her than me – she was pushing 70 and her memory wasn't what it used to be.

I looked down to see that I would be receiving a colour and restyle at Paul Sandford, the hairdresser of choice for the local over-50s. I accepted the style slap with grace and escaped into the marquee, which was hotter than a sauna. My father had taken off his shirt and tie and was walking around putting chairs out with his suit trousers undone and nothing but the hair on his chest (and back) to hide his marshmallow torso. I looked around for my mother, who, once again, would prove the least absurd person in my family. As far as I could see, neither of my siblings were in attendance, which suited me just fine.

"Darling!' my mum squeaked as she rushed towards me with streamers in her hands. The theme was pink and purple, much like everything I owned at the age of ten. She locked me in a hug with her tiny arms before I could get her attention focused on four potential disasters I'd spotted in the past 30 seconds. The first, and most pressing, was my father. "My friends are here, you have to make Dad put on a shirt," I whined, expecting a battle. But two minutes later he was even doing up the buttons on his cuffs, which up until this point I was fairly certain he didn't know existed.

Next I needed to figure out the temperature. It was around 100 degrees inside the marquee and, since my brother was nowhere to be seen, I assumed it wasn't in the interest of making women take their clothes off. Lisa finally made her way through to the 'main venue' with a customary, "Fuck me." She immediately removed her coat, which my father nearly fell over himself to take from her. I guided her away and we set about fiddling with the patio heaters, which were situated in every corner, on full-blast, and in danger of burning down half the street.

"Mum, they're supposed to go outside," I said as I tried to force the dial to budge from 'max'. "Well, what would be the use in that?" she answered puzzled, and walked off to consult with my DIY dodo of a father.

Denise and Leanne came in, looking unusually shy. Apparently my aunt had got to them, and Denise was now cursing her choice of dress, and Leanne was trying to take her hair out of the ponytail she'd spent all morning working on. "Ignore her," I reassured them. "She commented on my hair as well." They both tipped their heads to the side and didn't offer any positive response, so I gave up and headed to the huge pile of flaccid balloons on the floor next to what my dad was currently describing to Lisa as the "DJ booth".

After we'd huffed and puffed our way through hundreds of balloons – or, in fact, nine between us in 20 minutes – my father eventually walked over to ask why we weren't using the helium machine. Lisa went to the bar to get my aunt to rustle up a few mojitos while we worked, and Denise popped two balloons in a mini-rage before we got the helium on the go. My mother tried to join in, getting her head alarmingly close to the machine, before I slapped her with a health and safety warning. "Oh, but it's so fun," she said flicking her hair back. "I do it with the girls whenever we go to that nice Italian, Prezzo." I promised her a shot of helium later in the evening if it was taken with caution out of an actual balloon, and decided against starting in on "that nice Italian, Prezzo".

The next mission would be to sneak out front and remove as many of the giant face pictures as I could. I was just heading out, when I heard my brother's car pull up. OK, so I couldn't identify his specific car through the wonder of sound, but I could hear loud rude-boy music, tyres screeching and something hitting the curb at an alarming speed. I hurried along my wall of shame, grabbing at the most offending articles and collecting them under my arm. Andy trudged towards the house, carrying boxes of booze, with Stuart following obediently behind him. I stared at Stuart in disbelief. Hadn't our mini showdown in the pub implied he would not be top of the guest list at my party?

"Oh, hey," he mumbled in his Irish drawl. "I didn't know you'd be here." I eventually shut my gaping mouth and continued to glare at him until my brother stepped between us. "You are so full of yourself," he said, shaking his head. "*What?*" I screeched. He gestured to the photos under my arm and the remaining offenders still on the wall. Before I could assure him and my wholly unwelcome ex-liaison that I had nothing to do with this particular display of narcissism, they had both walked straight through into the lounge and were unpacking their goods in front of a stressed-out Aunt Mary.

It turned out the five drinks orders she'd already received this evening had sent her into a tizz, and part of me wished if one of my recent sexual encounters had deemed it appropriate to turn up, it could at least have been Paul, who had bar experience. I realised I was still clutching my photos, so I shoved them into the downstairs toilet, then rushed back out to deal with the next crisis.

It seemed my brother and Stuart really had been seeing each other behind my back, and their Beavis And Butt-head rapport suggested it had developed into a pretty serious bromance. Lisa walked into the lounge for a top-up, simultaneously greeting Stuart and raising her eyebrows in my direction, as if to say "What the hell?" I headed over, grabbed the drink my brother was holding out, and rushed Lisa back out to the marquee. "My bastard brother brought him!" I whisper-shrieked. Lisa tried to jam her drink in her mouth before a smile broke out, but failed miserably. I tossed my hair and walked back towards the front lawn to remove the remaining portraits.

Apparently I'd missed my opening though, and three more carfuls of people were walking in the direction of the house. I downed my drink and returned to the bar to try and make nice with my brother and his annoying new friend. Every drink was currently being termed a "Long Island Iced Tea", which essentially meant they were mixing anything that came to hand and topping it up with Coke. I reluctantly took the brown liquid and returned to the main venue, which was finally looking like the wedding/bar mitzvah combo my mother was clearly going for.

Streamers and balloons hung from every available wall and ceiling space, while my father was hooking up what looked like '70s-style disco lights. He had stacked a pile of old records in the corner next to the DJ booth and was inviting Nev, the alcoholic neighbour, to, I'll assume, "get the party started". Nev's mousy wife was scuttling around after my mother, helping with final details and occasionally enabling her husband by bringing him another beer whenever he barked in her general direction. She seemed nice and I felt bad, so I called Denise over and suggested we get her good and drunk so she could actually enjoy herself for once. It was the kind of intervention Denise loved, so she

179

rushed off to find a less potent cocktail for our new recruit.

I heard a commotion from the lounge, where my Uncle Roger had just arrived and immediately challenged Charlie's husband Tom to what looked like a standing arm wrestle. My mother's little brother had been a builder since the age of 16, and after an accident last year (while his company were renovating the local leisure centre to bring it bang up to the 1980s with a wave pool), lost the end of his left pinky finger. This had led to a few months off work and about a lifetime's worth of drama, before he finally returned, desperate to prove his manhood at every turn.

While Charlie tried to extract her husband from the long arm of my family, I was momentarily distracted by a collapsible table that had appeared next to the bar. My Aunt Mary was scrawling a sign that said "present table". I walked over, placed her IOU in the centre, smiled sweetly and walked away. Somebody had to go first. I watched for a while to see what would appear, before deciding to give the guests some privacy in the gifting suite. I grabbed Charlie and Tom before heading into the marquee and the relative safety of my mother.

There was a loud crack and a screech of ear-drum popping proportions, as my brother took to "the decks" (my father's 25-year-old record player positioned next to what was still referred to as the "boom box"). Now we were being subjected to a 'song' that seemed, between the swearing and grunts, to be solely about blowjobs. By this point Lisa and Denise had broken out in the hugest smiles, and Leanne just looked horrified. My mother furrowed her brow disapprovingly, but my father told her to "get with the programme" and moved to the centre of the floor to bust some moves. I assumed, like all his useless skills, they'd been picked up on late-night TV.

Andy left his playlist running and headed back to the bar. I looked at my empty drink and headed after him. It seemed like Stuart had done a good job holding the fort, and I started to wonder whether I'd been a little hard on him. Then he and my brother let out a synchronized burp, followed by a high five, and I looked around the room for something less depressing. I noticed two of my distant cousins had arrived. I could barely remember their names and I was still a little shaky as to how exactly we were related, so I went over to try and figure out which ones they were. I had 12, or was it nine? As long as they were far enough removed not to make the Christmas card list, it was fine by me. I'd spotted a pack in Selfridges that were £25, which worked out at £5 a card, so I was going to have to be frugal in the name of style.

The tall one with breasts, but no other indication of sexual origin, was called Melody. She was joined by Alfred. Alfred was dull. I'd never looked at my watch so many times within a two-minute period. We managed to cover all the university fresher questions in the first 60 seconds, before he started talking about his goldfish. What person over the age of eight actually has a goldfish? I might have been able to get onboard with some kind of exotic specimen – like Nemo, or perhaps a small ray or those ones that look like the flying dog monster in The NeverEnding Story, that suck onto the side of the tank with their mouths.

I decided since it was my party I had a good excuse to 'circulate', so I dumped the pair back into the questionable depths of our family gene pool and rushed over to Kiran, who had just arrived. As my father was taking her coat, looking sweaty and breathless after dancing for a good 30 seconds, he inquired where she was from. That makes it sound like he wasn't being mildly idiotic and hugely offensive. What he actually said was, "So, what are you then?" Apparently Kiran's exotic mix of Indian and Armenian had my father confused, and as he was telling her she was very attractive for an "Eastern", whatever he thought that was, and that she reminded him of Princess Jasmine, I grabbed her and rushed her into the main venue, apologizing profusely and trying to pass my dad off as a mentally challenged uncle.

She said it was nothing a glass of wine wouldn't solve, so I headed back to the bar to collect a drink and her sandwich guy date, who I'd left behind in the panic. Considering there were only a handful of people currently suffocating inside my birthday marquee, I was finding my 30th birthday pretty bloody stressful. By the time Selina and Matt arrived, I was trying to create separate areas for family and friends to mingle freely without danger of cross-pollination. This worked pretty well for a few hours as various factions of my family, our neighbours and random men from my dad's 'Club' (this could be anything from boules to AA for all I knew) milled in and out, and dangerously close to the more attractive end of my friendship offerings. After my thousandth cocktail I was actually starting to have

182

fun, and didn't even care that Lisa and Selina were dancing in the centre of a circle of uncles I wasn't convinced were even all mine. What I did care about was Stuart sat in the corner with his hand on some girl's knee.

Matt, ever the faithful sidekick, spotted it at the same time as I did and tried to throw himself casually in my line of vision, but it was too late. The self-loathing hit me like a punch from my Uncle Roger's fully working arm. I was 30, I had no men on the go and the one I'd stopped seeing just over a week ago was currently using my party as a pulling ground for a replacement. Matt led me under a flap in the marquee and sat me down on a freezing-cold stone next to what looked like the beginnings of a garden pond. It was currently a large puddle surrounded by rocks and my dad's gnome Osama (he'd named him after I'd called him a racist for the 10 billionth time, and kind of proved my point in the process). He crouched next to me and cooed to me about how wonderful I was and how Stuart, and every other man I'd kissed, touched or sex texted this year, wasn't good enough for me. I listened dutifully, wishing I could just find someone more like him. Hot, funny, clever, normal. These didn't sound like such big asks a few months ago, but now it seemed about as likely as finding a low-fat Black Forest gâteau. "At least don't let that asshole ruin what is otherwise only a mildly tragic party," he winked as we headed back inside.

I decided to throw myself head-on into the embarrassment instead. After all, what 30-year-old didn't want to spend her Saturday night in a dance off

183

with the drunken neighbour's even more drunken wife? It seemed Denise had gone to town and properly welcomed her into our fold. Her dick of a husband was passed out slumped against a speaker, no doubt on his way to a week's worth of tinnitus.

My beloved sister had appeared at some stage, making zero impact as usual, and was refusing to take part in the merriment, also as usual. Instead I grabbed her sap of a boyfriend and threw him into the centre of the circle. He busted a few ridiculous moves, that I think were intended to be far from funny, and scuttled back to my sister's side. In the meantime, she'd recorded the whole thing on her phone. It may well have been the most outrageous thing either of them had ever done.

I was starting to have fun by default. I was being handed drinks from all directions, and I particularly enjoyed the consumption of alcohol when it wasn't paired with any effort on my part. Supping merrily on my thousanth mojito, I let the potential horror wash over me, although I was still struggling to entirely ignore bastard Stuart's presence. When I spied a few cousins, or half cousins, or second cousins once removed and stuck back on, who I remembered being less annoying than most, I headed in their direction. One of these things was not like the others, so I immediately demanded to know the identity of the tall, dark and handsome with the George Michael stubble.

Apparently he was a hanger on. He'd come with my 'cousin' Max, who could usually be found smoking pot behind the shoddily constructed shed at any family event. I decided this friend seemed intelligent, witty and truly fascinating, so I resolved to speak to him to find out if that was true. I'd settle for one of the three at this point in the evening. I spied Stuart looking in our direction, or maybe he was looking at my Aunt Beverley doing the Macarena with her underskirt tucked into her belt, but I figured I might as well turn on full flirting mode to make the fucker jealous.

Around seven minutes later I'd dragged Richard/Robert/Raymond/Ronald (the '90s hits were pretty loud at this stage) into the garden and away from the suddenly protective eye of my father. I needed to enter my 30th year with a bang, and since that wasn't appropriate in my parent's garden, a teenage fumble behind the washing line would have to do. As I grabbed R by the shirt, I stopped mid-tonguing to assess the situation from the outside. Was I really snogging some random guy at the bottom of the garden? Had my approach to singledom really regressed to secondary school? I wondered whether we'd head back inside to find everyone waiting to play spin the bottle.

I decided then and there that my 30th year's resolution would be to have more fun and worry less. This was the resolution I made every year, but it was something I was still willing to work on in the interest of developing as a better human being. I reinserted my tongue into R's mouth and we remained locked there for some time, before I pulled away again. "We're definitely not related, are we?" I asked, to be sure. He just smiled and carried on. I took it as a no, but figured even if he was a second cousin, that's not actually related by blood, right?

CHAPTER TEN

Playing Dress-up

I awoke to a cold October morning and the screeching of a car alarm, which was making my head vibrate even through my bargain earplugs. I dragged myself into the lounge and twitched the curtains to locate the offender, but the only person out and about at 8.30am (in his dressing gown, no less) was Ronald. I didn't think we had an octogenarian crime wave on our hands, so I went and put on a frighteningly similar robe, and headed downstairs.

Ronald (who in my head I liked to call Smokey for no apparent reason) was stamping his feet and attacking the car door with a small black box. "There's no keyhole!" he shouted. I gestured for him to turn his hearing aid back up. My grandma had always turned hers off when it was too noisy or, in fact, the conversation was too boring, and I was not willing to show the same level of patience with someone I wasn't even related to. Once Smokey was back with the hearing elite, I took the smart key from his hand and showed, in helpful slow motion, how to press the button.

The screeching ceased and Smokey asked me in for a cup of tea. It was wholly inappropriate, since we were both in our dressing gowns and I really knew very little about my ancient neighbour, so I went ahead and said yes. I was 30 now, so surely I could protect myself against an old man who walked like he'd had both hips and most of his other main joints replaced.

Five minutes later we'd nearly made it through the front door. I wished he was slightly smaller, so I could sweep him over my shoulder, like our second year teacher did to us in junior school (he's since been relieved of his position). Eventually we were in the hallway, and I was half impressed, half scared out of my mind. Either I'd just stepped into The Texas Chain Saw Massacre or our friend Smokey loved him some Halloween.

The hallway housed a menagerie of bizarre monsters made from what I hoped were plastic parts of people. Picture the scary little boy in Toy Story who pulled his toys apart and reassembled them with the wrong heads and bodies, but times it by a million on the creepy scale. Smokey had human skeletons with pumpkin heads, giant spiders with skulls on upside down... He'd even created what looked like a whole family of animals out of parts of stuffed cats and zombie limbs. I scoured the rooms for any sign of the beloved feline he stroked on the porch, but decided some things were better left alone.

187

I ran back through the hall and wedged the door open with what looked like a spare fibula in case I needed to make a hasty retreat. In the kitchen, Smokey was pouring our tea into big, black goblets. I raised an eyebrow as an indication that now would be a good time to explain his house of horrors, so he beckoned me with a bony old finger into the conservatory. It hadn't occurred to me before that he owned the whole house, and that it was probably worth over a million. Smokey was more of a catch than I'd previously considered, and I wondered, now that I was 30, whether I was ready to take on an older man.

We sat down on the requisite wicker chairs and I waited for a story from my personal Old Bear. Apparently the morbid decor was courtesy of his son, who was visiting not from Transylvania, but from Devon. The screeching car on his doorstop also belonged to his son, who he referred to as Jimmy, but was actually called James.

Apparently James was recently divorced and throwing a big Halloween party in an effort to win the love of his seven-year-old son. Less creepy. Just slightly desperate. Smokey asked what I was doing for Halloween and said I was welcome to drop by. As curious as I was to meet Smokey Jr, I told him I was heading to a big Halloween party on a boat. This excuse was actually true. Lisa had blagged free tickets through work for some kind of Halloween cocktail bash and invited me, Denise and Leanne. Leanne was out with her new(ish) man, so instead I grabbed Matt, who was always on hand to make up numbers or act as a fake 'plus one'.

Lisa had phoned last night to say people at these parties went all-out when it came to costumes, so today was put aside to find an alternative to the plastic devil horns I'd purchased at the local card shop. Matt was due over at 11am, so we'd have plenty of time to avoid going for the black dress and child-sized witch's hat I'd opted for last year. Back when I was all coupled up, Halloween had a very different meaning. It was an evening of fun and scares with friends, and the best costume was literally the best costume – one that looked like it had walked straight off a movie set. Now I was spending Halloween with Lisa and Denise (and Matt) I needed to take more of a Mean Girls approach and slut it up.

I thanked Smokey for the tea and headed back home to try and get a couple of extra hours' sleep, but after waking with a start from the third House Of 1000 Corpses-style dream, I gave up and headed into the lounge to see if the Kardashians were cashing in with a Halloween special. No such luck. I had a shower then searched online for costume inspiration until Matt arrived. At which point we dragged Denise out of bed, chucked her in the bathroom and waited for her to stop swearing.

Given that the party was described as a candle-lit ball with a champagne reception, we decided our creatures of the night would need to be black-tie attired. After trying two shops, Matt took the typical male approach to shopping and gave up. He bought some zombie make-up and headed off to rent a tux, saying he was going as the undead James Bond. Denise and I had tried on a selection of scary vampires, angels,

189

pirates, Morticia Addamses and other queens of darkness. Denise decided on a Carrie costume, because she said her dress was pretty much a ball gown anyway. I got confused and stressed, and after the seventh shop Denise demanded I make a decision within the next ten minutes. I grabbed a long, red dress, which turned out to be the Winona Ryder character from Beetlejuice, tried it on, decided I looked ridiculous and bought it anyway. After all, it couldn't be more unattractive than the Chucky costume I'd sported in 2009 (a ginger-haired, knife-wielding psycho doll didn't exactly scream "single and ready to mingle"). I decided with some carefully applied make-up I could still look hot as the forced-bride of a decomposing comedian.

Denise was in the spirit by the time we got home, and started mixing up cocktails in the washing up bowl, which she referred to as her cauldron. They were green and seemed to have some kind of steam emanating from them, but I thought it best not to ask questions and scooped some into a coffee mug, adorned it with what looked like a goblin's penis straw and headed back to my bedroom to figure out what to do with my hair. I had a feeling Winona's was big and back-combed, but my hairdresser had warned me against that last time I'd gone to a party as Patsy from Ab Fab. I decided it might be better just to get some wax in it. It wasn't.

By 6pm I was getting increasingly drunk and increasingly freaked out by Denise's Halloween soundtrack, which mixed it up between Thriller, The Monster Mash and other Halloween favourites (The Purple People Eater?), as well as some pretty scary sound effects. Every time the CD player let out a blood-curdling scream I came running into the lounge to find nobody bleeding from random orifices, then stomped back to my room.

At this point I could see that the party next door was in full swing. Small children dressed as randomly fanged superheroes, a few babies adorned as pumpkins and one dressed as a zombie baby – I couldn't decide whether to take a photo or call Barnardo's – were gathered on the porch, their parents attempting to traumatise them with a selection of props and sketches. I tried to get a glimpse of Smokey's costume, but I couldn't spot him.

Eventually I emerged in the lounge to find Denise in what looked like a silk negligée. "Are you even wearing underwear under there?" I asked suspiciously, as I circled her, my nose two inches from her various areas. "It's Halloween!" she said, rolling her eyes. I assumed that was a no, and wondered whether I'd been too sensible with my layered lace dress – black shorts underneath in case, god forbid, the wind were to toy with my false modesty. The doorbell rang and we buzzed up Matt, as we poured three more mugs of witch's brew. I assumed it wasn't particularly potent, since all I could taste was lime cordial, but I would later realise that was just its playful costume...

When we arrived at the dock down by the Thames, we were more excited than anyone over the age of five should ever allow themselves to be. I looked around to see sexy vampires, evil fairy queens and what looked like man-eating call girls milling around the entrance to the boat. The vessel itself was draped in black netting and cobwebs, and through the window I could see old-fashioned chandeliers and sexy undead waiters that were already getting my blood pumping. This was clearly going to be the best thing *ever*, and I needed to get inside immediately. Mostly because it was freezing cold and I had to pee.

A wolf whistle noisier than a jumbo jet alerted us to Lisa's presence, so we scurried in her direction all wide-eyed and unsteady on our feet. The chain came down and we charged towards the door, clinging tightly to the rails so we wouldn't have to change our costume theme to It Came From Beneath The Sea.

Inside the boat was the adult version of a haunted house ride. Only instead of cold, plastic seats it had plush, red-cushioned chairs, and instead of crazy inbreds handing out scares there were hot vampires and zombie waiters handing out drinks. As a bone fide fan of Halloween since the age of seven, when I put on a ghost mask and scared the crap out of my sister, I was in seventh heaven.

"Let's get that table by the window," slurred Denise, who was failing to adapt to the sway of the river and seemed oblivious to the fact that every table was by a window. We sat down at one adjacent to the bar, rearranged our costumes into less wind-swept versions and sipped on champagne as the crew made various announcements about how the king of the vampires was loose onboard and we should all watch out because he was thirsty for blood. Denise looked mildly alarmed given, as Carrie, she was covered in the stuff, but I reminded her we were on an organized trip and that vampires didn't go for those who were 'impure' anyway. She'd definitely have nothing to worry about.

Matt was busy fiddling with his bow tie, while Lisa touched up her pasty face make-up. Her costume consisted of a tight-fitting black dress and foundation that was a shade lighter than usual. The overall result did nothing more than bring her down from a ten to a 9.7. She still looked incredible, and already our table was getting attention. I sighed and held my glass aloft to see whether a kindly vamp would refill it, but nothing seemed to happen, and my arm was aching, so I gave up and put it back down on the table. "Drink, anyone?" I asked as the boat took an alarming lurch to the right.

Matt came with me to the bar. We ordered four 'Blood Curdlers' that looked suspiciously like sangria (not really an appropriate winter beverage). The man next to us smiled and asked which Bond Girl I was meant to be. He was unoriginally dressed as one of 10 million vampires walking the streets of London that night, so I decided his query wasn't worth my well-dressed time. I gave him a scathing look and skulked back to our table. "I feel like I need a name tag or something," I said, scrabbling in my bag, which was blue and purple and didn't match my ensemble in any way.

I looked around the room to see how other people were dressed, and if anyone else was suffering from ignorant people's severe lack of film knowledge when I spotted him. Beetlejuice. There was nothing for it. I would have to stand next to him for the rest of the night so people didn't ask annoying questions about my costume. I noted his table and got started on my starter, which was a prawn cocktail made of fingers.

Matt bit down on one and furrowed a brow. We all followed suit. After a long debate with the table next to us we agreed they were not, in fact, human fingers, but some kind of reprocessed fish. We drained the remainder of our blood-curdling Spanish refreshment, before the vampire waiters came around with a thick, red cocktail that appeared to be based on tomato juice. I made Lisa try it, as I have very strict rules regarding mixing vegetables with alcohol. Although Matt pointed out that a tomato was a fruit, and we mixed fruit juice with alcohol all the time.

I reluctantly sipped on my drink, pulling a face, until Matt grabbed it, downed it, then returned to the bar to find something more to my liking. Who needed a boyfriend when you had such a helpful drink-fetching buddy? Especially one who looked so good in a tux. When I had something of a less gruesome consistency and a few bubbles in my hand, I relaxed. Just then, the professional vampires swooped through the room and opened some big, wooden doors, disappearing into a wall of smoke.

We sat, waiting for some indication that the boat wasn't on fire, until Thriller blasted into our eardrums – for about the hundredth time that evening thanks to Denise's pre-party soundtrack. We all got up and headed into what turned out to be the ballroom. It looked amazing, like the underwater ruins of the Titanic, but dried out and bathed in blood. We shuffled in and found a spot, again near the bar, and put our bags in a pile in the middle of our circle.

I scoured the room for my zombie groom, but

Beetlejuice was nowhere in sight, so I tried out what I could remember of Winona's dance moves from the end of the film. A few drinks went flying, and Matt asked me twice whether I'd taken something, but eventually I was pretty sure I had the style down, and broke away from our group into the centre of the dance floor. I was overcome with the spirit of Halloween and nobody was going to stop me having my moment. OK, so the wedding dress was red and I didn't have so much as a boyfriend, let alone a husband, but a circle was emerging around me and I was more than happy to take this first dance alone.

But before I could really get into the groove, there was a cheer, and the sea of scary faces parted to allow my fellow '80s movie freak to join me in a dance of love. We stomped and strutted until everyone got bored – which was approximately half a song – at which point he led me to the dessert table. I looked longingly at the bar. Then I spied the chocolate fountain and a weird vat which proved to be full of white candy floss that you put on a stick with a skull on the end. It was a firm second place.

Beetlejuice introduced himself, while I stuffed candy floss into my mouth like the fat kid at a funfair: Chris – 5'8" (with built-in heels), fuzzy blond decomposing hair, brown eyes, likes pugs, dislikes mountain bikes. I sensed a story there, but I wasn't yet invested enough to sit through it, so I tried to shove the remainder of the candy floss in my mouth as I dragged him towards the bar. His cocktail of choice would be telling enough. He asked for the menu, which I approved of. He was a man who took his drinking seriously. After careful deliberation he went for a Howling Wolf, which was murky black and, according to him, tasted like a whisky and Coke. I went for a Virgin's Last Song, which was cloudy and white and tasted like a vodka and lemonade.

Matt came over and asked us what was good, then whispered in my ear, "Need saving?" He looked smug, like he was about to help me out of yet another bind, so I said, "No," with a hiss – which was impressive since it didn't have an 's' in it. Lisa and Denise came over to congratulate him on his dancing skills, and he was soon inducted into our coven with a series of fairly gruesome jelly shots. I was impressed at how well he was holding his drinks, but not sure I was holding very tightly to mine. A lurch of the boat and a matching one from my stomach and it was time to get some fresh air.

I excused myself, grabbed my clashing bag, and headed out onto the deck. The breeze was Arctic, and I hadn't brought my coat, but the air was making me feel less like I'd been at sea for the past two weeks. I leaned over the edge for a bit in case I was going to throw up, but nothing seemed to happen. I figured I'd stay like it for a while just in case, and was just leaning down to put my bag safely on the floor next to me, when the boat tipped violently to the left and my feet left the ground. I was halfway over the bar when I heard footsteps, and felt someone grab my knee and pull me back to safety. I was dizzier than ever by this point, so I spun around slowly to catch a glimpse of my saviour. Tall, dark, shiny hair, kissable lips…

What the…? Either I'd fallen in and drowned and this was my version of purgatory, or I'd once again found myself faced with my nemesis, Not-Ben. Although now I knew his name was Liam, so it didn't sound quite so dramatic. He gave me a wry smile as he backed away. "Don't hurt me!" he said in mock terror. OK, so he'd saved my life and deserved a smidgen of credit. He also probably deserved an apology for the tirade I'd launched at him for ruining my life earlier this year, but I wasn't here to hand out sweets, and I was still feeling pretty disorientated, so I just stared. He raised his eyebrows. "You OK?" he asked. I nodded, then flung my head over the side of the boat again just in time to be sick down the side. This seemed to be a running theme with him.

When I finally sucked up the embarrassment (and a disturbingly long line of green spittle) he was gone, and replaced by Matt, who had brought me a glass of water and a coat. I sat down on a bench and he put his arm around me to keep me warm. I sipped at the water and started to explain to him that Not-Ben (whose name I had temporarily forgotten again) had just saved my life, but he recoiled at my breath and went off in search of mints. Not the perfect gent, after all.

Eventually I made it back inside all wind-swept (which Beetlejuice assured me helped define my character) and smelling of roses (well, Extra Strong Mints). I got back in on the action and put some spontaneous choreography to work on the dance floor. Beetlejuice was showing an annoying interest in Lisa and one area of her revealing dress in particular, so I decided I needed to put the moves on him now to secure my catch. Denise spotted my approach and pulled me towards the toilets. "I've got a toothbrush,"

197

she ventriloquised into my ear. "Why?" was all I could think of asking. Her bag was tiny. How did she have room for a toothbrush and I hadn't even managed to squeeze in my mini-hairbrush? "We may be going through a dry spell," she lectured, "but you should always be prepared." She fiddled with my hair and applied some make-up to my face, then sent me out to retract my partner from Lisa's gel-nailed clutches.

It only took a few arm tugs and he was mine again, all crispy hair and white melty make-up. He was my Halloween prince. At this point our coordination was failing us completely and our dancing became more a matter of moving our feet to avoid falling flat on our faces every time the boat tipped. There was some kind of creepy announcement over the intercom about vampires taking over the boat and us needing to dock in around half an hour, which would mark the end of our evening.

Between the throbbing in my head and the churning in my stomach, the only vaguely coherent thought I could muster was that if I took Beetlejuice home he'd get make-up all over my freshly washed pillow (the likelihood of me getting vomit on it first didn't really occur to me), so I dragged him to a corner of the room to get my money's-worth on someone else's furniture.

A few raised eyebrows from the barman sent me and my costume counterpart heading for the toilets. They were unisex, so we figured we weren't actually breaking any rules. A few minutes in, the dimensions of the room and the swaying of the boat were making it a little more effort than I'd intended, and when he started

198

demanding that I say his name three times I knew it was time to extract myself from this gruesome grope. I wriggled free and broke through the door, barging past a group of people who may or may not have seen at least half an ass-cheek.

I tried to rustle my outfit back into family-friendly mode as I squeezed down the corridor in the direction of the exit. We were pretty close to shore now and my stomach had had about enough of this sea-faring adventure. Lisa and Denise were already waiting by the exit rope, looking about as good as I felt. I scanned around for Matt, who eventually made his way in our direction under a pile of coats and handbags. The boat bashed against the dock, making me wonder whether the crew were as drunk as the passengers. One of the vampire waiters had just pushed past us looking for his shoe, which didn't fill me with confidence.

Once our feet touched dry land we decided to call it a night. Lisa stumbled into the road, hailed a taxi, got in, and as we all headed in her direction, sped off like she was in a chase movie. We looked at each other for a few minutes, then decided to see if the Tubes were still running. The cocktails had set us back a little more than we'd realised and as we checked our various purses/wallets/pockets, we discovered our funds were running pretty low.

An hour-and-a-half and two night buses later we arrived back at our flat, where we'd demanded Matt would be sleeping to protect us from the creatures of the night. The bus to Finchley had succeeded in scaring the shit out of us, regardless of the fact very few people were dressed up. We could hear music coming from

199

Smokey's place, and I wondered if he'd left his new CD player on, but I saw bodies milling around through the window. Could it be that our 100-year-old neighbour was having a later night than us? As my mum would say, awesome.

I stomped up to our flat, feeling like I'd wasted what was a reasonably impressive costume, when I remembered we were actually invited to the super-cool late-night party next door. All considered, it would be rude not to attend. I marched into the lounge, where Matt had already passed out on the sofa, and Denise was scrubbing off her make-up and downing what looked like half a box of Nytol. I casually asked if they wanted to go on to an awesome party. They both told me to fuck off, so I marched into my bedroom to grab my own make-up wipes. After carefully removing then reapplying my make-up, I sauntered past my loser friends and across the pavement to the old man's house next door.

I couldn't decide whether or not to ring the bell, so I tried the doorhandle and let myself in. After tripping over Smokey's array of graveyard memorabilia, I headed for the kitchen to see if there was any alcohol left. In my rush, I'd failed to bring a bottle, but since Smokey and I were such good pals, I figured it wouldn't be a problem. The party seemed to be acting as a respite for the over-50s. They were milling around, occasionally dancing, and sipping cautiously from what looked suspiciously like alcopops. I suddenly wondered what the hell I was doing there. Until I spotted a hot stranger in the corner.

He was likely on the business end of 40, but if my

friendship with Smokey had taught me anything, it was that I was more than open to the idea of an older man. And this man looked like a young Tom Selleck, but with Friends-era facial hair. I couldn't wait to get tickled by his whiskers, so I headed in his direction, a can of Thunderbird and a half-empty bowl of nuts in hand.

I introduced myself drunk-coyly as "the girl next door." Not much about my current get-up suggested that, but I was talking to someone with a Frankenstein mask casually strewn around his neck and what looked like the remnants of green make-up on his hands. At least my costume got an A for effort in comparison. He introduced himself as James – 5'11", brown hair, piercing blue eyes, loves beer, dislikes cuttlefish – which immediately rang a bell. It took me a few minutes and an assault of seemingly random questions to decipher that he was, in fact, Smokey's son Jimmy. It turned out Smokey had gone to bed around 9pm, but had taken out his hearing aid, so the party had just gone on around him. James was staying over, and said in no uncertain terms that he was just waiting for all the random old relatives to leave before he high-tailed it upstairs himself. Apparently his seven-year-old son had come down three times to complain about the noise.

"Is his mum up there with him?" was the question that popped out of my mouth before my brain could inject any subtlety. "No, she's not around," he said, shifting on his feet. I was about to play separated/divorced/widowed, when I remembered Smokey had said he was divorced. Interesting. I could see the family resemblance in the eyes, but thankfully the similarity ended there. Smokey had liver spots and

201

an overhanging belly. James had more than two teeth.

I wondered what it would be like to wake up in the morning to James waving at me sexily from his window. Then I immediately felt guilty that I was killing off my old buddy for the sake of a hot new peeping Tom. In the meantime, James had been talking about a movie he'd seen with Arnold Schwarzenegger in that sounded ridiculous. I abruptly changed the subject and asked how long he was staying. "I'm heading back tomorrow morning," he said with a yawn. Damn, that didn't give me much time, considering that technically it was already tomorrow morning.

If my drunken calculations were correct, I needed to make him fall for me, desperately want my body and take me roughly in the spare room within the next hour or so. I was going to need reinforcements. I headed back to the kitchen, grabbed a bottle of vodka and poured two measures (each the size of a tea cup) then attempted to disguise the taste with a selection of the remaining mixers. Was this about to count as date rape, I wondered as I walked back through and passed him the cup with a smile. He gave it a sniff, stepped back, then picked up another beer and carried on drinking that. Damn. I was going to have to rely entirely on charm.

But just as I broke the five-minute silence with the beginnings of a hilarious joke I'd just invented about lesbian penguins, James took the drink out of my hand and led me towards the hallway. I tried to tell him that if he'd just let me finish my joke, I was pretty sure he wouldn't find it necessary to evict me, but instead of turning left to the front door he turned right and

202

mounted the stairs, not letting go of my hand. I really hoped he hadn't decided his son would enjoy my politically incorrect zoo-bound reverie, so when he opened a door upstairs and pulled me in without turning on the light, I peered desperately into the darkness to see if there was a minor snoozing in a corner. The room was blissfully empty.

As soon as the door closed quietly behind us, James jumped into action like a mercenary. There was no drunken fumbling, no hovering while the other person removed their shoes or wrestled with clothing. This was box office-topping movie sex. From the moment he threw me against the back wall to the moment we lay completely naked, panting on the floor, James had it going on, and I was starting to visualize myself as step-mum to his absentee child (and Smokey's favourite daughter-in-law). It would involve a significant lifestyle change, but for the pleasure I'd just experienced I was definitely willing to make that leap.

I imagined our love affair developing over the coming months, with James visiting on a more regular basis and me being invited to spend Christmas with Smokey and the family. James' son would object to his new step-mother at first, but my young, hip ways would win him over until I was his special confidant and we were one happy Hallmark Channel family. I tried to remember where Smokey said James lived. Was it by the sea? I liked that idea. After all, I was 30 now and maybe it was time to leave my wild city living behind and retire into sleepy village life.

I rolled over and peered into James' eyes. He started to gather up his clothes, bumping into things in

203

the darkness. I wanted to tell him he was ruining the scene. Surely we should fall asleep in each other's arms, illuminated softly in the moonlight. Then I'd wake up to him kissing my forehead and sneaking me out of the front door, followed by a lingering kiss on the front steps, regardless of morning breath.

There was a knock at the door and we both froze. "Daddy?" said a little voice through the keyhole. James gestured for me to scuttle into the wardrobe. Really? I'd spent most of my life trying not to get caught by parents, and now I was hiding from a child? My happy family dream started to shatter as I tried not to bash into too many coat hangers. It was musty as hell and I was pretty sure I could see moths flying around, but I stayed as quiet as I could, my Winona dress stuck half-on, half-off, my underwear-free lower section feeling particularly exposed considering there was a youngster just meters away.

I heard the door close again, and I peeked out of my hiding place, hoping to God the little boy was gone and I wouldn't become the face of crazy lady monsters lurking in his wardrobe for years to come. I felt around for my underwear, but it was nowhere to be found, so I concentrated instead on arranging my outfit to cover the offending areas. I was going to have to start carrying spare pants in case of loss or sexual damage.

When James came back in to retrieve his top, he seemed surprised I was still there. "I'm not that easily scared off," I said with what I hoped was a sexy smile. "I'm going to have to go and sit with him to get him off to sleep," he said as he pulled me down the stairs and towards the front door. I grabbed a pen on the way past and wrote my number on the back of his hand, regardless of the fact he'd shown no sign of asking for it. It turned out James was somewhat less forthcoming outside of the bedroom.

I wouldn't discover why until the following morning. After not-so-casually checking my mobile from 7am, I wandered groggily over to Smokey's with some Halloween candy as an excuse to see if I'd missed James And Son. As I helped him clear up the remnants of the night before, I casually mentioned that I'd made it to the party and was really sorry to miss him, but that I'd met his son, and how was he doing this morning? Smokey said he'd left first thing. He had to get back home early because his new fiancée was coming out of hospital. I stared at him for a few seconds. His *what*?

I took a deep breath. Not only had I inadvertently had an affair, but with a person so terrible he would have sex with another woman while his fiancée was in hospital. I started to ask what she'd been in for, but decided I didn't need any further details. So, I wasn't going to be Smokey's favourite daughter-in-law after all, since he already had a new one lined up, and I currently had sore muscles all over my body from working some of my best moves on a man who thoroughly didn't deserve them. I couldn't believe I'd brought back the twist and slide, which my aching 30-year-old limbs were no longer comfortably capable of, for this bastard. I felt a weird mixture of guilty and excited that next time I played "I have never" I would actually have something to drink to, other than "had sex in a park." An affair with a married man (well, once-married and about-to-be-married-again) wasn't ideal, but it was one step

205

towards cultivating the misspent youth I'd always dreamed of. I couldn't wait until Matt left so that I could tell Denise that I was finally maturing into a well-rounded adult.

CHAPTER ELEVEN

'Tis The Season

I awoke to the sound of sleigh bells. I was slightly confused, given it was still the night before 'the night before Christmas'. Either Santa was suffering from a bout of Alzheimer's or it was coming from within the house. I tried to ignore it and snuggled further into my duvet – all too aware that, as of tomorrow, I'd be waking up back in my parents' studio apartment. Potentially with a car and/or sibling in tow. Somehow I'd been signed up to a full four days of family fun. My father had twisted his ankle tightrope-walking on a piece of low fence, which had caused my mother to remind us this could be our last Christmas together.

I wasn't sure whether she thought my dad's latest obsession with circus skills would become exponentially more dangerous, or whether the two weeks waiting on him hand and foot while his ankle healed had set the divorce bells ringing. Either way, she'd laid it on pretty thick and I'd only just managed to get what started off as ten days down to a more bearable single digit.

The sleigh bells eventually turned into Last Christmas, and I was pretty sure Santa hadn't added a George Michael impression to his résumé, so I dragged myself out of bed to find out who I would be required to punch. Leanne threw open my door with the festivities emanating from her phone like a teenager on the back of the bus. She was dancing along in what looked suspiciously like the Sexy Mrs. Claus costume we'd seen in the Ann Summers catalogue the week before.

"So?" she asked, twirling (and flashing). "Nice." Denise pushed past in her reindeer dressing gown to hand me a cup of coffee. I took a sip to find it was Irish, which was a much more pleasant way to start the day than the straight Tesco's own we'd resorted to after our credit cards had taken their latest beating in the Christmas markets. Mostly on mulled wine. Mariah Carey's annoying but catchy Christmas ditty came on, and soon enough we were all dancing around my room like assholes, Leanne forcing some red tinsel around my neck that would leave a garrote-like mark for the rest of the day.

Denise threw the curtains open to show me the 'snow' (which turned out to be half a millimetre of frost) and Smokey waved enthusiastically at us. He gestured for us to stay put, while he briefly exited, stage right, then came back wearing a Santa hat. It was his wink that reminded Leanne she was essentially standing in her underwear, so we waved back and quickly redrew the curtains and headed into the lounge.

Leanne was spending Christmas with her boyfriend, and had agreed to a whopping full-week stretch, even though they'd only been going out for a few months. Since she was heading there straight from work, we were swapping presents this morning (hence the enforced, and very early, merriment). We'd originally attempted to do a Secret Santa, but after I pulled my own name out of the hat seven times in a row, we gave up and set a £5 limit. In all likelihood we'd have confessed who had who within minutes anyway.

I whipped my presents out from under our 1.5 metre Argos Christmas tree. They were wrapped in red paper left over from a birthday, but I'd made the supreme effort of attempting to draw a reindeer in the corner of the white sticker I'd used as a tag on each. It looked more like a miniature schnauzer, but I was still experiencing a mild amount of creative smugness.

Denise topped up our coffees and turned Leanne's phone down so we could concentrate fully on the pleasure of giving and receiving cheap Christmas cheer. I looked inside a small, green bag to find a plastic lipstick that started buzzing when I twisted the lid. "If you're at home for Christmas you're going to need something to do while the turkey goes down," said Denise, as Leanne opened her matching pocket vibrator. "I know you think you're having a romantic week with the boyfriend," she said to Leanne with a pitying look, "but I bet you're on a sofa bed in the lounge. At least you can take this to the toilet alone."

I'd bought them each a wine glass that held an

entire bottle (although I now realised how jealous I'd be with my stupid regular-sized glass) and Leanne had bought us each a shot glass with our face on (stunning pictures snapped while we were sleeping, no less). We wondered briefly whether this is what thirty-somethings were supposed to exchange at Christmas, but a third Irish coffee stopped us caring and we headed back to our rooms to get ready for work.

As we left the flat, Smokey emerged from his porch (still in his Santa hat) with a giant box of holiday cookies. We thanked him profusely, while Denise rushed back upstairs, grabbed a bottle of whisky that was almost untouched, wrapped a red hair ribbon around it, and re-emerged with a pair of reindeer antlers on. Those were some slick Christmas tidings.

Since today was the last day of work before the holidays, I was hoping to do very little other than go online and complain that most of my shopping hadn't arrived. Thankfully by the time I got to the office people already seemed to be clocking off. We'd agreed that instead of Secret Santa we'd each just put £10 in a kitty for a 'drinks trolley', which Mark's assistant would wheel around while we 'worked'. We all knew getting anything done on the last day of term was a complete fallacy, and I could see the school's-out buzz already kicking in. Kiran was playing some kind of Santa race on her computer against Male Jody, who I could see was the reindeer and winning by a mile.

I plugged my mini Christmas tree into the USB port on my computer and took off my coat. There had been talk of decorating the office from around October onwards, but nothing had happened until Monday this week, when Mark's assistant had purchased a white tinsel reindeer and matching tree. She had immediately been requested to "get in the box" for half an hour as a punishment for her chavvy taste. Now, looking at this impressive winter wonderland between the lift and the drinks machine, I was glad for the sparkly white. Especially given the 'snow' from this morning had quickly turned into grey sludge by the time I'd hit central London.

I mooched through hundreds of Merry Christmas emails from clients and about ten times as many out of office replies. Clearly most people had had the sense to get out of London before the last working day. For once I was grateful my parents lived relatively close. Kiran had a train booked for 6pm that would get her into Liverpool to see her folks by 11.57pm. She didn't have a reserved seat. I shuddered at the thought.

As Mark's assistant came round with bottles of wine in place of any kind of Christmas bonus, I figured I'd give mine to Kiran to drink on the train. I took a plastic cup from the water cooler and wrapped her makeshift gift in a Christmas-themed plastic Debenhams bag I found under the desk. As I walked over to her I nearly tripped over Mark, who was playing Twister with the work experience girl. I thought how lucky he was that we still didn't have an HR department set up.

Kiran and I had been discussing New Year plans since the summer, but eight days before the big event we still weren't any closer to welcoming next year with anything more than a half-hearted fizzle. At one point we'd been on the verge of shelling out £200 each to go

211

to some kind of masquerade ball in Covent Garden. But by the time we'd done a rough budget for the evening we realised there would be no money left for a new outfit, alcohol, or so much as a bus fare, so the idea had been vetoed. Kiran said there was a party in the Docklands that would only be £50, including dinner, so I said I'd check with the rest of the New Year posse – which was getting bigger by the day. It turned out most of my friends were equally bereft of glamorous plans.

I texted all the usual suspects with the NYE plan, then followed everyone else's lead and shut down my computer at 11.30am, ready for the work Christmas lunch. We all piled out of the office, Kiran grabbing my hand and pulling me ahead of the crowd to make sure we didn't end up at the butt end of the seating plan. We hauled ass to the pub, changed a few name places around and sat down happily next to each other in the middle of the long table. I didn't notice until it was too late that I'd inadvertently put myself next to Mark, and that his sexy-sleazy smile and my alcohol consumption may not go well together.

By the main course his hand was firmly planted on my knee. I was trying to figure out what my action plan was, and whether I should get one more inappropriate liaison out of the way before I set any New Year's resolutions, when I saw him pinch the waitress's ass with his other hand and decided it was time to make my move – the hell away to the opposite side of the table.

Kiran came with me, and we shuffled some randoms out of their seats with two big festive smiles. The lunch was fairly uneventful from there, so we watched a man on another table play with his long, blond rat's tail for the next hour while we planned what we would wear for New Year. I realised it would mark the anniversary of the demise of my relationship and any potential I had for a happy future. I also realised that even in my most depressed moments at the beginning of the year, I'd still kind of assumed I'd have a date 12 months later. With eight days to go, this was looking most unlikely.

Kiran and I had gradually moved our chairs away from the table so we could whisper about Male Jody's bad haircut and what a slut the work experience girl was. We were now sitting equidistant between our colleagues and another table of what I assume were someone else's colleagues. We peered over to their champagne spread, then looked back at our measly offering of house wine and the remnants of the Christmas buffet selection.

Kiran kept nudging me to say it looked like Mark was going to give a toast, and it might be time for Christmas bonuses, so we stuck around expectantly, munching on three sausage rolls, a handful of crisps and a small, fishy vol au vent between us. After half an hour of looking expectantly at our great leader, we realised no lump sum would be landing in our laps (and paying off a small portion of our Christmas credit card debt), so we joined the first few evacuees and headed "back to the office," which involved picking up our stuff and getting the hell out of there.

By this point Kiran and I were starving, so we headed to Marks & Spencer's to get some proper food before we headed off. Never have we been more excited to discover that our favourite posh food shop also does takeaway. We each ordered a burger and went and sat under the ass end of the giant reindeer in Covent Garden, trying to work out which one it was and whether we could see any balls. We couldn't remember much of the song beyond Prancer, which everyone knew was Santa's equal-opportunity gay reindeer. Given this one's shiny white fur and glittery collar, we made the only assumption we could so close to Soho, and carved his name into his hoof.

"We just tagged a reindeer," said Kiran as we walked away nonchalantly. "We're 30 and we just tagged a reindeer." I was about to ask why the hell turning 30 meant you suddenly had to act like an adult, but between that and the Tiffany album that had been playing on my iPod for the past ten years, I decided to accept defeat. I was never going to be a grown-up and I didn't care. I stuck my tongue out at nobody in particular and we exchanged a festive hug, before heading off towards our own versions of personal hell. Although Kiran was only sentenced to one-and-a-half days... Her family didn't celebrate Christmas, but it didn't stop her mother demanding everyone's presence over the holidays.

I arrived back at the flat to see that Denise had already been and gone and left me a half-eaten elf cookie as a parting gift. I headed to my bedroom to start packing. I didn't really have anything clean to wear, but surely that was one advantage of going home? I tried to find some items in festive colours, because my mother had previously refused to cook Christmas dinner until the entire family were dressed in either red or green.

I located some socks designed like Christmas stockings and found a pair of pants with a penguin on and shoved whatever I could reach, including Denise's lipstick gift, into my roll-along suitcase. I realised I hadn't opened my Advent calendar for a week, so I opened all the remaining windows and shoved the cheap unbranded chocolate in my mouth all at once. It was pretty grim, but overindulgence was part of the Christmas spirit, and I was determined to be full of it by the time I arrived in the Buzzard.

On the way to the train station my suitcase wheel got stuck in a grate and as I simultaneously tried to extract it and send a tweet on my mobile, the wheel came flying off and rolled down the street under a pile of leaves. I looked at my watch and saw that I was likely to miss my train already, so I hailed a cab, which was celebrating the holidays with 'Do They Know It's Christmas?' on repeat. Luckily my journey was only long enough to sit through three renditions, but by the time I reached the station I certainly knew it was Christmas. It seemed everyone else at the station, however, did not.

I squeezed in and out of screaming children, grumpy businessmen, and what looked like teenage train conductors standing around joking under a departures board that primarily read "cancelled". True to the Christmas miracles I'd seen on TV, my train was only seven minutes late, so I picked up my pull-along and walked casually to my platform. It was chaos onboard, but I smugly held my reserved seat ticket aloft and ejected a smirking forty-something in high heels

215

from my window seat.

I sat back and watched the angry mob on the opposite platform, whose train had been delayed by two hours, so far. I strained to see the destination, but couldn't make it out. I did, however, notice two people standing very calmly at the end, gazing into each other's eyes and ignoring the apocalyptic behaviour around them. As I looked closer the man caught my eye. Before I could pretend I wasn't staring, I realised it was Paul. With the security of a pane of glass and a train track between us I lifted my hand in a finger-wiggle and he waved back, what I assumed to be his new girlfriend looking up and waving too. I watched them as the train drew out of the station and realised my happiness for him was only slightly outweighed by the question of whether or not she was hotter than me. I hadn't really got a close-enough look, so my brain suggested I dropped the subject before any Grinch-like thoughts ruined my Christmas spirit.

My phone beeped, and I looked down. It was from Paul. "Happy Christmas" it said, with two kisses. Why was he so damn nice? Even after my brutal rebuff, he was still wishing me holiday cheer. It made me feel all warm and fuzzy even though I was stone-cold sober. I drowned out the harried phone conversations and people being shouted at for standing in the aisles and got in the mood with the Santa race Kiran had shown me on my phone. That is, until my mother texted to say she couldn't pick me up from the station because they'd had almost two centimetres of snow. My father could walk and meet me or I could get a taxi.

It was Christmas, after all, and I was determined to

stay in the spirit, so I decided to arrive in style and get a taxi to the house. Then my mobile rang. "You have got presents sorted for your cousins, haven't you?" she asked. "What cousins?" "Sweetheart, I told you that Max and Robert were spending Christmas day with us…" "Robert's my cousin?" I screeched, alarmed, remembering our bottom of the garden tryst at my 30th bonanza. "Well, he's a second cousin by marriage, and he's adopted, but that doesn't mean you should love him any less." I let out a sigh of relief. I hadn't committed incest as well as adultery in the space of a few months, so maybe Santa was still coming after all.

I said I'd pick something up at the station and hung up. Once there, I grabbed two Jamie Oliver cookbooks that were on offer in the miniature WHSmith, lost another wheel off my case and shuffled to the taxi rank, where I stood for half an hour shivering until a taxi deemed it appropriate to drop by. The queue behind me was at least 20 people long and it had, finally, started snowing.

By the time I made it the five minutes around the corner to my house I was faced with near-blizzard conditions. I pulled my now severely disabled suitcase along the drive as my family waved from the lounge window, none of them offering to leave the radiator area to help. I scrabbled in through the front door as my mother finally broke into hostess-mode, trying to pass me a glass of wine and take my coat in unison. Wayne was sitting on the sofa in one of the ugliest jumpers I'd ever seen. It had an angry, staring human face coming out of an otherwise innocuous-looking snowman. He jumped up to show me, explaining that it

217

was my sister, her face forever captured in a Christmas jumper. "Don't worry, love, you're not that ugly in real life," my dad assured Laura, as he walked past shielding his eyes from the jumper with his hand. At least he'd relieved me of the responsibility of telling them they were ridiculous for now. I noticed she didn't have a matching one with *his* face, and wondered if there was trouble in the land of no awareness.

I walked into the kitchen to top up my wine, then sat down to watch a Wallace & Gromit special. There was currently no sign of the "cousins", including the one I'd accidentally liaised with, so I could relax for a while. My mother announced I wouldn't be sleeping in the garage/studio, but in the "library" (formerly the jungle room). My father offered to show me around. He said he'd top up the drinks on the way back in, but he'd only fetch a beer for Wayne if he removed "that fucking ugly jumper." That my father did a swear seemed to escape my mother's attention, so Wayne did as he was told and folded it neatly on the arm of the chair, where the cat immediately made herself comfortable, kneading her claws pointedly into my sister's face.

I followed my dad upstairs to the door of my new bedroom, which had a poster of a woman with her finger over her mouth and a speech bubble, saying "Shhh." I didn't bother to point out to my father that the person who makes by far the most noise in the family is him, so I turned the handle and, for some reason, half tiptoed inside. What I was faced with was a room with three mismatching bookcases, each with around five books on. A further three tomes were piled in the corner.

"Way to go Dad, you've really outdone yourself." He half-heartedly picked out a few books and spread them onto other shelves. One of them clearly belonged to another library, and from its February stamp, was long overdue. "I don't think you can just steal books from other libraries to start your own," I said, dumping my bag next to a flaccid blow-up bed in the middle of the floor. "They factor in a few lost books each year, love. Don't worry." "I don't think it counts when some old man steals them for his own collection," I said, wondering whether I should just go ahead and report him, to avoid this getting out of control. "I'll have you know I'm still very young," he said, ignoring my main point about him breaking the law. "Just yesterday a woman asked me to get a roll of wallpaper down for her at B&Q," "Was she a midget?" My father was hardly the tallest person in the world.

Thankfully my mother called upstairs to save me from mining the depths of my father's mind any further, and we headed back down, he assuring me it would be OK to borrow a book while I was staying for Christmas. Although I would have to finish it quickly, because he couldn't let people who lived "outside the area" take them "off-site". I turned down his kind offer, saying I would be much too busy with mum's back copies of Top Santé and House & Home to move on to any longer-term projects.

We returned to the lounge, where my mother was laying out what she referred to as "a spread". "It'll just be the three of us," she said, opening enough Marks & Spencer packets to feed a family of ten. "Your sister and Wayne are going to the pub quiz, but your brother should be here soon." "Come to the pub with us," Laura said smugly. I considered the offer for nearly ten seconds, before Wayne started trying to retrieve his festive jumper from beneath the cat and I quickly declined. Hopefully my parents could just sit in silence in front of the TV until bedtime like the normal families I'd heard tell of.

Tweedledum and Dumber left the building, and I lined up behind my father at the buffet table. That I had to queue for food when there were only three of us was absurd, but luckily my dad rushed off to the kitchen before he'd even picked up a plate, so I started piling mine high. "Don't go in the fridge!" screeched my mum, as she ran in after him. "I'm just getting some food," my dad replied through something he'd already managed to shove in his mouth. "Not the cheese!" my mother wailed.

I flicked through the channels, trying to find something that would be family friendly, but wouldn't make me want to kill myself, and settled on one of the hundreds of identikit comedy quiz shows. There was a fat hairy man, who mostly did jokes about how he couldn't get a date, a young Asian woman, whose material was exclusively about her family and periods, and a guy I hadn't seen before, who looked about 12 and seemed to be just pulling faces and making gestures with his arms to get attention. I put my paper plate on the arm of the sofa and got up to refill my wine.

My mother was carefully overseeing my father's cutting of two approved cheeses, whipping them out from under him and smothering them in cling film the

220

minute his child-friendly knife finally sliced through. I wandered to the fridge unnoticed until I opened the door. "Don't go in the fridge!" She came rushing over. "What do you want?" I gestured with my wine glass and she led me over to the 'drinks zone', where a bottle of white was bathing forlornly in a plastic washing up bowl filled with ice. It seemed like a waste of space, time and, in fact, ice, but I poured quickly and left the area. She was in 'Christmas mode' and I wasn't going to be the one to rile the beast.

In fairness she was incredibly calm, given it was the 24th of December already. Usually by now, Christmas had been cancelled at least twice, and my father had booked and cancelled a selection of local restaurants at least three times "just in case". I shooed the cat away from my plate as she grabbed a slice of ham and headed upstairs. I hoped she wasn't going to chow down in my library room. My phone beeped, and I rummaged in my bag, dropping a few grapes on the floor and kicking them under the sofa. I wondered what the hell my dad was concocting in the kitchen for both of them to be in there so long.

It was an unknown number, which I usually ignored, but it was Christmas and I had nothing better to do. When I answered, it was my brother saying he'd run out of gas on the M25 and couldn't find his credit card, so could I give my details to the nice lady on the other end of the phone. Before I had time to tell him to go fuck himself, an ancient-sounding woman asked for the long number across the front of my card. "Can I speak to my brother again please?" I asked. "Just the big one across the middle," was her response. I gave up and gave her my details. For all I knew my brother was in a strip club and I'd just paid for his evening's entertainment. "That's £110 gone through on your card," she said cheerily. "What?!" I screamed, as the line went dead. How the hell had I just paid over a hundred pounds to get my brother a couple of miles along the M25? Christmas or not, I was going to kill the bastard.

"Who was that?" asked my mum, momentarily taking my mind off a plan for an accidental hit and run that would have me firmly at the steering wheel and my brother firmly under the back wheel. "It was Andy," I spat. "Oh lovely. It's so good of him to come back for Christmas. Is he nearly here?" I gave her a puzzled look, wondering why nobody had said it was nice that I'd come back for Christmas, and at what point I had really been presented with a choice that didn't involve losing my inheritance. I nodded furiously. "I just had to pay for his petrol," I said, stepping into tattletale mode. "Well, it is Christmas," she replied gazing at a photo of him on the wall like he was George Clooney (pre-smug era – circa that hospital show). I gave up trying to bring down the prodigal son and downed my wine.

The doorbell rang and my father, unusually helpful, got up to answer it. Nobody emerged for a good five minutes, so I took inspiration from my mother and peered around the curtain to see him chuckling with a random neighbour. As I heard my dad start what would no doubt be a long story about the energy efficiency of different Christmas lights, I made a quick escape into the hallway, fleeing from the words "crystal ice bear".

Last year had been a traumatic time for my father.

The inflatable Santa that had been squatting on our roof for the past ten years was the victim of an aggressive pigeon attack, which left him somewhat deflated. My father had been on the hunt ever since for a new giant Christmas idol with which to upset the neighbours and had recently discovered a white LED polar bear in some kind of plastic-themed homeware catalogue. The description said "stunningly bright", and it was one of the most disgusting things I've ever seen. Surprisingly, yet thankfully, the high-quality item in question had sold out, and my father had been forced to welcome the holidays with nothing more than fairy lights in the windows and a "North Pole" sign pointing to our house from what turned out to be the boundary of the neighbour's garden.

I crept to the top of the stairs and took refuge in the library, where my inflatable bed was showing no sign of living up to its description. I was looking around for a foot pump hoping I wouldn't have to huff and puff my 20 per cent-proof breath into my bedding, when I heard the unmistakable screech of my brother's car.

I made sure I had a clear route to my library after I'd smacked him around the head, then hovered patiently on the stairs, snow blowing directly into my face through the open door. I spotted him meandering up the driveway. He appeared to have shaved his head and gained about a hundred stone since my birthday, which looked so ridiculous I decided it was punishment enough. I also wasn't sure I could take him in his current marshmallow form, and he wasn't known for taking it easy in physical fights. I have a vague memory

223

of being five, when he nearly drowned me in the swimming pool on holiday by standing on my head in the shallow end. He'd also used his plastic ride-on car to perform a hit-and-run on my Wendy house while I was still inside and tried to smother me in my sleep with a life-sized Sylvester toy within the same year. That's while he wasn't making a small graveyard for my Sylvanian families at the bottom of the garden. The raccoon clan rose from the dead at least ten times that year. My parents turned a blind eye to this, as with every other clue that pointed to their son being a psychopath. They obviously hadn't read We Need To Talk About Kevin.

I stomped downstairs just in time to see my mother thrusting a handful of cash towards him in the doorway. "Why are you giving him money?" I demanded. "I'm the one that paid for his petrol!" "Your brother has come all the way down from Edinburgh," was my mother's response. "Why are you giving him money?" I repeated, on the verge of stamping my foot. Nobody had given me any money... The beginning of a pout formed on my lips. "Sweetheart, he's had to drive hundreds of miles, have you any idea how much that costs in petrol?" I started to say that, as a matter of fact, I did because I had just paid for that amount in petrol, but my tiny mother was already laden down with my brother's suitcases and trying to feel her way through the hallway.

Five minutes later my brother started up a characteristically inappropriate conversation about a threesome with two girls from the field hockey team, which my butter-wouldn't-melt mother got confused with some kind of new sport, proceeding to ask some pretty intricate questions.

I decided at this point that the lesser evil would be joining my sister on her date night at the pub. It was still blizzard conditions outside, but with my mother's trusty BHS snood firmly in place I made my way down the road to The Golden Lion, the place where I'd been served my first-ever schnapps and lemonade at the age of 15. At the time, it was the place to be because it got raided by police at least once a week (usually in search of under-age drinkers such as myself), and also because it had a Blockbusters quiz machine, which was the height of zeitgeist technology at the time. I had invested many a 20p only to go down in flames at the last minute on the Gold Run.

I stomped in through the front door, past the local 17-year-olds in festive sequined boob tubes, and didn't take my snood off until I was safely by the precariously placed gas heater on the bar. I caught fright at my reflection, but figured I didn't know anyone, other than my family, who'd had the bad sense to stay in the area anyway. I ordered a glass of what was referred to as "champagne". It cost me a measly £5, so I severely doubted its bubble count. I looked around to see if I could spot the Tweedles. I scanned past the table where people actually looked like they were having fun until my gaze fell upon the outline of an old married couple in the far corner, which turned out to be my sister and Wayne.

They were clearly the only people in the whole place not drunk and/or having fun. I downed my drink, ordered another one, took a deep breath and headed to experience my death-by-boredom. As I sat down they immediately started complaining bitterly that the quiz had been cancelled and they would have gone to The Woodman if they'd known, because they did better crisps. Wayne said he liked the cheese and onion ones best. We sat in silence for a few minutes. He added that the roast chicken ones were a bit "too much". I mentally shot myself in the face.

As I chiselled what turned out to be a penis-shaped hole in the beer mat, Wayne finally offered to "get a round in," which seemed like a dramatic way of describing the purchase of two drinks. Laura had decided that a pint and a half of lager shandy was quite enough festive fun for her, so he headed to the bar to get me a white wine (after he'd nearly choked over the extra 50p for a 'champagne') and himself half a Foster's and lime. I checked my phone during the three-and-a-half minute silence that followed, as my sister gazed at the groves in the wooden table. I flicked through my texts. Denise had sent a picture of herself being mounted by three small children and a dog, what looked like the remnants of a glass of wine spilled across the carpet and a second dog licking it up. The message read, "Three days to go. Not enough alcohol in the world."

I felt sorry for her for a couple of seconds before looking at my evening's entertainment struggling to carry two glasses as he squeezed past merrymakers with an "Ummm" and an "Errrr" and the apologetic look of a dog that just peed on the floor. This is exactly the kind of situation where it's technically fine to revel in your friends' misery, because it makes you feel a tiny bit better about your own short straw. Apparently there had been a shorter one still left in the hat.

It's also nice to know that not everyone leaves London at Christmas to enjoy fabulous reunions with their fashionable, successful school friends during the holiday season. When people return to work saying something along the lines of, "Yeah, it was great. I think I'm still hungover," they mean from drinking alone in the laundry room, not from attending some kind of local holiday gala. Most people tend not to elaborate much, leaving that air of mystery that could either smell of being swept off on a Caribbean holiday or spending the day in the old folks' home with the grandma of a second cousin twice removed who you're not even sure knows who you are. Selina had tried to overcome this by applying a terrifying amount of fake tan over Christmas every year to imply she'd been living it up in foreign climes, but we all knew she'd been counting the hours until some quiet time during the Doctor Who Christmas special like the rest of us.

Eventually Wayne made it to the finish line and sat back down. His beer was now more like a quarter of a pint, and his shirt a little more tie-dye than it had started out, but he'd done the gentlemanly thing and protected my wine pretty well, so I grabbed it gentlemanly in return and downed half of it in one gulp. He and Laura started discussing how they'd forgotten to buy a present for Aunty Irene, who I assumed was his relative, rather than ours, since I was pretty sure I'd never heard of her before. I looked around the room like a bored teenager until my eye landed on a familiar face.

Ryan Philip – 5'11", super-gelled brown hair, blue eyes, likes his own reflection, dislikes beers other than Foster's and Stella. The first-name-last-name that sent a shiver down my spine from the ages of 13-15. I'd spoken to him on three very memorable occasions during the five years we were at school together. Once, he asked to borrow my pen. I rummaged in my B*Witched pencil case to make sure I offered him the full range of colours and nib types and, on looking at me like I should be in a special school, he took the green one and said, "Thanks." I had to wait a year for my next fix, which was when my friend Beth nudged me in the lunch queue and said right to his face: "Isn't that the guy you fancy?" Actually pointing with her finger. I managed to not speak for long enough for him to turn back around (and refused to speak to Beth for the rest of the week), but when I got to the checkout with my tray he turned around and said, "Don't worry, I didn't hear what she said anyway." Which kind of proved that he did, but was also a nice thing to say for someone so high up in the social ranks.

The last time I'd 'spoken' to him was at the Snow Ball in our final year. We hadn't really made the effort that some of the posher local schools had made, and there wasn't a ball gown in sight, but our identikit little black dresses were working pretty well for us and our wallets. I was at the bar ordering what in my memory was a wine, but what must have been a Coke considering we were all under age, and Ryan Philip was stood next to me. When I noticed him I dropped my purse on the floor in a panic and he bent down to pick it up for me, tilting his head to one side and saying,

"You've got quite nice legs, actually," as though this was a huge surprise. I ripped the compliment from the jaws of the cocky half-insult and proceeded to casually order my drink and walk away – strutting in what I imagined was a runway model gait, but was more likely the totter of me about to break my ankles on my cheap high heels.

Now, a million years later, here he was in the pub, and for some reason I desperately needed him to notice me. Pathetic? Yes. After all, I was now a mildly successful marketing something living a spontaneous single lifestyle in the big city. For all I knew he was a thrice married parking attendant who'd never left his hometown. As I followed my confident feet up to the bar to get a closer look and listen in to his conversation for old times' sake, I really hoped he was a massive loser. I wanted to feel the same exhilaration I felt when I'd been home two Christmases ago and walked into the local travel agents' with Ben to book a holiday, only to be served by a greasy haired Leanne Cooke, one of Ryan Philip's stream of girlfriends and voted most popular girl at the disco four years in a row (she lost her crown to a slutty new girl in the final year, but it was still a pretty impressive run).

I hovered for a while trying to hear what he was saying to a short stumpy guy I recognised as Lee Pewter, the annoying kid in the gang who was popular purely because he held the record for getting the most detentions without being thrown out of school (his dad was the Mayor). If he was still hanging with this goon, life couldn't be going that well. I caught Lee's eye and realised I was staring. I needed to at least make a pretence of trying to order a drink. The barman was over unusually quickly, and I panicked and ordered a bottle of 'champagne', which still cost less than three glasses of wine in London. I knew I was being a dick, but it was too late to take back the attention-grabbing gesture.

As I tried to scurry back to my table, the inevitable happened. Ryan Philip turned around. He saw me, tilted his head to one side like he had at the Snow Ball and grabbed my arm. "You went to our school, didn't you?" Yes, decades later it was still "their school", but I was pretty excited he'd recognised me (even if it meant I hadn't developed much from the sexy perm and braces combo I'd sported back then). I made a mild attempt to play him, with a squint of the eyes and an, "Oh, yeah, did we have maths together?" We actually had almost every class together. It was torture. "Yeah. Jessica, isn't it?" Holy shit. He even remembered my name! I went in for a final power play, tilting my head to mirror his and asking if his name was Philip. He seemed content that I'd remembered his last name and grabbed the ice bucket to help me back to my table. God forbid he should think I actually chose to hang out with the likes of Tweedledumb and Dumber, so I panicked and did what any sane woman would do in that situation. Told a white(ish) lie.

"I'm stuck on family duty," I said conspiratorially. "My sister just got engaged." It didn't reflect well on me that I had treated my sibling to a night out at The Golden Lion to celebrate, but it was too late to squirm out of it, and we were nearly at the table, so I spent the last few seconds of my walk getting into character. I swooped in and gave my sister a big hug while I whispered to her that she was now officially engaged, and to "just be cool". Unfortunately Ryan Philip had already got to Tweedledumber and was congratulating him. I just laughed really loudly to try and cover up the specifics of any communication, quickly pouring three glasses of champagne and trying to seamlessly top up my wine glass with bubbles. There was a silence that seemed to drag on for centuries and Ryan Philip started to look longingly back at his socially able friends at the bar, so I grabbed his elbow and suggested we leave the lovebirds alone.

"I had such a crush on you at school," he whispered in my ear, as we headed towards a small gap by the toilets, where I was starting to feel pretty at home. The overlooked teenager in me wanted to believe him, but I was pretty sure if I hadn't lost the braces, straightened the perm and bought some mascara I'd have been carrying my own damn drinks. Still, I had Ryan Philip's undivided attention. I was just savouring the moment, and wondering how long I could leave it before heading back to my newly engaged buddies when Ryan Philip stuck his tongue down my throat. Now, this was a moment I'd imagined on almost a nightly basis at the age of 14, but never had it gone quite like this. And never had it been anywhere near as unpleasant as the teenage fumbling that was currently occurring.

It turned out Ryan Philip's kissing technique had moved on very little from school. Maybe every woman he kissed since had been so grateful to have his tongue in their mouth that they didn't care what he did with it, but my bubble had been burst and was slightly leaking out of the left-hand side. Never had I been the victim of such a saliva-heavy onslaught. I developed half an ounce of self-respect and pushed him away with one hand, while forming a little plate with the other, like an old lady eating a biscuit. When I felt a moist string hit my little finger I knew it was time to remove myself from this dream-dashing disaster.

I casually wiped my hand on my jeans and said I needed to get back to my sister. He made a move to come with me, so I slapped the family card firmly onto his forehead, accepted his phone number with all the maturity and grace I could muster and ran back to the table, where my sister was looking disgusted and Wayne was looking out of it after consuming what looked to be around half the bottle. His out-of-the-blue alcoholism I could get on board with, even if I struggled with his choice of potential spouse. "What the hell was that?" demanded my sister. She clearly had no concept of the monumental shift in power that had just occurred as she had no idea who Ryan Philip was. Laura is so socially unaware that she probably thought she was the popular girl at school (which, I can assure you, she was not).

We'd all pretty much had enough of The Golden Lion at this point, so Wayne picked up the remnants of the bottle of champagne, which he hid none-too-subtly under his coat, and we made a dash for the door. I checked my phone to find a text from Lisa with a photo of her sitting in her lounge, next to her sleeping grandma, drinking directly from a bottle of whisky. I was reassured that at least I had a story to share about

Christmas, even if it was only a short chapter long.

We got home at 11pm (while the pubs were still open. Not cool) to find my brother alone in the lounge watching Die Hard. This was a bit of a Christmas tradition after our parents had gone to bed, so I grabbed a bottle of wine and joined him in an armchair a safe distance away. Tweedledumb said she was going to bed, but Tweedledumber said he'd stay and watch the movie because he'd never seen it before. Was it the one with the warring neighbours and the Christmas lights? None of us were quite sure what he was talking about, but I fear Danny DeVito may have been involved. He sat down casually next to my brother, who was disgusted enough with his lack of action movie knowledge not to acknowledge him for the rest of the holiday season, and I was stuck explaining John McClane's motives until midnight passed and I decided it was a less embarrassing time to head to bed.

I awoke Christmas morning to the sound of silence in my house. I looked at the clock to see it was 11am. Were those fuckers enjoying Christmas without me? I dragged myself out of bed and peeked through the door onto the landing. Also silent. The magic of Christmas was officially over when nobody in your family could be bothered to show any indication of excitement before midday. Last year I'd made it downstairs by ten, while my brother had dragged himself out of bed at 2.30pm, just in time for a very dry turkey.

I decided to break the habit of a lifetime and have a shower before I made my entrance. I was determined to facilitate at least one acceptable Christmas photo this year. I was halfway through tonging my hair into beachy waves when my mother tapped gently on my door, before flinging it wide open and rushing in in her red dressing gown. She'd brought with her what looked like a haggis, but on closer inspection was a stocking, created out of an actual stocking. I hadn't had a stocking since I was about ten, so this was a rare, and admittedly exciting, treat. That is, until I got halfway down and opened my third tampon directly after a small packet of cotton wool buds. I paused and looked around to see if I'd missed a saving grace like a small glass of Bucks Fizz, but there wasn't so much as a cup of tea to accompany the unwrapping of my personal pharmacy, so I battled on, trying not to think about how one side of my hair was finished to photoshoot-quality and the other was currently at a very precarious stage. I rushed through the remaining items – nail scissors, what looked like a trial-sized shampoo torn from a magazine, and, for some reason, a tiny water pistol – and got back to my mane maintenance.

By the time I made it downstairs, my brother and sister were sitting on the sofa surrounded by similar items – my sister had a small rubber shaped like a cat and my brother a pair of comedy glasses, but the remainder included tissues, combs and lip balm. My mother already had her head stuck in the oven. Not as any kind of suicidal gesture – that would come later in the day – just because it was a thousand years old and only reached its optimum heat right at the back, which was far from reassuring in terms of potential food poisoning. My father was ignoring the carefully laid-out Christmas glasses and drinking Tetley's straight from the can. I poured Bucks Fizz for myself and my nightmare siblings, with as little of the Bucks and as much of the Fizz as I could, and resigned myself to the sofa as my sister systematically sorted the presents into piles. It turned out our cousins weren't showing, thanks to a whopping three-and-a-half centimetres of snow in neighbouring Whipsnade, so I quickly re-tagged my Jamie Olivers and regifted them under the tree, snatching back the nail varnish I'd had my eye on since I wrapped it up for my sister last week. It was much too good for someone who still wore socks with individual toes anyway. I also decided that maybe the jumper I'd bought my brother was metrosexual enough for me to get away with.

Eventually we were all seated and we started ripping into our presents. These days they were usually chosen from a carefully stipulated Amazon list, so there could be no confusion or duplication. I opened my sad little pile, none of which looked big enough to be the 3D TV at the top of my wish list, but perhaps there was an IOU in there somewhere (I still hadn't used my free gay haircut voucher). My brother had bought me a copy of What Not To Wear, which must be pretty low down in the bargain bins these days. The accompanying message in the front simply read, "Take note." My sister had bought me a Mr. Bean board game. While she found this kind of bumbling British humour amusing, one too many holiday viewings had rendered Rowan Atkinson one of the most annoying people in the world to me and I couldn't think of anything I'd like to do less than lead his plastic avatar around a shoddy piece of cardboard.

235

I reached for my parents' present hopefully. Surely they'd at least looked at my list? After opening Nigella's Domestic Goddess cookbook and a pair of Bridget Jones-style pants, an offensive two sizes too big, I was fairly sure that Christmas was a complete bust. "Open that one," said my dad eagerly, pointing at my final gift. Here was my 'main' present. The one that would put all the little offerings to shame. As I pulled off the paper and opened the box, I saw that my father had been putting his lack of computer skills to good use with some kind of internet printout. It was for a year's subscription to a dating website. I turned to look at my entire family with contempt and retired to my library bedroom with a bottle of Cinzano in hand. I could hear my mother bristling that it had been very expensive and my brother saying something that began with, "Desperate times…"

I sat back on my blow-up bed and, as my ass hit the floor, I knew I was done with Christmas and all the forced merriment it entailed. Now I just wanted to focus my attention on New Year and all the false merriment that entailed. At least I would be back to civilization with friends who understood that it was not appropriate to give gifts relating to weight or relationship status and that wish lists were there for a reason. To save us all the hassle of returning our presents on Boxing Day. I went online and ordered some items from my Amazon list, hoping they might be in my flat by the time I got home (they weren't), drank half the bottle of Cinzano and passed out. I woke up in time for turkey sandwiches later that evening, at which point I decided to forgive my family due to mild starvation. The 'turkey' was more moist than the previous year, probably thanks to the pre-cooked chicken wrapper I spotted in the kitchen bin, and further Bucks Fizz was working quite well as hair of the dog. The rest of the evening was spent as it should be, watching The Sound Of Music and surrounded by seemingly unexpected levels of gas.

CHAPTER TWELVE

Full Circle

I awoke to the strong aroma of meat. I hoped it wasn't coming from within the bed. I'd been pretty slovenly since my return to London, and I may have taken a couple of meals "a letto", which Leanne claimed was Italian for "in bed". I removed the animal-print earmuffs I'd been sleeping in since I lost my earplugs and sniffed the air. Bacon. I quickly wiped the drool from my pillow and followed my growling stomach towards the kitchen. We still had one day before our New Year's Resolutions kicked in and I was determined to use it wisely.

I walked in to find turkey bacon sandwiches on wholewheat bread. Dry as a bone – not even a sliver of low-fat spread. I decided to make a pot of tea to try and help them down. Denise handed me organic Redbush teabags and a carton of almond milk. There was no sugar, and no sugar substitute (since Leanne had read

238

that all artificial sweeteners give you cancer). I took a deep breath. This was not OK, but if we made it through the day we could reward ourselves this evening. It was finally New Year's Eve.

The problem was, I was already exhausted. I'd stayed with my parents for the requisite time, then "borrowed" (although some would say "stole", since I pretty much took it and left a note) my mother's Peugeot 205 and drove around the country catching up with equally Christmas-jaded friends. Check-List Charlie had announced on Boxing Day that she was pregnant and wouldn't be coming out for New Year, so I decided to get in my brownie points and visit her before she got too fat to move and started whinging about her ankles, or piles, or some other reproductive drama. The evening mostly involved holding small sample pots while she painted lines on the wall in the spare room and asked whether, as a baby, that colour would make me feel calm.

Just when I'd been asked to decide between 'Atmosphere' and 'Lost Lake' (both of which just looked 'Blue'), I got a call from Lisa. She'd found herself in the typically plush position of house-sitting for her boss over the Christmas break, and was living in a multimillion-pound property with a swimming pool somewhere in deepest Sussex. I was there in a flash, albeit one that lasted nearly four hours since the Peugeot tops out at 45 mph. We watched The Kardashians in the mini movie theatre, then decided to go swimming. Just because we could. And also to work off the wine calories we'd consumed over the festive break so far. We'd fallen into our filthy rich roles pretty quickly and were soon supping cocktails in our fluffy bathrobes while we perved on the gardener, who was trying to chisel the frost off the flowerbeds.

Now that I was back in London there was only Smokey to look at through the window, but the pride he was showing in his new purple jumper that morning at least made me smile. He even did a dance. Well, kind of. Denise had been in London for the past two days and Leanne was scheduled to return just in time for the celebrations tonight, but had texted late last night to say she'd had a better offer with the new man. She'd communicated very little since being holed up with his parents, except for the occasional text saying how nice his family were and how much she was enjoying herself, which only served to convince Denise and I that she'd been drugged and joined a cult.

I shuffled through the pile of post on the coffee table. Maybe Ben had returned from finding himself to find that he couldn't live without me. Then I could return his note to sender and start the new year feeling fully satisfied that I was not the Aniston in this relationship. Or maybe a random great aunt or uncle had suddenly tracked me down on Ancestry.com and sent an enormous cheque to apologise for being so hands-off for the past 30 years. Five minutes later I'd found neither to be the case. But I did find around a thousand leaflets about sales. I made a note not to buy a load of crap that I didn't want this year – unless it was at least 70 per cent off.

In the meantime, our New Year buddies had been dropping like flies, each accepting better invites or deciding life was just too damn depressing to leave the house and celebrate the oncoming of yet another fucking year. We still didn't have a firm plan, which probably wasn't helping. Nobody was willing to sign up to what could turn into a murder mystery evening or a games night at the last minute. Denise and I hit Google while hitting our second turkey bacon sandwich. We alternated episodes of Sex And The City and Girls to inspire us to aim high, but ultimately remain realistic about how our night would likely turn out. Kiran's bargain evening had fallen through after the venue temporarily shut down thanks to a particularly heavy moth infestation and she was stranded in Glasgow (the hometown of the sandwich guy) due to heavy snowfall.

Between our budget and our unwillingness to travel further than 30 minutes from our front door, our options were fairly limited. We found a local pub with a fancy dress party, but unless the theme last year had been inbred criminals, the photos online suggested these were not our kind of people. Matt called and said his neighbour had told him about a party in an old cinema, which was only around 35 minutes from our front door, so we hung up on him mid-sentence and checked out the website. The cinema was known for showing pretty artsy films, but it did have three bars. The costume criteria was just "the movies", which at least meant I could whip out my Beetlejuice ensemble if things got tough.

We texted Matt and told him his pitch had been approved and contacted the remaining guest list (which now consisted of Denise, Lisa, Matt and myself – so essentially I texted Lisa). Together we voted to disguise our laziness in the costume department under a general

241

Hollywood theme, which meant we could just wear nice dresses and too much make-up. I gave up on my wardrobe pretty quickly and sat like a hopeful puppy begging for scraps as Denise went through her own collection and discarded most of it onto the floor. I rummaged through the rejects, but they were in the pile for a reason, so we sat back and cursed our bad planning and our friends and families for failing to buy a us a surprise gown for Christmas. Just as we were about to start rooting out the board games in favour of a New Year's Eve in front of the TV, Lisa texted an image of herself in two amazing dresses to ask which one we thought looked better.

Immediately after I'd suggested we review the plan, she sent ten more images of even more dresses and said, "Take your pick." It turned out the thought of spending the evening with us without so much as the new Mr. Bean game for company (it had gone straight in my parents' loft on Boxing Day) had made her pretty damn generous with her designer clothing. She none-too-subtly pointed us towards the dresses "with a little more room" in them and we each pointed at a picture and had our wardrobes rescued from their malfunctions within seconds.

Soon we were squashed into our most flattering underwear and weaving a selection of products and tongs through our hair to try and add a bit of Hollywood glam. My straightened locks had received a pretty disgusted look from Denise, so I was now attempting a mixture of curling and half up-do accompanied by some brighter-than-usual colours on my face.

The result was like a five-year-old playing dress-up, but I didn't feel invested enough in the evening to care. I was experiencing an early onset of New Year blues. Sometime during putting on my make-up I'd also put on rose-tinted glasses about this time last year. And particularly about that bastard Ben. Just as expected, I was heading into the New Year single. I looked out of the lounge window to see there were no Prince Charmings waiting to whisk me away in their big, white, horse-powered steeds. I couldn't think of a single New Year's resolution that would improve my chances of not dying alone.

Denise came into the lounge with two cocktails. "They were both for me, but you look like you're about to jump," she said, thrusting a mojito into my hand. Somehow she'd thought frozen spinach and mint liquor would work as a viable alternative to fresh mint leaves, but I wasn't about to complain, so I sucked on my twirly Christmas straw and tried to stop being such a dick.

Matt turned up in the same suit he wore for Halloween, minus the zombie make-up. He was, however, carrying the lamest prop ever – a small plastic clapperboard with his name on it. I almost disinvited him on the spot, but remembered there were only four of us now, and we didn't have the luxury of losing a member of the party just because they were ridiculous. Lisa turned up in a tight-fitting gold gown about 20 minutes later, with our dresses shoved elegantly in a Tesco bag. We wandered into our rooms to change, while she and Matt raided the kitchen in search of alcohol that didn't require frozen ruffage as an accompaniment.

When we returned to the lounge in our outfits – me in a little black flapper dress (I hadn't even begun to fight the holiday weight) and Denise in a red flamenco dress with a wildly clashing orange flower in her hair – we heard a spittly wolf whistle. It turned out Smokey had come over with a bottle of wine and made himself comfy on the sofa very close to Lisa. The sight of consumable alcohol had subdued her disgust for the time being, but we needed to get moving if we had any hope of staying sober enough to make it out of the flat before the bell tolled. I accepted a glass of wine and proceeded to down it as I none-too-subtly shoved my other arm into my coat.

The others casually followed suit, and soon we were ushering Smokey through the door. It turned out they were having a "do" at the community centre anyway. He stopped to flash us his new tie, which was bright green with purple spots, and asked us if we thought the ladies would "dig it". I was so sick of old people talking in antiquated teen mumbo jumbo, but I told him he'd definitely get some if he hurried along and made sure to get the ladies good and drunk. Matt looked at me like I'd just encouraged his grandmother to put on a condom in place of a washing-up glove and we all headed silently out of the door.

Travelling anywhere in London on New Year's Eve is one of the most annoying things in the world. It's like all the people that were teetering on the edge of being obnoxious suddenly get three pints down them and act like absolute assholes. By the time we made it to the bar/cinema I was about ready to shoot someone in the face. Then I spotted Not-Ben in the queue and decided he'd make a pretty good target. After unsuccessfully appealing to my three New Year buddies to show a little compassion and accompany me around the corner to the Old Nag's Head, I joined the queue (which I objected to – I wasn't 18 anymore) and pouted until we got inside.

I walked purposely to the toilets, keeping a steely eye out for Not-Ben as I went. Just on the night I was trying to forget about my disastrous start to this year I was being reminded yet again by the bastard who orchestrated it.

When I reemerged I headed for the main room, where the cinema seats had been swivelled around into little clusters leaving room for what I assumed would later be dancing. Lisa had grabbed a free table and flung a spare item of clothing (including her left shoe) on each chair to secure our location. As we sat down and she redressed, I scanned the room to see if I could spot Not-Ben. "You're seeing things," said Denise, rolling her eyes. "It's because you got all dramatic about Ben earlier and now your mind's playing tricks on you." "Stop being a dick and go and get the drinks in," added Lisa as she scoured the room for hotties. Matt dutifully stood up and accompanied me to the bar.

Everyone else had gone for a similarly vague theme with their costumes. A few people were wearing jeans and trying to pass themselves off as anyone they could think of from the Judd Apatow crew. A guy with Seth Rogen written across his T-shirt, but very little resemblance otherwise, was standing next to me, while a pregnant 40-year-old with a skirt over her jeans and a zip-up hoody, who I assumed had come as Juno, was inching carefully back to her seat. I was glad I'd just gone for glamour. At least there was the potential of decent photos on Facebook that might pop up more prominently than the ones of me doing a headstand in Charlie's garden with my skirt over my face and very little over my ass.

We ordered a couple of bottles of wine and headed back to our seats. Lisa and Denise were deep in conversation about a guy at the next table, who was stoically trying to act like he couldn't hear them. We poured the wine and raised a toast to a year where I'd discovered Denise and Matt discovered that England wasn't so bad, which had brought us together on this beautiful evening, blah, blah, blah.

We took a load of pictures, because we were all looking pretty hot, and we wanted to remember that in two hours' time when we looked like homeless prostitutes and their hobo pimp. I sat and reapplied my lipstick and eyeliner, determined not to let my standards slip. I wasn't entirely concentrating, because I was watching Matt, who was looking particularly cute tonight and being the perfect gentleman as usual. As he practically mounted the table to let a woman in a fat suit walk past, I thought about what a good catch he was.

There'd been a few drunken moments at uni when we'd nearly consummated our friendship, but mostly one of us had been dating someone when the other was single, or one of us had passed out long before the other had time to make a move. Now I wondered whether the time was right. We were both single. We were both still relatively sober. He was sweet, funny, good-looking and, from what I'd heard (when we'd shared a house at uni), not a sexual deviant.

I watched him walk back to the table with another tray of drinks. Whether it was New Year working its magic or the fact that he came bearing wine, I started to wonder how I would broach the subject of 'us'. Then immediately made a note never to use that term to broach the subject of anything.

I picked up a glass and stared at him dreamily, imagining us going for Sunday lunch in the country, walking our sausage dog (my current baby-surrogate of choice) through the park, going for romantic dinners, enjoying wild, steamy sex... At the last thought I nearly choked. Not through pure, unadulterated erotic desire, but because I thought I was going to be physically sick. I looked at Matt again. He was funny and great and the ideal man, but the idea of kissing him or seeing him naked made me want to get the disinfectant hand cream out and smother it all over my body. I guess a happy rom-com, marry-the-best-friend ending wasn't on the cards, after all. It would be like having sex with my brother. At this thought, I had to put my wine down completely and place my head inbetween my knees I felt so nauseous.

I sighed, and sat back upright as he handed me a napkin suggesting I "wipe that shit off" my face. I blotted my new bright-red lipstick. At least he was useful for something, even if it didn't involve a huge amount of satisfaction. Lisa was looking bored by this point, and was twitching like a hemmed-in animal. She'd been sitting in the same place for nearly an hour, so Denise suggested we hit the dance floor. A couple of enthusiastic singletons had already made their debut, so we joined them around a circle of bags and busted some moves to Cher's The Shoop Shoop Song. Over the next hour or so we were treated to everything from Gangsta's Paradise to Bohemian Rhapsody (the music was movie-themed but I had no idea which film either of those songs were in). At 11pm we decided to take a breather and save our energy for the lead-up to midnight. I was thankful nobody had pulled so far, so I wouldn't have to make a mouth with my fist and kiss myself when the bell tolled. We sat down at a table near the bar (despite Denise throwing a shoe in its general direction as we danced, we'd failed to save our original spot) and grabbed a few more bottles in the interest of consuming as much alcohol as we could before next year.

My resolution was to cut back on wine (although I hadn't specified any other types of alcohol, which left me a pretty solid get-out clause), so I knew I had to make the most of the next hour. I realised we didn't have any glasses, so I went off to the bar to grab some. One my way back I managed to drop one, which somehow toppled all four of them onto the floor. The entire room seemed to turn around, like when you walk into your classroom naked in a dream. I bent down to try and pick up some of the bigger shards of glass, but a man swooped in to stop me, moving me aside as he gestured for the barman to come and sort it out. "Surely getting stitches in your hand would be worse than last year?" he whispered as he handed me a napkin to brush off any remaining particles.

I looked up to see the raised eyebrow of Not-Ben still holding onto my arm. This was the second time he'd saved me from injury in the past couple of months, so I exhaled a well-deserved, "Thanks." "Well, you've dropped your only potential weapons, so I guess I'm safe to approach you?" he said with his big, full lips. Fine, thought my brain, my New Year's resolution is to forgive Not-Ben for ruining my life. I was getting bored of having to yell at him every few months anyway. "How's the gerbil?" I asked with a withering look. "Guinea pig," he said. "I don't have one, I was just trying to make conversation." "And the first subject that came to mind was your imaginary guinea pig?" "Just in case you haven't noticed," he said as we walked back up to the bar, leaving the poor barman to clear up my mess, "you're not the easiest person to get along with."

I gave in and cracked a smile. "Which is a shame," he said. "Because we got on pretty well from what I remember…" He immediately adopted the brace position and peeked over the top when I didn't strike. "I don't really remember," I said. "I was pretty wasted." Adding "pervert" for dramatic effect. "Well, I was pretty damn good, so I'm sorry you missed it." "Do you run marathons and do charity work?" I asked suspiciously. "Of course," he replied. It was my turn to raise an eyebrow. "No. Although I did help my sister with a bake sale a few years back… 15 years back."

He followed me back to the table carrying three of what looked suspiciously like five glasses with him. "Either or," I demanded. "A weekend building homes for starving Africans, or a weekend of Funniest Home

Videos on repeat?" He laughed. "Well, I'm not great at DIY."

As we sat down, Lisa gave a very obvious wink from across the table and Denise pointedly asked if I'd like to join her on the toilet (not even bothering to correct her drunken slur). I gave in and went with them, leaving Not-Ben to make it through Matt's weird big-brotherly questioning.

"Who the fuck is that?" demanded Denise as Lisa sprayed herself with an inordinate amount of perfume. "That," said Lisa, "is the reason Jess has been living an exciting single lifestyle for the past year." "Totally worth it," said Denise, and before I knew it they had high-fived and continued putting on their lipstick. "At least you're over blaming it all on the poor guy," Lisa continued like I was completely immune to the desire to hit her in the face. "And, if you're going to start yelling at him again, declare him fair game so one of us can have a go. He is super-hot."

Suddenly I felt pretty possessive over my previous nemesis. I decided to return to him as soon as possible to apologise for being a complete head case and try and charm my way into starting the new year with a hot new(ish) man on my arm. But I walked back over to the table to find Matt sitting by himself. "Where did he go?" I demanded. "He headed back to the upstairs bar. Nice guy – for a change. How do you know him?"

I sat and stared at the room full of people dancing and having fun and suddenly felt like getting the hell out of there. I scoured the dance floor to see if I could spot Not-Ben, but he'd clearly made a sharp exit before the crazy came out, and I didn't blame him. I picked up the wine bottle to pour another glass, but it was empty. Was it only now that I couldn't have him that I wanted him? He'd been relentlessly nice in the face of my insanity and I'd waited until he'd given up to decide I wanted to jump his bones (again). Great work. Matt, Denise and Lisa got up to dance, but I wandered outside to get some air and feel sorry for myself in the snow, which was coming down pretty hard.

"Thought you looked like you needed a drink," said a voice from behind me. And we all know who it was. I accepted it, tilting my head to try and establish what the hell was going on. He smiled. "It's called déjà vu," he whispered, just as Matt, Lisa and Denise came stomping outside shouting. I looked over to find they were accompanied by a bouncer. Apparently Denise had tried to keep my seat by throwing her bag at someone and it had knocked over a bottle of champagne and caused a chain reaction of general carnage. They were being thrown out before we even made it to midnight.

I tried to shoot Denise a look while I gauged Not-Ben's reaction. In the meantime Lisa barked down the phone at someone. Within seconds a taxi pulled up. She gestured for us to get in immediately or die a horrible death, but before I could weigh up my options we discovered there were only three seats. "It's fine, you guys go on ahead. I'll order another one," said Matt, taking out what turned out to be the same ancient mobile as my father's. There was no time to deal with that now. I needed my brain to react at a more sober pace to get this situation together. I looked at Non-Ben to see if I even had any options. His half-smile and

251

familiar raise of the eyebrow assured me I did.

"I need to grab a taxi to another party anyway, so I'll just drop Jess off on the way," he said, looking to me for confimation. Denise and Lisa stuck their heads out of the taxi and stared at me. "If I don't hear from her by 11.45pm, I'm calling the police!" said Denise as she pulled Matt into the taxi and banged the headrest as a message to go. The three of them pulled off with surprisingly little concern for my personal safety, or the likelihood I'd make it to the party before the ball dropped, but at least I had a few more minutes to suss out what the hell was going on. This situation was ridiculous. I hated this guy.

There was no time to make an educated decision before he smiled at me and scooped up my hand. Turns out I didn't hate it. Another cab pulled up and we both got in. He gave the address of my party then another one. "Mine's east as well. You're welcome to join me," he said casually. "You're welcome to join *me*," I said, unwilling to lose the first battle. It turned out his was right around the corner from his flat, so I looked at him to try and figure out exactly what his offer entailed. He rolled his eyes and put his arm around me. I sat back against it. Judging by the traffic I had around five minutes to decide. We pointed out random landmarks and people throwing up in the street while the driver turned up the radio.

As we approached my party venue, and I started to gather my stuff, the countdown began. Ten, nine, eight… I rummaged for a business card or another super-casual way to give him my number. Seven, six, five… We pulled up outside the party and I saw Denise by the door, wrapped around what looked like one of the men from the dating website. Four, three, two... Not-Ben reached over and brushed my chin. One. "Happy New Year," he said as he kissed me lightly on the lips. Again, I didn't hate it. "Happy New Year," I replied with what I hoped was the coy smile I'd been practising in the mirror. I opened my mouth to say goodnight. What actually came out was, "Drive on."

Acknowledgements

Thank you to all my friends and family who smiled resiliently every time I told them I'd nearly finished my book. Especially those who took time out of their busy schedules as superwomen to read it – particularly Liz, Kate, Lora, Alex, Rosie, Sian, Tori, Jo and Ruth. Thanks also to Steve for stepping in and rescuing me from potential artistic disaster, Jemma for your creative flair, Lisa for some speedy research and Belinda for your generous advice. Thank you to my mum and dad for being the most supportive and encouraging parents out there. Your warmth and wisdom will stay with me forever, and I'll admit your decision not to let me have a bar in my room as a teenager was probably a good call. To John for your kindness, generosity and ability to make my mother smile. To Alfie and Lola for providing incessant, but welcome distraction throughout the process. And finally, thank you to Ian, for your unwavering love and inspiration. For going on emergency wine runs and turning down the football to create the perfect working environment. And, of course, for helping me through a few morning afters of my own… I love you all.

11631538R00154

Printed in Great Britain
by Amazon.co.uk, Ltd.,
Marston Gate.